A
ROYAL
MURDER

A ROYAL MURDER

Elliott Roosevelt

SEVERN SH HOUSE

This title first published in Great Britain 1994 by
SEVERN HOUSE PUBLISHERS LTD of
9–15 High Street, Sutton, Surrey SM1 1DF,
by arrangement with St Martin's Press, USA.

British Library Cataloguing in Publication Data
Roosevelt, Elliott
  Royal Murder
  I. Title
  813.54 [F]

  ISBN 0-7278-4674-4

Typeset by Hewer Text Composition Services, Edinburgh.
Printed and bound in Great Britain by
Hartnolls Ltd, Bodmin, Cornwall.

A
ROYAL
MURDER

I

Unlike some of her successors, Mrs. Roosevelt preferred not to be made privy to state secrets. She was in fact uncomfortable with secrets and would rather not know, except only what it was necessary to know. She had an instinctive sense of the principle later encapsulated in the cliché phrase "need to know," and throughout her White House years she never asked to be told anything she did not need to know.

The President, on the other hand, frequently decided she did need to know. As she travelled during the war, often she was acting as the President's courier, carrying top-secret information for generals, admirals, and sometimes for the statesmen of other governments. Usually she carried the information in her head and communicated it verbally. Occasionally she carried a code.

When she went to London in October, 1942—on the occasion when she helped solve the mystery of the murder in Buckingham Palace—her visit with Winston Churchill at Chequers was not just a social occasion. She delivered to the Prime Minister some highly confidential observations and opinions which the President did not want to communicate in writing. When she returned to Washington, she carried Churchill's responses. She memorized all this. She did not make even a cryptic note to reinforce her memory.

In spite of her determination not to pry into state secrets, Mrs. Roosevelt was likely privy to more of them, and more important secrets, than any other First Lady before or since.

She would say later that she wished she had never heard of the distressing secrets she learned in September of 1940, when she travelled to the Bahamas Islands at the President's request and was received as the official guest of the governor—who was at that time no less a personage than the Duke of Windsor, the abdicated King Edward VIII who had given up his throne for the woman he loved.

What she learned and what she saw remained her secret for many years. Almost fifty years later the governments involved decided—or were compelled—to open their files. What Mrs. Roosevelt knew when she went to the Bahamas became public information. What she learned after she arrived there still has not been officially disclosed.

To understand the purpose of Mrs. Roosevelt's five-day visit to the Bahamas Islands in September, 1940, it is necessary to review a little history.

Hitler invaded Poland on September 1, 1939. Great Britain and France honored their treaty commitments and declared war on Germany. In May and June, 1940, the German blitzkrieg overwhelmed Allied forces in The Netherlands, Belgium, and France, and on June 22 France formally surrendered, leaving Britain to fight on alone. The English-speaking nations—and indeed all of civilization—faced a real and imminent danger of defeat and destruction.

At first, the greatest threat to Britain was German submarine warfare. The U-boats roamed the Atlantic, sinking merchant ships almost at will. Prime Minister Winston Churchill sent an urgent request to President Roosevelt—please lend or sell us fifty or sixty of the old destroyers the United States maintains idle in East Coast ports; these ships can be the key to our survival.

President Roosevelt wanted to send the destroyers, but he had to overcome isolationist resistance in Congress. After some months of complex negotiations, a deal was struck—the United States would send the destroyers, and in return Great Britain would lease to the United States a group of naval and air bases off the East Coast of North America. The destroyers were important to Britain. The bases were important to the United States.

Some of those bases would be in the Bahamas Islands.

Summer lingered long in Washington. By the middle of September, New Yorkers and New Englanders already enjoyed cool nights and days when every color was enhanced by the oblique sunlight of autumn. In Washington the days remained hot and damp, the nights warm and foggy. As Mrs. Roosevelt walked through the colonnade between the White House and the Executive Wing, she was pleased by the gusty wind off a tall gray thunderstorm that was brewing. A morning rain would cool the city.

It was an unusual morning. The President had asked her to join him for breakfast at his desk in the Oval Office.

Although the President had never in his life tied himself to a rigid schedule, still he did have his habits; and one of them was to take his breakfast in bed, usually with his Scottie, Fala, romping around the room, begging for bits of toast and bacon, while he ate, sipped his coffee, smoked his first cigarette of the day, and read the morning newspapers. The only person welcome to intrude on this private hour was Missy LeHand, his private secretary, who often came in with a few words about the day's schedule or with some report she knew he would want to read before his first appointment. The President disliked interruption in this hour, and this morning's sharp break from his routine suggested something important.

Likely something to do with the campaign, Mrs. Roosevelt speculated as she walked through the colonnade. The election was six weeks away. The President was a candidate for an unprecedented third term, and, although the President and Mrs. Roosevelt were confident of his reelection, his political enemies were being unusually harsh and bitter in their personal attacks.

Or it might be something personal that he wanted to talk about. Their son Elliott had enlisted in the United States Army Air Corps and had been commissioned a captain. Republicans had printed tens of thousands of campaign buttons reading "Poppa I want to be a captain, too," and Elliott had offered to resign his commission and re-enlist as a private, or, failing that, to enlist in the Royal Canadian Air Force. Maybe there had been some development on that front.

Or maybe—

No point in speculating. She hurried into the Executive Wing and to the entrance to the Oval Office.

President Franklin D. Roosevelt was at his desk, smoking a cigarette in his famous long holder and frowning over a newspaper. He had already drunk a cup of coffee; the empty cup sat on the desk. His wheelchair had been pulled out of the Oval Office, and he sat in his favorite comfortable chair, with a special wooden footrest below, for his legs he could not move.

"Good morning, Babs," he said to the First Lady. "Did you have a restful night?"

"Very restful, thank you," she said.

He grinned and shook his head. "You haven't had a restful night since we moved to Washington," he said.

For an instant she hesitated; then she spoke candidly. "I had rather hoped we would go home in January of 1941," she said. "I won't deny it."

"I know you had. So had I. But this fellow Hitler played a dirty trick on us. Anyway . . ." His voice, softly contrite for a moment, hardened. "Anyway, who would have taken over this job? Farley? Garner? Wallace?" He shook his head.

"You had no choice," she said. "I never questioned your judgment in deciding to run for the third term. And when I look at this morning's papers, I can't imagine leaving in any other hands the responsibility for what this country is going to have to do."

He glanced at the newspapers lying on his desk. "Which story troubles you most?" he asked.

"Oh, I was reading about the blitz," she said. "Poor London! The poor people of London! I know you read that a bomb hit Buckingham Palace itself."

He opened his mouth to speak, but he was interrupted by a discreet knock on the door between the Oval Office and the secretaries' office just outside. Missy LeHand opened the door and said quietly that the breakfast was ready.

The President nodded, and two White House ushers wheeled in carts carrying pots of coffee and tea, bacon and eggs, fruit, toast and jellies, and pitchers of orange and tomato juice.

Mrs. Roosevelt frowned at the service and said, "I believe I am not your only guest for breakfast this morning, Franklin."

"No," he said. "I'm afraid this is a business meeting."

"Are others waiting?"

"Yes, for a moment. Maybe we'd better ask them in."

"Perhaps we should," she said.

The President picked up his telephone and told Missy to send in this morning's guests.

There were two of them—

—Philip, Lord Lothian, British Ambassador to Washington. A natural aristocrat, aloof and dignified, Lothian had, nevertheless, a light humorous approach to life that had helped to endear him to the President.

—Adolf A. Berle, Assistant Secretary of State. Something of a prodigy and genius, he had graduated from Harvard College at seventeen, from Harvard Law at twenty-one, then had become a corporation lawyer and professor of law at Columbia University—before accepting appointment as one of the original members of the "Brain Trust" that came to Washington in 1933 with the body of ideas that formed the basis of the New Deal. A short, slender man, he continued after seven years to enjoy the President's complete confidence and reported personally to him at least once a week.

After the exchange of pleasantries, Lord Lothian and Adolf Berle sat down on one of the couches near the fireplace, and the ushers served breakfast on the coffee table. Mrs. Roosevelt resumed her seat, and her breakfast was laid out on a corner of the President's desk. The President urged the ushers on in heaping his plate, and he drank tomato juice with apparent relish and set to work on the bacon and scrambled eggs.

"Who starts?" the President asked when everyone had eaten a little. "Dolf?"

Berle nodded. He wiped his mouth with a napkin. "I suppose I can outline the problem," he said crisply. He nodded to Mrs. Roosevelt. "This has been discussed with the President and the Ambassador. We have agreed you should be asked to help deal with the problem."

"I am always glad to help when I can," she said.

"Yes, of course," said Berle. "Our problem has to do with the bases the United States acquired in return for the destroyers. Specifically, we are concerned about the situation in the Bahamas. As you well know, Mrs. Roosevelt, we very much welcomed the opportunity to establish an air and naval presence on some of the Bahamas Islands. Having bases there extends our defense perimeter four to five hundred miles east into the Atlantic."

"Let me add," said Lothian, "that His Majesty's armed forces are heavily burdened at present, and we cannot guarantee we could defend the Bahamas in the event Herr Hitler should elect to attempt a seizure of one or more islands. I need hardly tell you that a German submarine base or, worse, an air base only four hundred miles off the American shoreline would be an intolerable threat to the security of the United States."

"I well understand," said Mrs. Roosevelt. "German bombers could bomb . . . well, they could bomb Miami from the Bahamas."

"More likely," said Berle, "they could use the islands as a staging base for an invasion of, say, Cuba."

"In any event," said the President, "we cannot allow Hitler to establish a naval base or airfield in the Bahamas. The mischief he could do from there is incalculable."

"How very fortunate, then, that we are establishing bases of our own."

"Yes," said Berle. "But we have a problem. There is a definite pro-German faction in the Bahamas. I'm not sure I would go so far as to call it a pro-Nazi faction, but there is certainly a pro-German faction which may constitute a threat to the security of any base we establish there."

"I should rather express it a bit differently," said Ambassador Lothian. "My fear—the concern of His Majesty's government—is that everything done in the Bahamas will be reported to Berlin. Perhaps directly. Perhaps indirectly. But reported. What is more, there may be efforts to resist the establishment of the American bases. Obstacles may be put in the way, to make everything more difficult, to delay construction, and so on."

Mrs. Roosevelt frowned and shook her head. "But the islands are a British colony," she said.

"A majority of the population are of African ancestry," said Lothian. "Unfortunately, they live in poverty and must concern themselves almost exclusively with eking out a living. The islands are governed, actually, by the business community—and, unhappily, many of the leading businessmen, including the bankers, are decidedly pro-German."

"Why?"

Berle answered. "For the same reason that a man like Henry Ford is pro-German," he said. "For the same reason that Alfred Sloan, chairman of General Motors, is pro-German. Their eyes are on their profit-and-loss statements, and there is more money in doing business with a triumphant Germany than with a prostrate France or an embattled Britain."

"Besides," said Lord Lothian, "a number of European businessmen, including some outright Nazi sympathizers, use the islands as their headquarters for the present."

"Well . . ." said Mrs. Roosevelt. "You opened the discussion by suggesting that I might be able to do something. Just what can I do to help cope with this situation?"

The President spoke. "The Duke and Duchess of Windsor arrived in the Bahamas only a few weeks ago," he said. "As you know, the duke has been appointed royal governor. Both he and the duchess have been pressing the Foreign Office and the State Department to arrange an extended tour of the United States, including a reception here at the White House. We have resisted. We are thinking, however, that if *you* were to pay them a visit in the islands— You see the point."

"I do," she said. "A bit of diplomatic soothing of ruffled feathers. But I don't see what this has to do with the problem of German sympathizers in the islands. Also, frankly I should like to know why we don't welcome the Windsors to the United States. They are very popular here, very well thought of."

The three men exchanged glances.

"Some time ago I received a confidential telegram from Prime Minister Churchill," said the President. He picked up a file folder, took out a sheet of yellow paper, and handed it to her. "Please read it, Babs."

The telegram read—

THE ACTIVITIES OF THE DUKE OF WINDSOR ON THE CONTINENT IN RECENT MONTHS HAVE BEEN CAUSING HIS MAJESTY AND MYSELF GRAVE UNEASINESS AS HIS INCLINATIONS ARE WELL KNOWN TO BE PRO-NAZI AND HE MAY BECOME THE CENTER OF INTRIGUE. WE

REGARD IT AS A REAL DANGER THAT HE
SHOULD MOVE FREELY ON THE CONTINENT.
EVEN IF HE WERE WILLING TO RETURN TO
THIS COUNTRY, HIS PRESENCE HERE WOULD
BE MOST EMBARRASSING BOTH TO HIS
MAJESTY AND TO THE GOVERNMENT.

She handed the telegram back to the President.

"I have another telegram for you to read," said the President. "This is from Claiborne Pell, our ambassador to Portugal. He sent this telegram, top secret, to Secretary of State Hull."

Mrs. Roosevelt read the second telegram the President handed her—

DUKE AND DUCHESS OF WINDSOR ARE
INDISCREET AND OUTSPOKEN AGAINST
BRITISH GOVERNMENT. CONSIDER THEIR
PRESENCE IN THE UNITED STATES MIGHT BE
DISTURBING AND CONFUSING. THEY SAY THEY
INTEND REMAINING IN THE UNITED STATES
WHETHER CHURCHILL LIKES IT OR NOT AND
DESIRE APPARENTLY TO MAKE PROPAGANDA
FOR PEACE.

"They want to work with our isolationists," said the President. "They want us to keep away from the conflict and let Britain lose the war. Am I stating it too strongly, Lord Lothian?"

"Not too strongly," said Lothian.

"But surely," said Mrs. Roosevelt, "you are not suggesting that the Duke of Windsor is a traitor to his country?"

"Let me respond to that," said Lothian. "No, I don't think the duke is a traitor. He simply thinks Germany is

going to win the war—a prospect that is not unwelcome
to him. He is not a great admirer of Herr Hitler, but he
doesn't think him a villain, either. What he wants is a
negotiated peace that would leave Germany in command
of Western Europe and the United Kingdom reduced to
dependency. He thinks we should acknowledge our in-
ability to defeat Hitler and should buy peace by conceding
him a lot of colonial possessions."

"Some of our isolationists believe essentially the same,"
said Mrs. Roosevelt.

"The difference," said the President grimly, "is that *we*
are not at war with Nazi Germany. If we were, I would call
a man a traitor if he tried to enter personally and independently into peace negotiations with an enemy who is
bombing the hell out of—My syntax has gone awry. But
you see what I mean."

"I do see what you mean," said Mrs. Roosevelt.
"Still . . . Do we define the Duke of Windsor as a—"

"Not a traitor," Lothian interrupted. "But . . ." He
paused for a brief moment. "He was king. He is a member
of the royal family. It is not easy for me to say this, Mrs.
Roosevelt, but the truth we have to face is that the Duke
of Windsor is a man of . . . of decidedly limited intellectual
capacity."

"Let me relieve the ambassador of a bit of this embar-
rassment," said Adolf Berle. "And let me be specific, Mrs.
Roosevelt, about what a dangerous couple the Duke and
Duchess of Windsor can be."

"They were *ordered* to go to the Bahamas Islands," Lothian interjected. "There were those who wanted to send
them to the Falkland Islands."

"For good reason," said Berle. "We are indebted to Sir
Robert Vansittart for certain information. And, once

again, let me be specific. Early in the war the Duke of Windsor asked for—in fact, demanded—a significant role in the British war effort."

"Understandable," commented Mrs. Roosevelt.

"Yes, of course. And he was given a role. At one point in 1939 he was allowed to sit in on discussions at the highest level, about the Allied strategy for the defense of Belgium and France. Within a short time Secret Intelligence Service learned that a detailed account of what was said in that meeting had been received in Berlin."

"Mr. Berle . . . !"

"We know what happened," said Berle. "Among the closest friends of the Duchess of Windsor are some French and Spanish people who are not just sympathetic to Hitler; they are fanatic Nazis. Some of these people were under constant surveillance by the *Deuxième Bureau*, French intelligence, as well as British intelligence. Their reports to Berlin followed immediately on lunches and dinners with the Duchess of Windsor. Obviously the duke confided in her, and she repeated everything he had said—whether intending to serve as a Nazi spy or just to impress people with her knowledge of Allied plans, we don't know."

"We had supposed," said Mrs. Roosevelt, "that the highly publicized visit of the duke and duchess to Herr Hitler was of a purely casual nature."

"I rather think it was," said Lothian. "I don't believe the duke and duchess have been recruited as Nazi agents. I would rather think they are exceedingly naive people, harboring a great deal of resentment against the present king and government, and ambitious as well."

"The fear is," said Berle, "that they will fall into the hands of the Nazi sympathizers in the Bahamas and will serve Hitler's purposes—albeit unknowingly."

"We must, unhappily," said Lothian, "even acknowledge that it might happen knowingly, given, not just their tolerance for the Nazi political philosophy, but their sympathy for it as well. The duchess has been quoted as saying that the fall of France was inevitable, since France was not as committed to its cause as Germany was."

"I return, then," said Mrs. Roosevelt, "to the question of just what contribution you think I might be able to make."

"It is not easy for you," said the President, "to practice deception. Yet, I am going to ask you to do so. The Windsors will happily receive you, as a guest of honor, at Government House in Nassau. You will be accompanied by a staff—a secretary, a—"

"The Windsors," Lothian interrupted, "keep at all times a staff of at least fifteen people. If you arrived without a staff, they would wonder at your simplicity."

"Your staff," said the President, "will be intelligence officers. Men and women. It will be their duty to assess the situation."

"And mine," said Mrs. Roosevelt dryly, "to facilitate their work by being determinedly charming, totally diplomatic, and apparently totally naive."

"You understand the assignment perfectly," said the President.

II

Mrs. Roosevelt left Washington three days later, by train. She had by then read the entire file on the Windsors and had found it one of the most distressing collections of reports she had ever seen. She all but wished she hadn't read it.

For example, while Great Britain was fighting for its life and the Prime Minister was burdened with the heaviest responsibilities any one man had ever borne, the duke bombarded Winston Churchill with telegrams demanding he give personal attention to finding suitable servants to accompany him and the duchess to the Bahamas. The duke wanted a soldier from a Highland regiment to serve him as batman. The Prime Minister replied that able-bodied soldiers could not be spared from their soldierly duties to function as servants for anyone, even members of the royal family.

"Consider, Sir, how the public will receive such a request from you, such an assignment of personnel," Churchill had written.

At the same time, when Britain was fighting for its very

life against Hitler's Germany, the duchess was in contact with the German government, asking to be allowed to return to German-occupied Paris to pick up her personal possessions from her Paris home. Hitler's foreign minister, Joachim von Ribbentrop, ultimately allowed one of the duchess's maids to travel to Paris and return to Spain with several trunks of clothing and bibelots.

These were petty items. Some of the other reports were far more damaging.

Mrs. Roosevelt decided she would reserve judgment on the Duke and Duchess of Windsor until she had met them and had some opportunity to study them in person. After all, if one believed much of what was published about her and the President, one would gain an impression of two evil, destructive people. She would let the duke and duchess make their own case.

Similarly, she withheld judgment on the staff assigned to her—a naval attaché, a personal aide, a bodyguard, and a maid. Each of them was in fact an intelligence officer.

The naval attaché was Commander Wilson MacGruder, a somewhat formidable man of forty-five—broad-shouldered, bulky, with a big head set on a bull neck. He wore his black hair slicked down with hair dressing, and his black mustache was neatly trimmed. Mrs. Roosevelt observed in him, almost from the moment she met him, an active, imaginative sense of humor.

The man designated as her personal aide was a protégé of Adolf Berle, a young lawyer from Ohio. His name was Kenneth Krouse, and he was an elfin man, no more than five-feet-four, with a round and happy little face. He, too, had a pronounced sense of humor, though his was dry and reserved, and you had to listen well to hear his trenchant observations of people and things. Mrs. Roosevelt soon appreciated why Berle had such confidence in him.

Krouse was astute; his intelligence was of a practical nature.

Her bodyguard was a Secret Service agent named Alexander Zaferakes. At thirty-five, Alex was prematurely balding, prematurely gray. He was capable of fastening on people a hard, skeptical gaze that all but the boldest found disconcerting. There was no question of his position. He was Mrs. Roosevelt's bodyguard, and no one came close to her unless he knew who it was and knew she was willing to talk to that person.

Finally, the personal maid was a civilian employee of the Department of the Navy. Jean King was only twenty-eight years old, but she was an experienced agent of Naval Intelligence, and she was in no sense a subordinate of Lieutenant Commander MacGruder. She was thin, yet hard-muscled; in fact, her body looked hard all over, as if she trained like an athlete. She wore her light-brown hair short. Her face was freckled. She was amused by her position as Mrs. Roosevelt's personal maid, since she had no idea of the duties of a personal maid. Mrs. Roosevelt was amused, too, since she had no wish to be served by a personal maid.

Each of these people carried a pistol, the men in holsters inside their jackets, Jean King in her handbag.

Besides these people, Malvina "Tommy" Thompson, Mrs. Roosevelt's personal secretary, went with her.

Mrs. Roosevelt had a roomette on the train, which chugged south, drawn by one locomotive then another as her car was switched from one railroad to another. Because her trip was confidential, she did not travel in *Ferdinand Magellan*, the private armored railroad car assigned to the President of the United States, but in a car she shared with a number of wealthy people who were on the way to their estates in South Carolina and Georgia for the autumn season.

When the car was switched from one railroad to another in Atlanta, Mrs. Roosevelt was aware of a clamor outside as—apparently—some celebrity came aboard. That night at dinner in the dining room she was told by the waiter that the wonderful young actress Judy Garland occupied a roomette in the car. Mrs. Roosevelt said she would be pleased to receive Miss Garland as her guest for dinner, and a few minutes later the eighteen-year-old performer came to her table, accompanied by a gruff, burly man who was conspicuously her bodyguard and was unwilling to let her sit down at anyone's table until he was certain who it was. When he was satisfied, he sat down at a nearby table, where he could keep a close eye on his charge.

"Hired by the studio," said Judy Garland wryly when the man was out of earshot. "To guard my body in more ways than one."

The young woman was a contrast. On the one hand, she flaunted her youth and innocence. On the other she forswore them by smoking cigarettes and drinking two double Scotches before dinner.

"I enjoyed your performance in *The Wizard of Oz*," said Mrs. Roosevelt.

"It's a real honor to hear that from you," said Judy Garland as she tapped the ash from her cigarette on the edge of a glass ashtray. The Scotch and maybe the cigarettes had made her voice throaty and liquid. "It's the picture I'll be remembered for."

"It's a fine picture," said Mrs. Roosevelt. "But there will be others—perhaps even better."

"I'll be singing 'Over the Rainbow' for the rest of my life," the girl said.

"I hope so," said the First Lady. "But of course many other songs, too."

Judy Garland smiled wistfully and shrugged.

Commander MacGruder came in and joined them, and when he ordered a Scotch, the girl said she'd have one, too.

Juan Trippe, president of Pan American World Airways, had arranged for the First Lady and her party to be flown to Nassau, Bahamas, on a twin-engine Pan Am amphibian. A crowd had gathered to watch her board the big airplane and take off, and a score of newspaper reporters were there to report the event. She held a brief, impromptu press conference.

"Is the visit official, Mrs. Roosevelt?"

"It is official. I am going to the Bahamas Islands to meet with the governor, the Duke of Windsor, on my husband's behalf, to express our thanks for the cooperation we have had from Great Britain in the matter of establishing bases in the Bahamas and to assure him that we will reciprocate with good will and cooperation. Also, Commander Mac-Gruder will inspect the sites where the bases may be located."

"There have been reports that the duke and duchess would like to visit the United States this fall. Will you extend an invitation to them to visit the White House?"

"It is my understanding that the Duke and Duchess of Windsor would like to visit the United States, and I will of course assure them that they will be very welcome. On the other hand, the duke has said that he feels he cannot leave his post as governor so soon after his appointment, so we expect the visit will not happen this year."

Her eye fell by chance on the face of Kenneth Krouse, and she had difficulty suppressing a smile or even a laugh as she gave this answer. Secretary of State Cordell Hull had reinforced the President's caution to her to resist every suggestion on the part of the duke and duchess that they visit the United States any time soon. Ken Krouse knew this, of course, and the amused expression on his chubby, ruddy face all but defeated her determination to speak with solemn sincerity.

"Are you concerned about German submarines operating in Bahamian waters?"

"No," she said.

In fact, six United States destroyers were operating in the waters around New Providence Island, and today, in advance of the departure of the Pan Am flying boat, twenty navy airplanes had flown patrols over the waters and islands between Miami and Nassau. The Duke of Windsor had cabled London that German U-boats were operating in Bahamian waters, but there was no confirmed sighting.

A small chartered plane took off just before the amphibian, carrying four of the reporters to Nassau. There was no room for them on the amphibian, and they wanted to arrive at Nassau ahead of the First Lady and her party, to photograph and report on her arrival.

The Pan Am airplane was a medium-range airliner, of the type the airline used for its service to Havana. With a flying-boat hull, it was also equipped with retractable wheels. At the waterfront base south of Miami, passengers boarded as the amphibian sat on the concrete near the terminal building, and when they were aboard, the airplane was towed to a ramp and slowly descended into the water.

As it lay in the water, wallowing in the gentle swell of

Biscayne Bay, the engines were started. Then the pilots taxied out and turned into the wind for takeoff.

Some of the First Lady's party were nervous about flying, particularly in a flying boat. The seats were wicker chairs—wicker for its light weight—in two rows, one seat on each side of a narrow aisle. Each seat was by a window, and Tommy Thompson and Kenneth Krouse watched apprehensively as the engines roared, the propellers spun faster, and the airplane surged forward, gained speed, and began to bounce across the waves.

A flying boat did not roll on rubber tires. The hull slapped the water hard, making loud, disconcerting noises heard inside the cabin. Just when the jolting and banging reached the point of being alarming, the amphibian abruptly staggered clear of the water and all noise but the roar of the engines stopped. For perhaps half a minute the plane flew level above the water, gaining airspeed; then it began to climb, and a minute or so later it was high above the boat-filled waters of the bay, giving the passengers on the left side a spectacular view of downtown Miami.

Mrs. Roosevelt was elated. This was an adventure. The sea was a gorgeous blue-green. The boundary between land and sea was a gleaming strip of white: the surf. The plane continued to climb. Looking back, one could see Florida, flat and green; and beyond Miami a group of tall gray clouds stood over the Everglades: a thunderstorm that would reach the coast and ground air traffic half an hour or so later.

A pleasant young woman in a light-blue uniform came along the aisle, offering glasses of champagne. She was followed by another who offered canapés. The first young woman, who had served the champagne, returned a little later, carrying a small chart of the Florida–Bahamas area, with their route of flight marked in pen.

Their route was direct. They would pass over Cat Cays, then the northern tip of Andros Island, just beyond which was New Providence Island and Nassau. The pilot had written his estimate of their flying time at the bottom of the chart: one hour and forty minutes.

The roar of the engines and the gentle rocking of the airplane were soporific. In spite of her determination to remain wide awake and see everything, Mrs. Roosevelt dozed. She awoke when she became aware of a change in the pitch of the roar. She looked out to see that they were descending.

New Providence Island is about twenty miles long and about seven miles wide at its widest point. The only town, Nassau, is on the northeast tip of the island. The airport is about ten miles west of Nassau, on the northern shore.

As the amphibian flew over the western tip of the island, on what pilots called a left downwind for the runway, the landing gear came down and locked with a bump. The welcome was visible even from the air—a hundred cars lined up on the roads around the little airport, a crowd on the field, a band in red coats. The airplane passed by the airport and out over the southern shore before it made its turn. The sea was that vivid blue-green that had surprised Mrs. Roosevelt when they took off from Miami. The sun burned on sand beaches. A large lake occupied a major part of the island, and she wondered if it was fresh water or salt. Before she could focus any thought on that, or in fact on anything else, she saw the tops of tall palms, the roofs of tiny houses, the cars, even now the people, and the airplane crossed one end of the lake and touched down on the runway.

Mrs. Roosevelt already knew that a dignified arrival by airplane was no easy task. One exited an airplane only by ducking through its low and narrow little doors, then by

descending awkward little stairs. She was determined, nevertheless, to bring as much dignity as possible to this official diplomatic visit.

She wore a silk dress, suitable for the tropical climate. It was blue and violet and white, and loose sleeves covered her arms. She also wore a broad-brimmed straw hat. Landed, the airplane sat at a sharp angle, nose high, tail low, and she had to make her way gingerly down the aisle toward the door, her head down to clear the ceiling. For a long moment she stood inside the door, while the two hostesses and the copilot stared out the window, then struggled with the latches.

They pushed the door open, and she was simultaneously pleased and distressed. She was pleased to see that a red-carpeted wooden platform had been drawn up to the airplane so that she would not have to turn sideways and work her way down narrow steel steps. She was distressed by the oppressively hot and humid air that immediately blew into the airplane.

Two men waited for her on the platform, one a British officer in red and gold uniform, the other likely an American from the look of him, in a white suit.

She stepped out onto the carpeted platform. A small military band to the side struck up "The Star-Spangled Banner." The officer turned and saluted an American flag carried by a uniformed bearer, and the civilian put his hand over his heart. Mrs. Roosevelt put her hand over her heart and faced the flag.

The heat was truly oppressive. She could not help but feel it. As her eyes glanced around, she spotted the Duke and Duchess of Windsor. They waited for her on another red-carpeted platform, this one shaded by a red and gold canopy. They were some twenty feet away, but she recognized them easily: the duke a slender, blond man, the duchess a slight, dark woman. The duke was in the uniform of a British general, complete to an ostrich-plumed hat which he had removed and held under his left arm. The white plumes stirred on the lazy breeze. The duchess wore a navy-blue suit, with a white orchid on her shoulder.

The national anthem came to an end. Mrs. Roosevelt looked to the two men to introduce themselves, but before anyone could speak a word the band broke into "God Save the King," and again everyone stood at salute.

The British national anthem was much shorter, and when it ended the officer introduced himself. "Brigadier Sir Edmund Hilary-Percy, Ma'am. I'm commander of His Majesty's forces in the Bahamas Islands." He was an archetypal career officer, British army—ruddy of face, with a thick gray mustache.

The white-suited civilian then introduced himself as John W. Dye, American consul.

The two men escorted Mrs. Roosevelt down the platform steps and along a red carpet that extended the twenty feet to the platform where the duke and duchess and other dignitaries waited. Ranks of red-uniformed soldiers presented arms to either side. Behind them ranks of police kept the crowd back.

The Duke of Windsor stepped to the front of the platform as Mrs. Roosevelt climbed the two steps. He was smiling. He was a handsome man, beyond any question: trim, square-shouldered, erect, with cool blue eyes.

"A great pleasure, indeed, Mrs. Roosevelt," he murmured. "Welcome to the Bahamas Islands."

Now a question of protocol. She had been advised that she could, if she wished, curtsey to the duke but in no circumstance was she to curtsey to the duchess. The duke was royal. The duchess was not. The British government insisted on the distinction. The duke, even so, insisted that women *must* curtsey to the duchess, or he would take offense. Mrs. Roosevelt had solved the problem her own way. It was inappropriate, she had decided, for the First Lady to curtsey to anyone, royal or otherwise; and if she didn't curtsey to the duke she could hardly curtsey to the duchess. She beamed a warm smile at the Duke of Windsor and extended her hand.

She saw him hesitate for the briefest instant. Then he seized her hand and shook it. On the tarmac below, cameras clicked.

Holding her hand, he firmly turned her toward the duchess. "May I present Her Royal Highness, the Duchess of Windsor," he said.

Another sticky problem. Officially, the duke was a royal highness. And just as officially, the duchess was not. Officially, the duchess was "Her Gracè," nothing more. The dispute over this mite of protocol was charged with emotion—so far as the duke was concerned.

Again, Mrs. Roosevelt had resolved the problem in her own mind. "A pleasure and honor, indeed," she said to the duchess—and extended her hand.

The duchess seemed unfazed. "I've looked forward to meeting you," she said.

The duke then presented the other officials on the platform—the chief justice, the commissioner of police, the colonial secretary, the commander of the naval squadron (who would later admit he commanded nothing but a score of tiny patrol boats), and the speaker of the Bahamian Assembly.

Introductions completed, the officials began immediately to leave the platform. The duke pointed toward the stairs at the rear, suggesting that Mrs. Roosevelt should now leave, too. She turned around to see what had become of her staff and saw that they were now among a group assembled at the foot of the platform.

A carriage waited. Drawn by two gray horses, it had room for two people only, and was attended by two uniformed men on the high box at the front and by two standing on steps behind. A similar carriage waited just behind it. The Duke of Windsor escorted Mrs. Roosevelt to the first carriage. She climbed in and sat down, and he followed. The driver moved forward a few feet, and the second carriage drew up. The duchess and Brigadier Hilary-Percy took places in its seats.

Mrs. Roosevelt looked back. Alex Zaferakes was conspicuously unhappy with the arrangements. If he could not sit in the carriage with the First Lady, then he wanted to ride behind in place of one of the lackeys, and he was expressing himself vociferously. She lifted a hand toward him, as a signal not to be upset. He frowned and shrugged and allowed himself to be ushered into a Rolls-Royce that would follow immediately behind the two carriages.

The procession set off for Nassau and Government House. Four policemen on motorcycles rode ahead. Eight others, mounted on horses, rode to either side of the carriages. Four cars followed the carriages, and they were followed by two open trucks packed with soldiers.

"We've forty-five minutes' ride ahead of us," said the duke. "And really stifling, this climate, isn't it?"

"Unpleasant," she said.

It had to be more unpleasant for him. His uniform was wool. He had replaced his plumed hat on his head, and sweat streamed down over his forehead. He wiped at it with a handkerchief he pulled from his sleeve.

"I'm pleased you've come," said the duke. "I have some things to tell you. I should be grateful if you would communicate them to the President."

"I shall be glad to."

"There is only one way to preserve democracy," said the duke. "That is to terminate this war. I mean, terminate it immediately."

"And how can that be achieved?" asked Mrs. Roosevelt ingenuously, as though she had no idea what he might say.

"By negotiating a peace," said the Duke of Windsor. "Herr Hitler is a villain, but he leads an inspired, united people, as none of the other national leaders do. Nations like France, which is weak and corrupt, or Britain, which is divided and dispirited, can't defeat him. We should have recognized that a year ago. We should have let him take Poland. He offered peace. We should have accepted it."

"What will he demand?" asked Mrs. Roosevelt.

"A great deal, I'm sure," said the duke. "Colonies. And more."

"And how will democracy survive if he gets all he wants?"

"It must survive in the United States," said the duke. "And that is my message to the President. The United States must *not* become involved in this war and have to share the defeat."

"We in the States think otherwise," said Mrs. Roosevelt with a measured, cool smile.

"I want to come to the United States with my message," said the duke. "I have a great popular following, you know."

"I am sure we will be glad to hear your opinion. The President will of course welcome you. He will do all he can, I'm sure, to facilitate an early visit by you and the duchess."

The Duke of Windsor smiled and nodded, filled with satisfaction.

Mrs. Roosevelt looked up at the sky—from which no righteous lightning came to punish her for her lie.

III

It was not until they were inside Government House, the official residence of the Governor of the Bahamas Islands, that Mrs. Roosevelt had the chance to talk one-on-one with the Duchess of Windsor. She found her a more charming, accommodating person than she had expected.

"My husband is governor," she said, "of twenty-nine islands, almost seven hundred cays—whatever cays may be—and something like twenty-five hundred reefs and sandspits, populated by about eighty thousand people, five-sixths of them Negroes. And seriously said, Mrs. Roosevelt, most of the Negroes live in wretched poverty. We are going to see what we can do about that."

The duchess was smaller than Mrs. Roosevelt had expected. Personalities you read about in the news often turn out to be smaller of stature than you expect. Fame, or notoriety, exaggerates one's notion of physical size. Anyway, the duchess was petite. She was thin—thinner than usual that autumn of 1940. She wore red lipstick, rather more of it than would flatter her, in the First Lady's judgment. And she wore glittering jewelry, even in the daytime.

In one respect, the duchess had Mrs. Roosevelt's entire sympathy. Neither of them had ever been known as a glamorous woman. The girl Eleanor Roosevelt had in fact been brought up to think of herself as the ugly duckling of the family, better not too closely observed. Something of the like had been the fate of the girl Wallis Warfield. Eleanor Roosevelt had earned love and respect through qualities other than conventional beauty. Wallis Warfield, now Duchess of Windsor, still strove to be admired at a distance. The First Lady could relate to the duchess's disappointment with herself. She could understand, even if she could not approve of, the way that the duchess sought to win the world's esteem.

"The house is impossible," said the duchess as she led Mrs. Roosevelt on a brief tour.

It sat in the center of a fenced garden of ten acres, with beach and surf behind. The entrance gate was guarded by stone pillars capped with lamps and by two dilapidated ancient cannons that threatened to fall out of their rickety naval carriages. The grounds grew thick with tropical flowers and foliage, the sweet odor of which was cloying. The architecture of the house was, to give it its best, colonial: aspiring to a sort of provincial grandeur.

Even though recently refurbished, Government House was in disrepair and disarray. The interior walls were painted with shiny blue enamel, which caused the state rooms to look like oversized bathrooms. Woodwork sagged, eaten half away by termites. The swimming pool, with ER VIII painted on the bottom, was dry and littered with garden debris.

"We are lucky to have it, I suppose," the duchess said bitterly. "There were those in London who wanted us sent to the Falklands."

In Mrs. Roosevelt's own bedroom, though grand in size,

the paint was peeling from the walls. There was no closet. In the bathroom, the black-stained toilet was flushed by pulling a chain. When she entered, huge insects skittered around inside the rust-stained bathtub, and some took refuge from her intrusion by sliding down the drain.

"Paradise compared to the broom closet they've assigned to your personal maid," said Jean King. "Do you mind if I take a bath in your rusty horse trough? Otherwise—would you believe this?—I'm supposed to trot down to the waterfront with my towel and a bar of soap, strip starkers, and do my bathing in the great briny. The household staff does it that way."

"Use the tub, of course," said Mrs. Roosevelt. "I'm anxious to see if water really comes from those corroded old taps. I'm sure all of us need a bath. The heat—"

"The Brits are paid a hardship allowance above their pay, for serving in a primitive environment and a tropical climate," said Jean King. "You suppose . . . ?"

"Certain congressmen," said Mrs. Roosevelt, "will suggest you should not be paid at all, since you are spending your time in a tropical paradise."

Jean King laughed. She sat down without being invited, spread her legs wide, and used a woven fan to blow air up her skirt. "One of the locals told me a joke," she said. "It seems some prominent businessmen wanted to erect a statue in the middle of town—to honor, guess who? To honor Senator Volsted. Prohibition made just about every substantial fortune anyone has in these islands. From the passage of the Volsted Act to the repeal of Prohibition, the traffic in liquor from here to the States was worth tens of millions annually. In fact, during the twenties, the Bahamas imported more Scotch whisky than any other nation in the world. They ran it across waters in fast boats and—"

"And sometimes," said Mrs. Roosevelt with a smile, "made rendezvous with my husband's yacht, the *Larooco*, and delivered the liquors and wines he and his friends would enjoy until the next rendezvous could be arranged."

"They made huge fortunes," said Jean King.

"But sold at reasonable prices," said Mrs. Roosevelt.

The welcoming dinner that evening was served, not in decrepit Government House, but at the Diamond Beach Club, the most prestigious social club in the Bahamas. Everyone who was anyone in the Bahamas Islands was invited, and Mrs. Roosevelt stood in a receiving line for a full hour, shaking hands, smiling amiably, and chatting with ten times as many people as she would ever remember.

She noticed—since the duchess had said that five-sixths of the population was Negro—that every guest at the cocktail party and dinner was white. The whites were dressed in white—white dinner jackets, white tropical uniforms with decorations, the women in white gowns. The Duke of Windsor appeared in the white dress uniform of a British admiral, the duchess in a stunning gown of white silk, with diamonds set in white gold lavishly displayed on her ears, at her throat, and on her wrists. Most of the women here curtseyed to the duchess, and Mrs. Roosevelt—two places away from her in the receiving line—could hear that in this crowd she was "Your Royal Highness."

Kenneth Krouse slipped up to the First Lady's side after the receiving line disbanded. "The Bay Street boys," he muttered to her. When she looked down into his cherubic face, he supplemented the statement. "This crowd. Two kinds, and watch out. The old money was made smuggling booze from here to the States during Prohibition. The new money is making it now—from the war."

Mrs. Roosevelt smiled at him. "There will be time later for you to expand on that," she said.

At the dinner table Mrs. Roosevelt found herself seated between the duke and duchess. They were pleasant company. The duke spoke of visits to the States when he was Prince of Wales.

"I might have met the duchess ten years earlier," he said. "She was in San Diego when I visited there in 1920. An interesting town, incidentally. But she saw me from afar. If only—Well . . . Probably, if truth be known, I could have done nothing about it then. But it *is* distressing to think of the years we spent apart, that we could have spent together had the fates been kinder."

Mrs. Roosevelt saw in the duke, no matter what the conversation, an undeviating disposition to wistful reflection. It was as though his mind was always half occupied with what might have been. She could not say he was unhappy. To the contrary, he seemed profoundly happy with the duchess, and the two of them constantly exchanged little tokens of affection: glances, touches, soft words. But he did not seem ever entirely focused on the here and now.

"You realize," said the duchess to Mrs. Roosevelt, "that this war need not have been, *and would not have been*, if my husband had remained on the throne."

"His Royal Highness explained to me his theory of how the democracies must cope with Mr. Hitler," said Mrs. Roosevelt.

"As Prince of Wales," said the duchess, "he was at pains to cultivate the friendship of Signor Mussolini. If Mussolini had allied himself with Britain, instead of being driven into the hands of Hitler, there would have been no Axis, and Hitler would never have dared his major adventures."

"An interesting theory," said Mrs. Roosevelt.

"Not a theory," said the duchess, not sharply but with firm conviction. "Those who drove my husband from the throne are responsible for the war. *He* could have prevented it."

Mrs. Roosevelt did not comment. Certainly she would not argue the point. It was apparent you couldn't disabuse the duchess of her conviction, and to try would have risked a rancorous argument.

"The local government," said the duchess, "has appropriated money for the refurbishing of that ghastly house. Obviously we will have to spend five times as much from our own funds. I do have hopes, though, of making it a livable home for the duke. We'll be moving out soon and will be living with friends until the remodeling is completed. I am sorry you have to endure the place in its present state."

"I am sure," said Mrs. Roosevelt, "it can be made into a lovely home."

"Fortunately there are people with money in Nassau," said the duchess. "You met Gunnar Torstenson in the receiving line. As soon as this dinner is over, we'll walk down the dock and go aboard his yacht for a party. A charming man. Very wealthy and very well connected."

Mrs. Roosevelt was no expert judge of the size of yachts, but she estimated the length of Torstenson's *Christina* as more than two hundred feet. Steam powered, it was in every respect a small ship; and it was substantially larger than any other yacht in the harbor.

The *Christina* was painted white. A fat yellow funnel

stood amidships, and two vestigial masts stood on the fore and aft decks—not tall or strong enough to carry sails but ample for pennants and flags and for the radio antenna that was strung between them. Four big, canvas-covered lifeboats rode atop the aft cabin, roped to davits that could swing them out and lower them. The blue and yellow flag of Sweden hung above the stern—a somewhat bigger flag than a yacht would normally fly there, apparently meant to give prominent notice to anyone who saw the yacht that it was from a neutral nation.

The duchess's girlish enthusiasm was conspicuous as she climbed the gangplank and received a courtly bow and a kiss on the hand from Gunnar Torstenson. He extended the same courtesies to Mrs. Roosevelt.

"I am honored," he said, "to welcome you aboard my little boat."

Torstenson, if Mrs. Roosevelt judged correctly, was about fifty-five years old. He was short and compact, a very small man actually. No one would have accused him of being handsome—his nose was sharp, his lower lip tended to form a point like the lip of an elephant, his jowls and the flesh under his chin were loose and shook when he talked—but there was in the man something engaging, appealing, that augmented the weak impact of his unprepossessing appearance.

It would have been easy to like the man, except that Mrs. Roosevelt recalled vividly, almost verbatim, an intelligence report on him, provided by Ambassador Lothian. The report had been transmitted to him by the foreign secretary, Lord Halifax, who gave him the authority to pass it on to the State Department. The significant words were:

Mr. Gunnar Torstenson is director-in-chief of Vellinck-Torstenson Associates, Ltd., a Swedish company engaged principally in the manufacture of high-quality steel machined parts, in particular ball bearings important in the manufacture of aircraft engines. Germany has no internal source of this type of bearing and relies on companies like Torstenson Associates to provide them. Although the Swedish government, anxious to maintain its neutrality, is doing everything reasonably within its power to prevent the exportation of bearings to Germany, they are nevertheless being supplied to German factories by Torstenson and other companies, through smuggling aboard fishing vessels, personal pleasure craft, ferry boats, etc.

Mr. Torstenson is widely understood to be a confirmed Nazi sympathizer. He is a long-time personal friend of Hermann Göring, through Göring's first wife, the Swedishwoman Karin Krantzow. When he visits Germany he is invariably received by Göring and other high-ranking Nazis.

We are also concerned about his operation of a large yacht in Bahamian waters. The yacht carries far more radio equipment than is appropriate for a pleasure craft, and monitoring stations have picked up transmissions from the yacht in a code which it has not been possible to break. It is not unlikely that observations of shipping and particularly of the movement of naval vessels are transmitted to German submarines lying off the North American continent. Communicate to the State Department our concern that the Torstenson yacht may be used as an observation vessel to watch American naval movements in and out of the Bahamian and West Indian bases we have newly leased to the United States.

One member of the crew of the Torstenson yacht

has been identified as a German naval officer. There is reason to believe several other members may be German nationals.

Finally, we are concerned about the close personal friendship between Mr. Torstenson and the Duke and Duchess of Windsor. It is not beyond the realm of possibility that the duke and duchess might be carried to the United States aboard the Torstenson yacht, in spite of our firm orders to the duke that he is to remain at his post as governor until he has specific authorization to leave. You will recall that when the duke was posted as a liaison officer to the French army in the early days of the war, he abandoned his post whenever he wished, often to return to Paris for dinners and parties with Nazi sympathizers. We are not certain what mischief resulted, but his social life at that time was to the distinct disadvantage of his country—which, let me hasten to add, he probably did not realize.

Torstenson led Mrs. Roosevelt and the Duchess of Windsor through the yacht's midships saloon, then through the dining room, before emerging into the big aft lounge, the site of the gala party.

Except for being long and narrow, the lounge could have been situated in any first-class hotel. It accommodated perhaps fifty guests comfortably—a selection from those who had attended the dinner at the Diamond Beach Club, plus some others who had not. A long bar, tended by a pair of young men in white jackets, was covered with bottles of liquor and wines, with bottles of champagne standing in silver buckets of ice. A table was spread with a lavish supper. In spite of the fact that most of the guests had just left a complete dinner, preceded by a cocktail reception, almost everyone was eating hungrily and drinking thirstily.

The Duchess of Windsor swept into the crowd as though all of them were her lifelong friends. The men bowed to her, and most of the women curtseyed. The duke beamed. This was the kind of honor he wanted the duchess to receive.

Commander Wilson MacGruder, who looked something like Ernest Hemingway, was drinking like Ernest Hemingway, and Kenneth Krouse seemed to have no inhibitions on that score, either. Only the Secret Service man, Alex Zaferakes, seemed to feel he was on duty; he stayed near, but inconspicuous, and kept a wary eye on the people who approached the First Lady. Of Mrs. Roosevelt's staff, only Tommy Thompson and Jean King had not been invited. Tommy was, after all, just a secretary, and Jean, ostensibly, only a maid.

Though not invited to the party, the ostensible maid was also aboard the *Christina*. Wearing the uniform of the catering service that was serving the supper, Jean King was working in the kitchen of the yacht, on the waterline deck, below the dining room and lounge. As personnel from above came down with trays of empty platters and dirty glassware, a fat black woman named Hannah expertly refilled the platters, and Jean King inexpertly washed the glasses.

The job had been arranged for her by Lieutenant Kevin Hammet, Royal Navy, an intelligence officer working incognito and in mufti—nominally a clerk in a Nassau solicitor's office. He was her confidential contact.

"Ah don' think you wash many dishes befo'," said Hannah.

Jean, affecting a persona wholly alien to her, chewed

gum vigorously. "Gotta make the dough to get back to Miami," she said.

"Hee-hee. Boyfriend abandon you, I bet."

Jean nodded. "Yeah. High and dry. And took everything I had."

"Men," grumbled Hannah.

Jean disliked her uniform—gray dress with an unstylishly short skirt, starched white cap, white apron. She also disliked the one she wore as the First Lady's personal maid, which she'd had to put on as soon as she was established in Government House. That was a black dress, again with white cap and white apron. Mrs. Roosevelt told her not to wear it if she didn't want to, but it was a part of the deception, and Jean wore it.

She was a graduate of Smith College, with a major in modern languages. She spoke French and German fluently. Also, she had been a hurdler and might actually have competed for a place on the Olympic team, except that the 1940 Olympics had been cancelled because of the war in Europe.

"Hannah, I'm going to have to make a visit to the ladies' room," Jean said. "Back in a jiff."

"Take time fo' a cigarette, honey," said Hannah amiably.

Jean nodded and smiled her thanks, then left the kitchen, carrying a straw bag, supposedly her purse.

The head for crew women was forward. They had been shown where it was when they came aboard. The radio shack was on the top deck, between the funnel and the bridge. Jean walked forward, along a narrow passage. Amidships she found a ladder, and she climbed out of the hold of the yacht and to an open deck. She was forward of the funnel, well forward of the party in the aft lounge; and she paused and lit a cigarette. She leaned on the rail and pretended to stare across the harbor at other yachts.

A crewman walked past. She was a dishwasher from the catering service, on deck for a smoke, and as he passed her he gave her a light but bold slap on the rear. She pretended not to notice.

When the crewman was out of sight she flipped her cigarette overboard, turned to a ladder she had spotted, and climbed quickly to the upper deck.

The lifeboats were aft, the funnel was amidships, and the radio shack and bridge were forward. Dim lights burned behind portholes. The sharp odor of cigar smoke told her someone was inside one of the open doors—not in the radio shack, she hoped.

She heard a voice. A screen door opened. The man with the cigar stepped out on the deck, continuing his conversation through the screen.

It was in German. Not Swedish: German; and she understood it easily—

"As soon as the caterers are off the ship, we can start filling the lockers. The ice—"

"Has been ordered," said a voice from inside the screen door.

"To be delivered when?"

"As soon as we call for it. Within ten minutes."

"I don't want to stay at sea all day tomorrow. Herr Torstenson doesn't want us to stay at sea all day. I'd like to finish the business before dawn. But—Those drunken fools will be aboard too long, I am afraid."

"I think so," said the voice. "I think we'll have to make the run to Miami and then make the rendezvous tomorrow night."

"Risky," said the man on deck. "I don't like it. The *Christina* should not be used as a tender."

"Well, I feel sorry for the poor devils. Maybe you don't

realize, Herr Captain, what a load of fresh fruit and vegetables means to them."

"We could lose the ship," said the captain. "Very easily. There's a British cruiser between here and Bermuda. If he discovers what we're doing, he'll fire on us. He'll sink us, without hesitation."

The man on the other side of the screen door laughed. "Too bad we couldn't take the duke and duchess with us. And Mrs. Roosevelt. They wouldn't fire on us then. Or if they did—" He laughed again.

"Speaking of the duke and duchess and Mrs. Roosevelt," said the captain, "I am required to put in an appearance. A brief one, I hope. Stay awake, Lieutenant."

Jean hurried to edge her way around the funnel, to stay on the opposite side from the captain as he strode aft and went down a ladder to the main deck.

She crossed to the port side of the yacht, the side opposite the screen door where the lieutenant sat in a room behind the bridge—probably a chart room where the yacht's courses were plotted. She slipped along the bulkhead and risked looking in through a porthole. The lieutenant sat in fact in the captain's day cabin. An open bottle of brandy and two glasses sat on a table. The lieutenant's glass was full, and he was absorbed in a magazine.

Jean was confident she knew the location of the radio shack. It was identified by the wires extending from its roof to the antenna stretched between the two masts. She walked back and looked in another porthole. Though a small bulb burned in a socket on the ceiling, the radio operator was not there.

"What are you doing here?"

She spun around. A sailor stood staring at her accusingly, legs apart, hands on his hips.

Jean leered suggestively and tipped her head toward the door of the day cabin. "The lieutenant," she whispered.

The sailor shook his head. "I don't believe that," he said in a Swedish-accented voice.

"But—"

Her right hand shot forward, held rigidly flat, and three fingers plunged into the soft part of his throat, below his Adam's apple. The sailor choked, his breath stopped. He gagged. Her fist cracked him on the temple. Stunned, he staggered back against the bulkhead. Jean yanked the .38 snub-nosed revolver from her straw bag, raised it high, and brought the barrel and trigger guard down on the man's skull. He dropped and lay silent on the deck.

She had little time. The upper decks of the yacht were not deserted. She hurried around to the door of the radio shack. It was locked. She had anticipated that and set to work on the lock immediately with a steel pick designed for just this purpose. Fortunately, the lock was not complex. In half a minute it yielded, and she opened the door and entered the radio shack.

She found what she had been told to expect: sophisticated and powerful radio equipment. The *Christina* was equipped to transmit to receivers anywhere in the world. It was equipped also to transmit on the special low frequencies used by submerged submarines. A small but heavy safe, far too secure for her to attack, sat in one corner—the repository, obviously, of the operator's codes.

Jean tucked her pistol into the waistband of her apron. If she were caught here she might have to use it.

She set to work. With a screwdriver from her straw bag she removed the screws that held in place the covering panels of the biggest radio transmitter. In that floor-to-ceiling cabinet, scores of fist-sized vacuum tubes glowed with an eerie purple light. Their filaments glowed orange.

Jean had been trained in radio telegraphy and knew what the various circuits of the big transmitter were for. It was a straightforward layout, looking much like the big navy transmitters she had been shown in Washington.

She set to work. From the straw bag she withdrew several small packages, each one wrapped in a coil of wires. She also had two independent coils. She used those first. Locating the leads from the telegrapher's key that the operator would use to transmit his signals, she attached her wires to those leads with alligator clips. She snapped the bare ends of the wires together to be sure she got no spark. She unwrapped the first package from its coil of wires. Those wires, too, ended in alligator clips, and she attached the clips to the bare ends of the wires that led to the key leads. Then she pushed the little paper-wrapped package back among a rank of vacuum tubes.

She repeated the process until four packages were distributed throughout the big transmitter and their wires were attached to the key leads. Finally, she closed the cabinet and tightened the screws.

On the deck the sailor she had slugged was up on his hands and knees, crawling toward the door of the day cabin. Jean went down a ladder, passed through the saloon, and came out at the gangway that led down to the dock. She hurried down the gangway and crossed the dock into the shadows.

In the lounge, Gunnar Torstenson had introduced Captain Eric Lindeblad to Mrs. Roosevelt and to a few of the other guests. The Duke and Duchess of Windsor had already met him.

The duke had suggested that Captain Lindeblad and Commander MacGruder might have things to talk about, and he had more or less pushed them together.

"I am pleased, Commander, that your country will increase its naval force in Bahamian waters. I have been much concerned that *Christina* should not find itself in the middle of a contest between British destroyers and a German submarine or surface raider. We cannot afford to be misidentified. That is why we repainted the yacht white. We run with all lights blazing at night. Even so, we are nervous. Having a neutral naval force in these waters will do much to reassure us."

Captain Lindeblad spoke heavily accented English, but Commander MacGruder understood him. He understood more than the words.

"If the United States declared all waters within five hundred miles of its coastline a neutral zone and forbade the armed vessels of every nation from entering that zone, you would be even safer," said MacGruder.

"Ah. Is the United States considering doing this?"

"When our forces are in place," said MacGruder dryly.

"It will take a substantial squadron to enforce such a zone," said Lindeblad.

"A task force," said MacGruder. "Two carriers. Four or five cruisers. Maybe a battle wagon."

"You will put such a force in the West Indies?"

MacGruder shrugged. "If we're serious about our neutral zone," he said.

Mrs. Roosevelt was chatting with the Duchess of Windsor and a businessmen identified by Ken Krouse as one of the Bay Street boys. His name was Henry Chapman, and he was a rotund, flush-faced sixty-year-old, anxious to cultivate the image of businessman, all businessman, always

the businessman. He was a Canadian, and it was ru-
mored—said Krouse—that he had established his headquarters in the Bahamas to avoid Canadian wartime taxa-
tion.

"Your naval personnel may be assured," he said to Mrs.
Roosevelt, "that Nassau will see to it they have everything
they need for comfortable living when they're off duty. I
mean, we'll see to it that American movies are run, American food is available, and all like that. I've been in contact
with the Coca-Cola Company, to be sure we can import
enough Coke for the American boys."

"That is kind of you, Mr. Chapman," said Mrs. Roosevelt, even if she did wonder what kind of profit the man
hoped to make when he sold Coca-Cola to American naval
personnel.

"Mr. Chapman and Mr. Torstenson," said the Duchess
of Windsor, "are looking into the possibility of building
some houses for the wives and families of American naval
officers. That is important, I can tell you from experience.
I was a young navy wife back in the twenties."

"I can see," said Mrs. Roosevelt, "that the Bahamas Islands will really take our boys to heart."

Ken Krouse saw Captain Lindeblad smile and bow at Commander MacGruder, then hurry purposefully across the
lounge and out the door. Krouse checked his watch. He
stepped out on deck and stared down at the light and
shadow on the dock. The captain strode along the gangway and mounted a ladder to the upper deck. Krouse
checked his watch again and returned to the lounge.

Captain Lindeblad reached the day room. He found Lieutenant Valentin hovering over a crew member, holding a
wet towel to the man's head. The sailor clutched a snifter

of brandy between his hands and tipped it back for a great, noisy gulp.

"Was ist los, Herr Leutnant?"

Lieutenant Valentin replied in German, and the conversation was in German.

"Horn was attacked," said Valentin. "A woman tempted him, then he was struck by a man."

"Why?" the captain demanded curtly. "What is out of order on the ship?"

"Everything is in order," said Valentin. "I've had men checking everything."

"The radio room?"

"The safe has not been touched, Captain."

Lindeblad was known as a man with a formidable frown. Furrows appeared between his brows. His lips whitened and twisted. His tall forehead flushed, making a pronounced contrast with the cold pale blue of his eyes.

"Have another brandy, Horn," said the captain to the dazed sailor. "You come with me, Lieutenant."

Lindeblad led Valentin out on the gangway and to the radio room. Inside, he closed the door. He knelt before the safe and twisted the dial. In a moment he had it open, and he withdrew a blue-covered book with the swastika emblem of the Third Reich imprinted on it in gold leaf.

"I have obtained some information that must be transmitted to Berlin immediately," he said. "It must be encoded."

The process of encoding Lindeblad's report took a full ten minutes, and only after it was finished could Lieutenant Valentin sit down at the desk and face the telegrapher's key. He pulled a pair of earphones over his head. He listened for a moment, twisted a dial on the big cabinet beside him, then twisted another dial. He looked up at the captain, nodded, and put his right hand on the key.

Blinding white light escaped through the cracks and vents of the transmitter cabinet, followed instantly by choking white smoke. The two men scrambled backward, Valentin pulling the wire to his earphones with him, until the plug popped from its socket. Lindeblad fumbled awkwardly with the door knob, twisting it back and forth until it released the latch, and he threw his shoulder against the door and staggered out onto the gangway. Valentin followed, pushing the captain out of his way.

Backs to the rail, they stood open-mouthed, staring at the white and orange fire inside the transmitter cabinet.

"Fire alarm . . ." muttered Valentin.

"No! Get fire extinguishers. We put it out ourselves. No one must see what is being destroyed there. *No one!"*

"Someone knows," said Valentin grimly.

"Oh? Who?"

"The saboteur," said Valentin simply.

IV

Mrs. Roosevelt was ready to leave the yacht. She had stayed long enough to satisfy the demands of courtesy, and it was time to make a graceful exit. She could see that the duke and duchess were not going to leave soon; both of them were enjoying themselves, drinking, nibbling, chatting, laughing. It would be well, however, to tell them she was leaving, and she watched for a break in their conversations. Courtesy required, too, that she express her thanks to Mr. Gunnar Torstenson, and she looked around for him and didn't see him. He had left the lounge suddenly, a few minutes before, and had not returned.

Kenneth Krouse slipped up to her side. "There's a fire on board," he said very quietly.

"Serious?" she asked.

He shook his head. "They're trying to keep it secret. I don't know if they've got it out yet, but I suggest we stand close to the door."

Mrs. Roosevelt laughed. "Really, Mr. Krouse . . . Is the matter serious, or isn't it?"

Krouse sighed and glanced around. "It's up on the

bridge somewhere. Not spreading apparently. Nowhere near the fuel tanks. I don't think we're in any danger—unless someone sees smoke and panics."

"How do you know about this?"

"I stepped out for air. I could see them carrying fire extinguishers into a cabin behind the wheelhouse. There was fire inside it, and thick smoke. An officer saw me looking and made a point of running down and telling me it was nothing, a small fire, not to worry."

"That perhaps explains the sudden departure of Mr. Torstenson," said Mrs. Roosevelt. "I noticed that a sailor came up to him and that he hurried away from the party."

Krouse nodded.

Alex Zaferakes stepped closer. "Problem?" he asked.

Mrs. Roosevelt shook her head, conscious that the Secret Service agent was deeply concerned for her safety.

"I am thinking, Mr. Zaferakes," she said, "that I would like to return to Government House and go to bed."

"Transportation is thanks to the Windsors," said Zaferakes. "I'll ask if they have a car on the dock."

"Well, Mr. Krouse," said Mrs. Roosevelt as they watched Zaferakes walk purposefully toward the Duke of Windsor, "have you learned anything that Mr. Berle wanted to know?"

"We're in a nest of vipers," said Krouse.

"Surely, Mr. Krouse . . ."

The young man nodded. "No immediate danger," he said. "But a nest of vipers."

"Ah . . ." murmured Mrs. Roosevelt. "The duchess."

She had seen the Duchess of Windsor tilt back her head, emit a peal of laughter, and walk off toward the bar with her champagne glass extended toward the bartenders. Mrs. Roosevelt walked toward the duchess, meaning to speak her thanks and good-night.

"I really believe I should return to Government House," she said. "It has been a long day."

"Of course," said the duchess. "Forgive me if I've been preoccupied for the past half hour. These people—Well, you know. They *are* our subjects, as the duke puts it."

"Of course," said Mrs. Roosevelt

"We seem to be condemned to spend the next several years in their company," the duchess went on, "so we are under some obligation to make the best of it."

"I should like to thank Mr. Torstenson."

"Yes." The duchess looked around. "Hmm. Gunny seems to be absent. I'll give him your thanks. You will see a lot of him during your visit. He's been a godsend to the duke and me. I mean, there are *air-conditioned* state-rooms aboard this boat. I only wish we could somehow commandeer it and make it the governor's residence for the remainder of our stay here."

"Mr. Zaferakes went to inquire if there is a car on the dock," said Mrs. Roosevelt.

"Of course, yes. Let me show you. I'll take you to the car and give the driver orders to take you to Government House, then to return."

"Thank you."

Mrs. Roosevelt glanced around. It was plain that Commander MacGruder was not ready to leave. Kenneth Krouse was. Alex Zaferakes would of course accompany her. She nodded at Krouse and Zaferakes.

"David! Mrs. Roosevelt is leaving. Come say good-night."

The duke obeyed the summons. He broke away from a group of men and came across the lounge to smile and bow.

"We shall walk Mrs. Roosevelt down to the car," said the duchess.

They left the lounge and stepped out on the deck in the still, fragrant air of a tropical night—Mrs. Roosevelt and the Duke and Duchess of Windsor, followed by Krouse and Zaferakes. It was impossible not to stop and savor the black, starry night and the odor of millions of lush blossoms borne on a gentle breeze. Somewhere a Bahamian band made raucous music, but distance softened the sound and left only the beat, another evidence of the character of the islands.

Mrs. Roosevelt glanced to the upper deck, where Kenneth Krouse had said there had been a fire. She saw no evidence of it. An officer at the rail above saluted them insouciantly.

The duke stopped at the top of the gangplank to light a cigarette. Then the party began to make its way slowly down.

"I would like to—" The duchess had begun to speak, but abruptly she stopped. She clapped her hand to her mouth, and her eyes widened. *"My God!* What is that?"

She was pointing down, toward something floating in the water forward of the gangplank, where the hull curved away to the bow, leaving open water between the yacht and the dock. Mrs. Roosevelt looked. She had no doubt of what it was. A body floated facedown in the water: the body of a man in white dinner jacket and black trousers.

The Duchess of Windsor screamed.

The man was pulled from the water by two uniformed black officers of the Nassau police. When he was identified, he was carried on board *Christina* and laid out on the dining table. He was Gunnar Torstenson.

The cause of death was no mystery. Gunnar Torstenson had been struck on the back of the head with the cliché blunt object. It could have been a hammer, a wrench, a ball bat, a billy, a blackjack, a length of pipe, a maul, the butt of a pistol . . . He had been standing at the rail probably; and, having been struck and stunned, he was hoisted over the rail and dropped into the water. It had to have happened near the bow or stern, where the hull of the yacht was not hard against the dock.

"It happened aboard ship," said Captain Lindeblad, "and is therefore a matter of maritime law, within the jurisdiction of the captain."

"It happened in the harbor of the port of Nassau," said Chief Justice Sir William Melbourne, coldly and forcefully, "and is therefore a matter of Bahamian law, within the jurisdiction of the colonial courts."

"And within my jurisdiction," said Edgar Hopkins, Commissioner of Bahamian Police, a formidable black man whose broad face gleamed with sweat. He wore a white, tropical-weight suit, complete with vest, and he had put a white Panama hat aside on a table.

"I beg to differ," said Captain Lindeblad.

"Beg as you wish," said the police commissioner. "I have fourteen officers aboard. If you want to argue my authority in court, feel welcome to do so. In the meantime, jurisdiction is mine—*de facto* if not *de jure.*"

"Perhaps the governor has a word on the subject," said the captain.

They were standing in the dining room, with the ghastly corpse lying on its back in their midst. Mrs. Roosevelt was there, with Kenneth Krouse and Alex Zaferakes. The Duke and Duchess of Windsor hung back, obviously unwilling to confront the body. Besides Captain Lindeblad, Lieutenant Valentin was in the room.

"David!" the duchess hissed, more audibly than she had intended.

"Uh, yes . . . uh," the duke muttered.

"Jurisdiction, Your Royal Highness," said Sir William.

"Uh, yes. Well, of course. It is . . . as you say. You are the chief justice. And, uh—" The duke displayed a small, toothy, nervous smile. "The commissioner does have his officers on board. And, uh, the crime was committed in— In, uh, how would you put it?"

"Within the territorial waters and the jurisdiction of the colonial government," said Sir William with scornful precision.

"Quite so," said the duke.

"Then seek the woman," said Captain Lindeblad to Commissioner Hopkins.

"What woman, Captain?"

"One of my crewmen, a sailor, was assaulted and injured this evening, in a matter not unlike what happened to Mr. Torstenson. That is to say, he was struck from behind with a blunt object. *He* survived the attack, possibly because she attacked him on an upper deck and was unable to heave him over the rail."

"A woman . . ." the commissioner mused. "How do you know it was a woman?"

"My sailor," said the captain, "was struck first in the throat, then on the side of the head, finally on the back of the head with some sort of bludgeon. He said at first that a man hit him, because he was ashamed to admit a woman had knocked him senseless. He has since admitted it was only a woman. Find that woman, Commissioner, and you have found the woman who murdered Mr. Torstenson."

"Not necessarily," said Mrs. Roosevelt. "Mr. Torstenson was first struck, one would assume, then lifted over a chest-high rail. I should guess his weight at one hundred forty or fifty pounds. We may assume he did not struggle, so he was—forgive this if it sounds like a pun; it is not so intended—dead weight. I am not sure *I* could lift a hundred forty pounds that high."

"I know I could not," said the Duchess of Windsor in a strained, high voice.

"Then our crime is not so easily solved," said Commissioner Hopkins. "Anyway, who is this woman, and where is she?"

Captain Lindeblad shook his head. "My crewman describes her as of medium height, perhaps less than medium weight, with short hair, and oddly dressed—that is, she was wearing a white cap and a white apron."

"Less than medium weight," said the chief justice quietly. "Too slight, then, to have heaved a man of Torstenson's size overboard."

"A facile inference, if you don't mind my saying so," said Mrs. Roosevelt. "I suggested we should not jump to the conclusion this woman committed the crime. I now suggest we don't jump to the conclusion she did not."

"Are we to understand that Mrs. Roosevelt is a detective?" asked Captain Lindeblad.

"As a matter of fact," said Kenneth Krouse, "Mrs. Roosevelt has made very useful contributions to the solution of some difficult murder mysteries in the States. Last autumn she literally saved the life of a young Englishwoman who was all but convicted of murder until Mrs. Roosevelt took an interest in the case and demonstrated that she could not have done it."

"Indeed," said Commissioner Hopkins. "Well, for my part, I should be happy to have your assistance, Mrs. Roosevelt. If you have insights that can help me, please feel more than welcome to communicate them to me."

Mrs. Roosevelt smiled. "I don't want to intermeddle," she said. "I must confess, though, that mysteries like the one that seems to confront us are fascinating intellectual challenges. If I can help—"

"Ah, but—" the duchess interjected. "We have a schedule of diplomatic engagements for you. It—"

"I shall not neglect my official duties," said Mrs. Roosevelt.

The body was covered, but it remained on the dining table, under a white sheet, a gruesome reminder of the gloomy duty that now had to be performed: an inquiry into murder.

Mrs. Roosevelt remained, so the Duke and Duchess of Windsor remained, both of them sitting on chairs they had dragged away from the table, she sipping champagne, he sipping whisky.

It had occurred to everyone that the woman who had struck the sailor on the upper deck was wearing the uniform of the caterers who had brought tonight's supper aboard *Christina.* The police commissioner had sent a man below, and he had returned with Hannah.

"She nevah work for us befo'," said the chubby black woman. "She ain' work for us no mo', either, I say sure. She walk off, leave a *ton* o' deeshes to wash."

"Who was she?" the commissioner asked.

Hannah shrugged. "Say her boyfriend, he done went off an' left her, took her money, too. Say she gotta work to pay her passage back to Miami. That all she say."

"Describe her."

"She 'bout so high, not much taller'n me. Skinny li'l thing. Brown hair. Got them spots white folks gits on they face—what y' call freckles. Jus' walk off. Went out to go bathroom and fo' a smoke, an' nevah come back."

"Would you know her if you saw her again?"

"You bet."

The sailor, Horn, didn't add anything to the description—except he suggested his attacker was maybe a man in woman's clothes. A woman, he said, couldn't hit that hard.

"I am most curious," said Mrs. Roosevelt, "to know why someone should have attacked you, Mr. Horn. Do you have any idea?"

"She was where she shouldn't have been," said Horn.

"Yes, on the upper deck," said Mrs. Roosevelt. "Where there was a fire also. Tell us about the fire, Captain."

Lindeblad shrugged. "A minor incident. A short circuit in one of the radio transmitters."

"Much damage?"

"Well, it destroyed the transmitter."

"I believe I'd like to see that," said Commissioner Hopkins. "I mean, the damage done by the fire."

"A matter of no consequence," said the captain firmly.

"Ah, but if this woman attacked a sailor, perhaps killed Mr. Torstenson . . . perhaps set a fire . . ."

"She did not set a fire," said the captain.

"Even so, I should like to see the scene of the fire," said the commissioner, rising from his chair.

"I must protest," said Captain Lindeblad. "This is a neutral vessel. I—"

"We shall see it," said the commissioner. "Mrs. Roosevelt? Would you like to see the damage to the yacht's radio room?"

"Well . . . yes. I would."

"So would I," said Kenneth Krouse.

"I protest!"

The commissioner smiled and nodded. "Your protest is noted."

"Actually, perhaps . . . ," the duke ventured. "It is, of course, a neutral vessel. Perhaps international law—"

No one was listening. Commissioner Hopkins, with Mrs. Roosevelt and Krouse, had already left the room.

"More forceful, damnit!" the duchess growled to the duke.

The big steel cabinet that had held the powerful transmitter had partially collapsed from the intense heat generated by Thermit. The radio inside was totally destroyed—tubes exploded, wires burned, chassis warped and melted. It was obvious that the radio had not been destroyed by a fire that resulted from a short circuit, so obvious the captain had lied that no one mentioned it.

"I cannot but be curious," said Commissioner Hopkins to Captain Lindeblad, "as to why a pleasure yacht should have carried what was obviously an extremely powerful radio transmitter."

"Mr. Torstenson had worldwide business interests," said Captain Lindeblad. "We received and transmitted business communications of all kinds. We could talk to Stockholm with this radio."

"Word of his death," said Krouse, "will have to be transmitted by regular radio-telegraph service."

The captain laid a cold, even hostile glance on Krouse. "I am afraid so," he said.

"What will you do now, Captain?" asked Mrs. Roosevelt. "Where will you take the yacht?"

"Back to Sweden as soon as possible," said the captain. "I think I should take the body with me—if it can be immediately embalmed. Vellinck-Torstenson Associates will want the yacht returned to Stockholm."

"I am afraid you cannot leave Nassau for a few days at least," said Commissioner Hopkins. "Until we have learned who killed Mr. Torstenson. And why."

"That could take weeks," the captain protested.

"I think not. But if it does, we will reconsider."

They did not return to the dining room and the presence of the corpse of Gunnar Torstenson but went instead to the lounge, where now no one was left but the duke and duchess and Henry Chapman, the Bay Street businessman who had promised to import Coca-Cola for the Americans who would be stationed in the Bahamas. Commander MacGruder and Consul Dye had left the yacht, as had the chief justice. Mrs. Roosevelt, Krouse, and Zaferakes were all that were left of the American party.

Although the duchess watched with tight-lipped disapproval, the duke was filling a plate with crackers and caviar, bits of smoked salmon, and a few smoked oysters. He had poured gin over ice.

"I say, Hopkins. Isn't there some principle of international law involved here? *Christina* is a neutral vessel, after all."

Commissioner Hopkins nodded at the captain. "So Captain Lindeblad is constantly reminding me," he said. "But a crime has been committed—the most serious crime: murder. Anyway, Captain Lindeblad is of course as much interested as I am in learning who killed the owner of this fine yacht, and why. We will expedite the investigation, Your Royal Highness, so that the vessel may not be impounded any longer than necessary."

"We are impounded?" asked Lindeblad.

"Yes," said the commissioner.

"Your Royal Highness," said the captain, speaking directly and exclusively to the duke. "What is happening here is a serious breach of Swedish neutrality. My government will protest in the most strenuous terms."

"We should take that very seriously," said the duke to the commissioner.

"I do, Sir. You may feel assured."

"It should be possible to release *Christina* tomorrow, don't you think?" said the duke.

"I shall ask for instructions from London," said Commissioner Hopkins.

"You can take your instructions from the governor," snapped the duchess.

The commissioner bowed slightly to the duchess, then to the duke. "Have I instructions, Sir?" he asked. "Or just a suggestion?"

"Uh . . . well—Consider it a firm suggestion," said the duke.

"Thank you, Sir," said the commissioner. Then he spoke to Captain Lindeblad. "Consider the vessel impounded. I will release it as soon as possible."

"You can obtain a court order for the release of the yacht," said Henry Chapman to the captain.

"Ah," said Commissioner Hopkins. "Yes, of course. In which case I shall be required to ask for instructions from London."

"Keep London *out of it*," protested the duchess.

Commissioner Hopkins poured a generous splash of rum over ice. It was his first drink since coming aboard, and he took a big swallow and stared into the glass with discernible satisfaction. "We shall remove the body to the hospital for an autopsy," he said to Captain Lindeblad. "After that process is complete, we will follow your instructions. You say you want it embalmed?"

"And sealed in a suitable coffin," said Lindeblad. "We will take it home."

The commissioner finished his drink. "Then we are finished for tonight," he said. He nodded at Mrs. Roosevelt. "I am grateful for your help. I am honored to have met you."

* * *

It was almost two in the morning when Mrs. Roosevelt accompanied the Duke and Duchess of Windsor to their car, which waited on the dock. Alex Zaferakes took a seat in front with the chauffeur. Commissioner Hopkins offered to drop Kenneth Krouse at Government House, so the commissioner's car followed the governor's.

A heavy glass separated the passengers in the rear of the governor's Rolls-Royce from the chauffeur's seat in front. Even so, the duchess spoke in a low voice, as if she thought the men in front might hear.

"I can tell you who murdered Gunnar Torstenson," she said to Mrs. Roosevelt. "I can tell you also that the identity of the murderer will never be revealed."

"Indeed?" asked Mrs. Roosevelt.

"I don't think we can be certain," said the duke.

"I can be *quite* certain," said the duchess crisply. "He was murdered by the British government, probably on specific orders from Winston Churchill."

"Oh, I don't think so, darling," said the duke quietly.

"*I* think so," the duchess insisted. She turned to Mrs. Roosevelt. "We are in fact prisoners on this wretched island. Gunnar Torstenson had offered us his yacht, to take us anywhere we wanted to go. One day we would have gone to Miami, then to Washington and Baltimore—which is my home town—and New York. We have a message to deliver to the people of the United States, and the British government will do anything to prevent us."

"Not including murder, my dear," said the duke.

"Not excluding anything," said the duchess. "So there is no point in trying to find out who killed Gunnar Torstenson. It was an official assassination, and it will be adroitly covered up."

*   *   *

Though it was very late and there was a breakfast meeting to attend, Mrs. Roosevelt did not find it easy to sleep. After only a few minutes in bed, she rose and went to one of the tall windows of her bedroom. She looked up at the moon, then down at the lawn.

In the pale, cold light, the bright and friendly flowering shrubs took on a new and spectral look. A small animal scampered across the lawn, barely escaping the huge owl that swooped down for it and missed it as the little creature darted into the cover of a shrub.

Then she noticed someone standing in the shadow of a tall hedge. In a moment another person appeared, and the figure in the shadow stepped out into the moonlight. It was Kenneth Krouse. And the person who had come to meet him was Commander MacGruder. They stood for a moment, talking, then a third person appeared. That was Jean King!

Mrs. Roosevelt could not hear a word they said, of course, but from their choppy gestures she guessed that they were discussing something that excited them.

A . . . A slight woman with short brown hair—With freckles. Mrs. Roosevelt shook her head, trying to dismiss the thought. Still . . . A young woman with short brown hair . . . and freckles. And not just a maid. An intelligence officer attached to the United States Navy.

They talked intently for five minutes, then slipped away into the darkness of the shadows. A conspiratorial meeting in the middle of the night. Oh . . . Oh, let there be an innocent explanation!

V

The breakfast was for Bahamians, a few of them black, who had not been invited to the dinner at the Diamond Beach Club the evening before. Either they were not wealthy or they were not at the highest rank of Bahamian society.

Government House was in truly sorry state, and the household staff were not trained to the standards of the Duke and Duchess of Windsor; even so, the duchess was able to arrange an elegant buffet breakfast, introducing in fact a style which she could be confident would be mimicked by every hostess in the islands.

Because the swimming pool was empty of water and littered with debris, the buffet and tables were arranged on the lawn in front of the mansion. Immense watermelons had been scooped out and filled with balls of the red, orange, and green flesh of three kinds of melons. The flavor of the fruit had been subtly enhanced by pouring over it a sauce of melon juice into which a tiny quantity of raspberry brandy had been stirred. Besides fruit, breakfast was oysters and smoked salmon. And champagne. There was no bacon, no eggs, no toast, no coffee or tea, no orange juice.

"And no porridge," the duchess said with a sly smile. "It's not an American breakfast or an English one."

"Thank God for small blessings," said Ken Krouse, who had overheard her.

He was talking with Kevin Hammet, the Royal Navy intelligence officer who was working under cover in Nassau. Ostensibly he was a clerk in a solicitor's office. In fact, he was the man who had arranged for Jean King to go aboard the *Christina* as a dishwasher for the caterer.

Hammet—who saw nothing wrong with English breakfasts, or American ones either, for that matter, and who had no understanding of the American sense of humor—frowned curiously, then smiled as if he understood and agreed. He was a handsome, typically English young man—thin, blond, apple-cheeked, with the serious mien of an Eton and Cambridge man.

Krouse knew Hammet's real identity, as did Jean King and Commander MacGruder.

"Floating in the water, facedown, skull caved in," said Krouse quietly to Hammet, resuming the conversation he had interrupted by his comment on the breakfast.

"Yes, I know," said Hammet. "The governor issued an order this morning that no word of the murder was to be published in the island newspaper or broadcast on the radio station. But he was too late. The Nassau *Intelligencer* headlined it. Every literate person on the island knows about the murder. There is, I might tell you, a great deal of distress."

"More than normal?" asked Krouse dryly.

"More than you might expect," said Hammet. "A great many people were expecting big things of Gunnar Torstenson. Neutral investment, you know. We're awfully short of hard money at home—and spending what we've got to buy American manufactures. A few Swedes, though, are profiting immensely from the war. Companies like Vellinck-Torstenson. I suspect, though I can't prove it, that Torstenson intended to use Bahamian banks to conceal illegal transactions."

"Deals in machine parts?" Krouse asked. "Bearings?"

"Things like that. And outright sales of arms and ammunition. Swedish law prohibits sales of that sort of materiel to the belligerents of either side. Swedish companies engaged in such sales have to conceal the proceeds somehow."

"So they . . . ?"

"The Germans pay in dollars, which they obtain from the sale of German manufactures to American corporations. The Swedes bring the dollars here, deposit them, and later withdraw them—calling them the revenues from business done in the Western Hemisphere. The Panamanians and Cubans, to use two examples, cooperate with them in this. I mean, those countries allow Swedish businessmen to show on their books huge profits from Swedish investments there, when in fact the businesses are marginal at best."

"Why the Bahamas?"

"What better place?" asked Hammet. "A British colony. But one with a business community that is generally sympathetic to the German cause—simply because the war costs businessmen money. I would remind you, Mr. Krouse, that your own Henry Ford is but one big American businessman sympathetic to Germany—again, just because he makes a lot of money trading with Germany."

"Germany is not our enemy, don't forget," said Krouse. "Not officially. Not yet."

The young naval officer had some training in diplomacy, too, and did not respond to the comment. "Even so," he said, "it is difficult to imagine who might have killed Gunnar Torstenson."

Captain Eric Lindeblad, in civilian clothes—a light-blue suit—tipped the shell of an oyster and poured the succulent meat into his mouth. The Duchess of Windsor watched, with a conspicuously critical eye on the technique with which the captain ate an oyster, and waited for him to swallow it and a following sip of champagne.

"Oh, Mrs. Roosevelt," she said, seeing that the First Lady was approaching, accompanied by Commander MacGruder. "I hope I haven't been neglecting you."

"Not at all," said Mrs. Roosevelt. "I have met many interesting people."

The duchess smiled wryly. "In the Bahamas? Surely—"

Mrs. Roosevelt ignored the comment, as did Captain Lindeblad, who bowed to her and used a napkin to wipe his mouth.

"I hope your repairs are going well," said Mrs. Roosevelt to the captain.

"The radio is irreplaceable," he said. "That is to say, it cannot be replaced in the Bahamas, nor indeed I think in the West Indies."

"Perhaps in the States," said Mrs. Roosevelt.

"Yes. As soon as we are released from the custody of the Nassau Commissioner of Police—"

"That is intolerable!" shrieked the duchess. "My husband will issue firm orders to Commissioner Hopkins."

"I should be most grateful," said Captain Lindeblad with a small bow.

"In any case," said the duchess, some of the wind gone from her sails, "I would be grateful to you, Captain, if we can continue to use the *Christina* for parties and the like.

Mr. Torstenson had put the ship at the complete disposal of the duke and me."

The captain bowed to her. "Until we are authorized to return to Stockholm, *Christina* is at your disposal, as Mr. Torstenson wished," he said.

"My husband," said the duchess to Mrs. Roosevelt, "has always wanted to own a fine yacht. Unhappily, his mother and brother have left us so poor we cannot afford it."

The publisher and editor-in-chief of the Nassau *Intelligencer* was a tall, long-faced, black man named Junius Gerald. His skin was walnut-colored, his hair short and kinky, his eyes calm and penetrating, his mouth wide, his lips thick. Characteristically, he clasped his hands before his face, with his two index fingers extending upward and pressed to the tip of his nose, as he turned down the corners of his mouth and frowned and pondered.

"They had just as soon you not meet me," he said to Mrs. Roosevelt as soon as they could have a word apart. "On the other hand"—he shrugged and showed her a small smile—"they could not omit my name from the invitation list. Not this morning."

Mrs. Roosevelt could not respond to that. She, too, smiled; and she said, "In any event, Mr. Gerald, we have met. I understand you have published a full account of last night's tragedy."

"You might think," said Junius Gerald, "that we never experience murders in the Bahamas. As a matter of fact, we do. Poor Negroes, you know, often settle their little personal differences with knives or spears. I—"

"Mr. Gerald, it can—"

"And," he went on forcefully, "the whites in the big houses do succumb to the tropical heat from time to time and use their pistols. Why, only eight months ago a charming English matron named Lydia Gloucester shot her husband in his bed. She was taken back to London, tried there, and hanged. They would like to have you believe it never happens."

"I cannot be cynical about such a terrible tragedy," said Mrs. Roosevelt.

"It is unfortunate," he said, "that this bit of nastiness should have occurred during your visit."

"That thought occurred to me, Mr. Gerald."

"It is not impossible that it was arranged to happen during your visit."

"Indeed? Why?"

Junius Gerald accepted a glass of champagne from a tray, took an experimental sort of sip, and frowned as if he did not find it acceptable. "A significant state visit," he said. "The investigation will be kept as unobtrusive as possible. The inquest will be postponed until after you have left. In the excitement of a visit by the First Lady—only a little short of the excitement that would be produced by a visit from the King—much may be overlooked."

"And someone wants something overlooked?"

"There is much to be overlooked in the Bahamas," said Junius Gerald. "A small, tight community—but one with many scandals." He shrugged. "Like any small community."

"Be specific, Mr. Gerald," said Mrs. Roosevelt.

"Mr. Torstenson was introducing a great deal of money into the islands," said Junius Gerald. "Big money outbids lesser money. Business opportunities go to the highest bidder. People who are outbid, who lose big profits they had dreamed of, become bitter. Even hostile."

"Even capable of committing murder?"

"Even that," he said grimly.

"Do you have someone in mind? A specific suspect?"

"I have, but since I haven't the evidence to make the case, I won't say who it is."

"In any event, Mr. Gerald, do you feel the Bahamas Islands are fortunate in having the Duke of Windsor as governor?"

"We might be if it weren't for the war."

"How is that?"

"If not for the war, he would be a tourist attraction," said Junius Gerald. "Otherwise . . ." He shrugged.

"I find you a bit cynical, Mr. Gerald."

"Forgive me, I don't mean to be cynical," said Junius Gerald. "May I ask if you would be willing to attend a party given by—How shall I call us? The native citizens of Nassau?"

"I should be pleased to attend," said Mrs. Roosevelt, "so long as you don't insist the Negro citizens are the native citizens. Africans and Europeans are equally newcomers here."

Junius Gerald smiled. "Let me put it differently. The majority citizens of Nassau."

"I shall be honored to attend your party."

Jean King, wearing a black dress, white apron, and starched white cap, carried a tray of champagne glasses. The duchess, complaining of the inadequacy of the household staff, had asked Mrs. Roosevelt to allow her to borrow her maid to help serve at the breakfast party. Mrs. Roosevelt had felt she had no option but to comply, although she was apologetic to Jean when she asked her.

"You look fetching," said Ken Krouse ironically.

"Go to the devil," she muttered.

He shook his head and grinned. "It is *so* difficult to get good help these days."

"Well, see if you can find out something, you or Mac-Gruder," she said quietly and out of one corner of her mouth. "Who is the man talking with Henry Chapman over there?"

Krouse glanced at Chapman and the other man. "Okay," he said. "But why do we want to know?"

Jean sighed. "Tell you later. I've got to move. That skinny bitch the duchess is giving me a hard stare. I'm not supposed to talk with the guests."

Krouse watched her walk away, carrying her tray and offering champagne to guests. Then he ambled over to Chapman.

"Good morning, Mr. Chapman," he said. "Have you recovered from last night?"

Chapman tipped his head to one side and stared at Krouse as if for the moment he could not quite remember who he was and was in any event faintly annoyed. "Oh yes, Krouse," he said finally. He spoke to the other man. "Mr. Krouse is a personal aide to Mrs. Roosevelt," he explained.

Krouse extended his hand to the other man. "Kenneth Krouse," he said. "Department of State."

The other man hesitated for a perceptible instant, then said, "Curtis Wyler. I'm pleased to meet you."

"Mr. Wyler is a business associate of mine," said Chapman.

Krouse guessed Wyler was about forty years old. He was an exceptionally handsome man, with striking blue eyes, features strong and regular, a cleft chin—and a complexion that the tropical sun had not tanned but had turned a glowing pink.

"You are . . . English?" Krouse asked.

"Irish," said Wyler. "I don't spend much time in Ireland

of late years, but I am a citizen of the Republic of Ireland and carry an Irish passport."

"My curiosity was prompted by the accent," said Krouse conversationally.

"It does confuse people," said Wyler.

"Anyway, it's a pleasure to meet you," said Krouse. "Everyone I've met this morning has a theory as to who killed Gunnar Torstenson. Do you have one?"

Wyler shook his head. "I have not the faintest notion."

Ken Krouse walked into the mansion and through the hall toward the kitchen. Jean King was there, pouring champagne into a score of glasses on her big, round tray. He tipped his head toward the door that led out to a porch and to the empty swimming pool. She put down the bottle and went out.

"His name is Curtis Wyler. Chapman calls him a business associate."

"Ask Kevin Hammet who Curtis Wyler is."

"What's the difference? Why the interest in Curtis Wyler?"

"He was aboard *Christina* last night."

"A lot of people were aboard *Christina* last night."

"A lot of men in white dinner jackets," she said. "A few men in the uniforms of the crew. One man in blue-gray dungarees. I set the Thermit and started down toward the gangplank, and I almost got stopped by the man in dungarees. I ducked inside a doorway just in time. And . . . Something more important. He was in a hell of a hurry, wherever he was going. If he hadn't been, he would have noticed me."

"Significant . . . ?"

"*Ken!* A businessman, huh? In dungarees aboard the yacht, when Chapman and the others were partying in white dinner jackets? He was aboard the yacht when Torstenson was killed. Why? Ask Hammet who the guy really is!"

Commissioner Hopkins had watched for some time for an opportunity to approach Mrs. Roosevelt and have some conversation with her alone. Now he saw her chatting only with a Nassau merchant, one of the Bay Street boys, and he walked purposefully across the lawn and greeted her. The merchant, who had made it plain a long time ago, not only that he was uncomfortable in the presence of the commissioner of police but was unwilling to engage in any social intercourse with a black man, excused himself to Mrs. Roosevelt, nodded curtly at Hopkins, and strode away.

Hopkins had managed somehow to obtain a small glass of rum over ice, in preference to the champagne being constantly offered by two maids with trays. He sipped sparingly and said, "I should like to have your opinion of something. A confidential matter, of course."

"Having to do with the murder of Mr. Torstenson?" she asked.

He nodded. "Having to do with the murder of Mr. Torstenson. I have something in my pocket that I will hand to you in a moment. I would be grateful if you would examine it, tell me what you think it is, and return it to me—without anyone else seeing it."

She glanced around. "Well . . . This is not a very private place."

"I don't think we'll be interrupted. Most of the people here openly dislike me. They won't come near."

"Really, Commissioner—"

"I am the only Negro holding high office on this island," said Hopkins. "I was appointed because eighty per cent of the population is Negro, because Negroes commit their fair share of the crimes—which means eighty per cent at least—but mostly because it was assumed my appointment to so conspicuous a position of authority would do something to settle the unrest among the Negro population."

"I didn't know about the unrest," she said.

"Eighty per cent of the population owns six per cent of the wealth," said Commissioner Hopkins. "If you'd like to see squalor, I can show it to you. I doubt the governor will take you to see it."

"I should like to see," said Mrs. Roosevelt. "I should like to be able to help."

"Your presence will help," said Hopkins. "Those American newspaper reporters who came out with you will have to follow you and see, too. They will see that the Bahamas are a tropical paradise only for the wealthy— and a tropical hell for most of the population."

"Distressing . . ."

"Yes. Anyway, no one is looking. Let me hand you the object I should like for you to examine."

Commissioner Hopkins reached into the copious jacket pocket of his white double-breasted suit and withdrew an item of jewelry, which he handed to Mrs. Roosevelt. She gasped from surprise.

It was a platinum clip set with scores of tiny diamonds and sapphires, plus several larger stones. The design was three feathers—the heraldic emblem of the Prince of Wales. On the back it bore a date: 28/8/34—August 28, 1934. Also, it bore the tiny mark of its designer: Jacques Cartier.

"What is it, Mrs. Roosevelt?" asked Commissioner Hopkins. "What can you tell me about it?"

She drew a deep breath and shook her head. "In 1934 the man we now call Duke of Windsor was Prince of

Wales. There were stories that he gave Mrs. Simpson, as the duchess then was, gifts of valuable jewelry. This— Well . . . The three feathers are the emblem of the Prince of Wales. The date—He was by 1934 already in love with Mrs. Simpson. The signature is that of Cartier, the world-famous jeweler. The prince—the duke—is well known to be a frequent client of Jacques Cartier. So I have to guess that this is a gift from the present Duke of Windsor to Wallis Warfield Simpson, now Duchess of Windsor. How does it come to be in your jacket pocket, Commissioner?"

"*My* jacket pocket is not the question," said Commissioner Hopkins. "It was in the pocket of the water-soaked jacket of Gunnar Torstenson. It was in his pocket when he was killed."

"Or placed there by the someone who killed him," said Mrs. Roosevelt.

"Your mind works very rapidly in these matters," said Hopkins with a smile. "That is, of course, another distinct possibility. But, in either case, *why?*"

"Or placed there," said Mrs. Roosevelt, frowning, "while the body lay on the table in the dining room of the yacht."

"A third possibility," said the commissioner. "I like the first one best. In any case, *why?*"

"I'd like to know," she said.

"What would you estimate as the value of that piece?" he asked.

She handed it back to him. "Oh, I am no judge," she protested. "But . . . In sterling, I should estimate it is worth £5,000 at a very minimum, more likely £10,000—in my own terms, $25,000 to $50,000."

"And casually carried in Mr. Torstenson's jacket pocket," said the commissioner.

"Or planted there," said Mrs. Roosevelt.

"Yes. Or planted there."

"What will you do with it?" she asked.

"Obviously, I must return it to the duchess sooner or later. But not immediately, I think. I shall be curious to see whether or not she reports it stolen."

"Commissioner! Whatever do you have in mind?"

Commissioner Hopkins let a smile gradually develop on his broad, sweat-gleaming black face. "Nothing specific," he said. "But who knows what the duchess's action, or failure to act, may suggest?"

VI

Tommy Thompson caught up with Mrs. Roosevelt just at the end of the party, when she was shaking the hands of departing guests.

"Important," she whispered close to the First Lady's ear.

Mrs. Roosevelt excused herself and stepped aside. "What's important?"

"A coded wire from the President," said Tommy. "I, uh, took the liberty of decoding it."

She handed Mrs. Roosevelt a sheet of paper torn from a stenographer's pad, on which she had printed the message in crude capital letters as she had undertaken the laborious process of decoding. It read—

WORD RECEIVED OF MURDER OF SWEDE STOP
IMPERATIVE YOU NOT TAKE PART IN
INVESTIGATION STOP MATTER MAY
BE EXTREMELY COMPLEX AND
SENSITIVE STOP MUCH INVOLVED
THAT I CANNOT COMMUNICATE
BY WIRE STOP

Mrs. Roosevelt tore the sheet of paper into tiny bits, then stirred the bits around in the water in an ice bucket.

"The next item on the agenda," she said to Tommy, "is a tour of some of the government offices in Nassau, followed by a luncheon party at the Emerald Beach Club. I will advise the duke and duchess that I need a few minutes to bathe and change. Find Mr. Krouse, Commander MacGruder, and Miss King. I want to meet with them in my room."

A few minutes later the three were in her room, together with Alex Zaferakes who guarded the door to see that no one eavesdropped. Mrs. Roosevelt told these people about the President's wire.

"I should like to think—although I am not certain of it—that I was made privy to essentially the same information as you were, before we left Washington. We are all aware, I believe, of the possible pro-German sympathies, not only of the duke and duchess, but of a substantial part of the business community here in Nassau. I understand, too, that Mr. Torstenson shared such sympathies. Our concern is whether or not these islands swarm with Nazi spies. If Mr. Torstenson was suspected of being one, then who killed him? The duchess thinks the British government had him killed."

"The Duchess of Windsor," said Ken Krouse, "is obsessed with her bitterness toward the British government and the Royal Family."

"Even so . . . Is it possible?" asked Mrs. Roosevelt.

"Anything is possible," said Jean King.

"I must ask you a question, Miss King," said the First Lady. "Where were you last night about the hour when Mr. Torstenson was killed?"

Jean King smiled. "Do you suspect *I* killed him?"

"No. No, I don't. But where were you?"

Jean's smile broadened. "I was taking a bath in your rusty bathtub," she said.

Mrs. Roosevelt, too, smiled. "Good," she said.

"It will be necessary," said Commander MacGruder, "to report to the President that the Bahamas *are* swarming with German spies and that it may be necessary to do a thorough housecleaning job before American forces are stationed here."

"I know little about radio equipment," said Mrs. Roosevelt. "A little more about yachts. The radio that was destroyed on *Christina* last night was far more powerful than anything needed for business communication."

"A very large amount of ice melted on the yacht club's dock last night," said MacGruder.

"What is the significance of that?" asked the First Lady.

"*Christina* would have gone to sea today if Commissioner Hopkins had not impounded it," said the commander. "The ice would have been packed around a cargo of fresh fruits and vegetables that would have been carried in special ice boxes in the hold."

"Whatever for?"

"That yacht has powerful engines," said Commander MacGruder. "It moves fast and has long range. A twelve hours' cruise out of Nassau puts her on the Cuban coast. In the same twelve hours, she's well out in the Atlantic, beyond the Bahamas. Or in Biscayne Bay, Miami. In twenty-four hours she's off Haiti. Or far enough out on the Atlantic to be out of range of aerial surveillance. So—" He shrugged. "She makes rendezvous with German submarines and supplies them with fresh fruits and vegetables. What's more, she pumps diesel oil from her tanks into theirs. *Christina* has been serving as a German submarine tender."

"A neutral vessel owned by a citizen of a neutral nation?"

"Ma'am," said Ken Krouse. "In this war there are no neutrals."

"The United States is neutral, Mr. Krouse."

"Yes, Ma'am. I stand corrected. That's why we're trading fifty destroyers for the possibility of setting up naval bases on certain islands."

For a moment Mrs. Roosevelt frowned at Kenneth Krouse, uncertain how to respond. Then she smiled. "Yes, of course. Strict neutrality," she said.

"In any case," said Jean King, "the *Christina* was scheduled to go to sea today and to make a rendezvous with a German submarine."

"How do we know that, Miss King?"

Jean King glanced at Krouse, then at MacGruder. "I'm sorry," she said. "We have ways of knowing."

"Was Mr. Torstenson killed to prevent that rendezvous?" asked Mrs. Roosevelt.

"No," said Krouse emphatically. "Torstenson wouldn't have been aboard. He never went on those missions."

"There is a possibility," said Jean King, "that on one of those rendezvous missions the Windsors would have been transferred from the yacht to a submarine."

"You mean . . . ?"

"Kidnapped," said Jean King. "I mean, they would have gone to sea on the *Christina* voluntarily, then would have been put over onto a submarine without their consent. And taken to Germany."

"Why?" asked Mrs. Roosevelt. "I think I know, but— Well . . . say it, one of you."

Jean King answered. "Hitler expects to defeat England, then to return the Duke of Windsor to the throne. In the meanwhile, he thinks it would be a good idea to have the duke in Germany as head of a British government-in-exile. He thinks a certain portion of the British people would rally to such a government."

"Oh, surely this is fanciful!"

Ken Krouse spoke. "British intelligence doesn't think so. Winston Churchill doesn't think so."

"That is to say," said Jean King, "it's not fanciful to think Hitler has some such idea in mind—though it is wholly fanciful to think any significant element of the British public would accept it."

Mrs. Roosevelt shook her head. "But the duke and duchess would never—"

"Forgive me," said Jean King. "If the Duke and Duchess of Windsor are kept luxuriously housed, amply fed, their jewels are kept well polished, and they are amply assuaged with flattery—they will happily support any cause, any government, any ideology, with absolutely no exception."

"I believe you exaggerate," said Mrs. Roosevelt.

Jean King shrugged. "Maybe. A little. But I do not lie. That's the way it is."

Mrs. Roosevelt walked to the window of her bedroom and looked down. The governor's limousine waited, as did undoubtedly the duke and duchess, just inside the door.

"None of this explains the death of Mr. Torstenson," she said.

"Oh, it does," said Ken Krouse. "I'm sure it does. We just don't know how."

"You said we are in a nest of vipers, Mr. Krouse. Whom do we trust?"

"Commissioner of Police Edgar Hopkins," said Krouse. "He is not commissioner because the Bahamian establishment wanted him. Nor because he is a Negro, which he may offer as an explanation. He was appointed on the recommendation—let's say insistence—of British intelligence, who wanted a man they could trust. That's who we can trust."

"That's why he impounded the yacht," said Jean King. "He welcomed the opportunity. Otherwise, it might have been necessary for a British destroyer to sink it. And how do you explain that—*Christina* flying a Swedish flag and sending out frantic calls on that big radio?"

"I must go," said Mrs. Roosevelt. "You have given me much to think about."

It was true. More than they knew.

The governor's Rolls-Royce, flying flags on the front fender, was preceded by two motorcycle policemen and followed by a police car as it sped through the streets of Nassau. A white midday sun blazed in a pale-blue sky, and the wheels of the hurrying vehicles stirred a thin cloud of dust that hung for a moment, then quickly dispersed on the sea breeze.

The luncheon, the duchess explained to Mrs. Roosevelt in the car, was being given by the Bahamian Assembly in her honor. They would visit the chamber of the assembly, then the courtroom of the Bahamian Court, and finally the Royal Council Chamber, before proceeding on to the Emerald Beach Club.

The Duke of Windsor wore the khaki uniform of a general of the British army. The duchess was in style, in a white silk frock, with glittering jewelry at her throat and on her wrists. Mrs. Roosevelt wore white, too, with a broad-brimmed white straw hat. The windows of the car were closed against the dust, and the heat was cruel.

"I am a bit concerned about something," said Mrs. Roosevelt. "I am embarrassed to ask, but—"

"Don't be embarrassed to ask anything you like," said the duke in a kindly, sympathetic voice.

"Well . . . When I travel I carry with me a jewelled bracelet my husband gave me many years ago. It *is* rather valuable, but its value to me is chiefly sentimental. I was wondering—your household being so new—if you think there is any problem with keeping it in my room."

The Duke of Windsor chuckled. "We have to think about that wherever we go," he said. "Her Royal Highness is fond of jewels, and I am fond of giving them to her. But, no, we've had no problem with the household staff at Government House—though I will admit the thought occurred to us when we arrived."

"To have to carry a safe around is really too much trouble," said the duchess. "But fortunately, we've never lost anything."

"Yes," said Mrs. Roosevelt. "That is fortunate."

Kenneth Krouse, Commander Wilson MacGruder, and Alex Zaferakes followed the governor's motorcade and would accompany Mrs. Roosevelt on her midday schedule. The Duchess of Windsor felt some obligation to provide diversion for her guest's private secretary and arranged for the duke's equerry and his wife to take her shopping in Nassau, or at her option to a beach for swimming. Jean King remained at Government House—the uniformed maid whose presence at official functions was neither appropriate nor required.

Within ten minutes of the departure of the official party, Jean had changed out of her uniform and was on the road toward the center of town.

By the time she reached the offices of Wait & Harrington, solicitors, she was dusty and sweaty—and angry. She climbed the narrow wooden steps from the street to the offices.

"Mr. Hammet, please."

"He is engaged at the moment. Is he expecting you?"

"Yes, he is. Tell him Miss Queen is here."

"Miss Queen? Are you a client?"

"I may become one, if someone will stop asking questions and tell Mr. Hammet I am here."

A moment later the solemn young intelligence officer appeared. "Uh—Miss Queen?"

He knew very well who she was. It was important that no one in the offices of Wait & Harrington know who either of them was.

"Yes. I require the advice of a solicitor," said Jean King. "I was told I should present the matter to you first."

"Of course," said Hammet.

He offered her the best chair he could, a straight-backed wooden chair in a tiny office where an oscillating fan stirred the damp air.

"We've played too boldly," she said, as soon as she was seated.

He had a pitcher of iced tea on the desk, and without asking if she wanted any, he poured her a glass and added ice from an insulated bucket. "The death of Torstenson changed everything," he said. "What wasn't too bold suddenly became too bold."

"The duchess is saying that you killed Torstenson—that is, that British intelligence did it."

Hammet all but ignored the information. He changed the subject. "This afternoon," he said, "Mrs. Roosevelt is going to meet another good friend of the Windsors. Isidro Gutiérrez. Does the name mean anything to you?"

"The Mexican," she said.

Hammet nodded. "We are not sure why he has come to

the Bahamas, but you can be certain it is not for a vacation in the sun. In fact, I think we are about to see some other visitors."

"I am not certain. I don't want to speculate. But something interesting is going on, which may or may not have anything to do with the murder of Gunnar Torstenson. I should like to tell you what we know about Isidro Gutiérrez. I doubt that Mrs. Roosevelt was informed about him before she left Washington. I hope you can warn her."

"Warn her . . . ?"

"The Germans have always thought of Mexico as a fertile field for conspiracy. They thought so during World War I, you'll recall. They read about how Mexicans despise *gringos*, and they scheme to turn that hatred into an asset for their ambitions. Gutiérrez is a very wealthy man—which of course automatically wins him the sympathy of the Windsors. We have intercepted some correspondence that suggests that a consortium of American, Mexican, and German businessmen may be in the process of formation. The purpose would be to fund a pro-Nazi movement, not just in Mexico, but throughout Latin America. It is possible that Torstenson was a member of this consortium. It is also possible that he was somehow blocking it and was killed to put him out of the way. He—"

"But what has this to do with the Duke and Duchess of Windsor?"

"The duke might be elected chairman of the consortium, to give it a prominent name and an appearance of respectability."

"Has the duke been approached with this proposition?" Jean asked.

"Maybe. In any event, the duchess almost certainly has."

"Will it be the policy of your government to try to prevent the duke's name being lent to this scheme?"

"Of course."

"I need to know something else," said Jean. "Who is Curtis Wyler?"

"He carries an Irish passport," said Kevin Hammet. "It's genuine; that's been checked. He has no criminal record that we've been able to discover."

"In other words, you suspect him. Suspect him of what?"

"It's a little difficult to discover how he makes a living," said Hammet. "He showed up here in January and has left the island only occasionally since then. He lived in a hotel for a time, then rented a house just outside town. He seems to have substantial funds to invest and has purchased some property."

"He was aboard *Christina* when Torstenson was murdered. Wearing dungarees. He damn near caught me."

"Actually, he probably feared you might catch him."

"Why wasn't he invited to the party?" she asked. "Chapman was."

"Good question. Maybe he was invited but chose to come aboard surreptitiously, for some reason we can only guess."

"He's my suspect-in-chief," said Jean.

Hammet nodded. "Mine as well, then."

The luncheon party at the Emerald Beach Club bore a monotonous resemblance to the breakfast party at Government House only a few hours earlier—champagne and food served from tables under the palms to many of the same guests—but the duke and duchess were conspicuously pleased.

Although a man who reputedly was a friend to many of

these people lay in the morgue, no one showed any sign of distress. Even those who had insisted on their close friendship with him—Chapman, for example, and the duke and duchess—circulated among the guests, glasses in hand, smiling, chatting, laughing. Mrs. Roosevelt was reminded of accounts she had read of the court of Louis XV, where it was considered bad style to allow any misfortune, including death, to interrupt the gaiety of Versailles, where a brief, quiet word of regret was all that fashion allowed, even when the deceased was a spouse or parent.

Indeed, Nassau society reminded Mrs. Roosevelt a great deal of the courts of the last kings of France, where food and drink and conversation were life and the reality beyond Versailles was determinedly ignored. A major war was being fought in Europe. The world was in chaos. But here, attention was focused on the quality of the wine and caviar, the wit displayed in conversation, the clothes on women's backs.

"Ah, Mrs. Roosevelt," said the duchess. "I would like to present a new but very dear friend, Señor Isidro Gutiérrez. He is a Mexican financier who has achieved remarkable success."

The Mexican bowed deeply and kissed Mrs. Roosevelt's hand. "A very great honor," he murmured in accented English.

Gutiérrez was a short, plump, happy-looking man with a gleaming olive complexion, dark hair and dark eyes, and a ready smile that suggested an obsession with ingratiation.

"The honor is mine, Señor," said Mrs. Roosevelt.

"Señor Gutiérrez is the owner of a very fine boat," said the duchess. "Knowing your interest in the island of Eleuthera, he has offered to run us all out there this afternoon—meaning, yourself, the duke and I, and obviously Commander MacGruder."

"Eleuthera?"

The duchess smiled. "It is no secret that Eleuthera is where President Roosevelt wants to establish a naval base," said the duchess.

"It is but forty mile to Eleuthera," said Gutiérrez. "My Chris-Craft runabout, he can run on the smooth sea at almost forty mile the hour—and today the sea is smooth. We can see the island after a pleasant journey and return in time for the dinner, of the which I hope you will be my guests. Also, I should say, between here and the there, it is never out of sight of the small islands. The journey is perfectly safe."

"And very pleasant," said the duchess. "You can see beautiful reefs between here and Eleuthera."

The Chris-Craft runabout could carry six people. Mrs. Roosevelt had to choose between taking Kenneth Krouse or Alex Zaferakes. She chose Zaferakes, her Secret Service bodyguard. She and the duchess left their broad-brimmed hats in the governor's limousine and accepted white yachting caps from Gutiérrez, as did Zaferakes also.

The runabout, named *Maria*, was an exceptionally handsome boat, twenty-six feet long, with a gleaming hull of light mahogany. It had two cockpits, one in the front and one behind the big engine compartment. Gutiérrez sat at the controls, with Mrs. Roosevelt and the Duchess of Windsor beside him in the first cockpit. The duke sat with Commander MacGruder and Alex Zaferakes in the rear. The flag of Mexico flew on the staff behind the rear cockpit, a yacht-club pennant on a short staff in front.

The seats were of soft leather. Canvas convertible tops lay folded behind each cockpit in case there should be rain. Green champagne bottles lay in ice, in chests in each cockpit, as did small plates of crackers spread with caviar.

Maria was sleek and heavily powered with two big marine engines in the compartment. As Gutiérrez guided it away from the dock and out into the bay, the boat seemed to wallow in the swell. But when he was clear of the docks and moored boats and need not be concerned about his wake, he shoved in his throttles and the runabout roared to life. It rose from the water and planed across it, banging loudly on the waves.

When he swung out into the open Atlantic, the sea he had described as smooth turned out to be gently rolling. The runabout bucked and plunged as it rose over wavetops and charged headlong into the troughs. Mrs. Roosevelt was glad she was not susceptible to motion sickness.

The duchess had been right, though, about how beautiful the ride would be. The route between Nassau and Eleuthera followed a line of tiny islands guarded by coral reefs. The water was blue, white surf broke on white coral, and a bank of gray storm clouds hung over the sea at a safe distance. Gutiérrez sped along the north side of the reefs until he came to a channel, and then he passed through and sped along the south side. They were hardly out of sight of New Providence Island when the low profile of Eleuthera appeared on the horizon.

Conversation was limited by the roar of the engines and the banging of the hull on the water, but the duchess initiated a conversation anyway—

"Señor Gutiérrez is establishing a new bank," she said. "In Mexico City perhaps, or in Vera Cruz. The duke and I very much hope the death of Gunnar Torstenson will not discourage him from continuing with the project."

The words were spoken to Mrs. Roosevelt but were of course meant to produce a response from the Mexican.

"It is the great loss, Torstenson," he said. "Much of the capital for the new bank was to have come from him.

Even so, I think we will be able to continue, perhaps on a more modest basis."

"When did you arrive in Nassau, Señor Gutiérrez?" asked Mrs. Roosevelt.

He shrugged. "Oh, I have been here since February. There are the great investment opportunities here perhaps. I return to Mexico only twice since February. My government there, you see, is hostile to me."

"When were you last there?"

"Uh . . . In July. I returned for a meeting of the board of directors of one of my companies."

"I see," said Mrs. Roosevelt. She wondered where he was last night. She had been told that Gunnar Torstenson had invited all his friends and business associates aboard his yacht for the party that turned out to be his last.

"Mr. Torstenson," said Gutiérrez, "was a fine man. I can think of nothing of his person and character that was anything but of the best."

"An aggressive businessman, I understand," said Mrs. Roosevelt.

"Uh, aggressive . . . The word has of positive and negative connotations," said the Mexican. "I should perhaps have called him forceful and, uh, vigorous."

"He was a good friend," said the duchess.

"Ah, but Your Royal Highness has many good friends," said Gutiérrez. "Of course . . . one can never have too many."

"I am grateful for your friendship," said the duchess. She turned to Mrs. Roosevelt and explained, "Señor Gutiérrez is helping us with some of our money problems."

Mrs. Roosevelt only smiled and nodded, though she wondered what those money problems were. She need not have wondered; the duchess went on to tell her—

"Currency restrictions, you understand. The duke is a

subject of his brother's, you know, and all subjects of the King are restricted in moving their assets out of the United Kingdom. Wartime restriction, they call it. We are fortunate to be able to secure the assistance of neutral businessmen to avoid some of these irrational impediments."

Gutiérrez seemed anxious to change the subject. "Zat island is call Current Island," he said, pointing to a low gray shape they were approaching.

It was wearying to converse over the roar, and they fell silent now. The duchess opened a bottle of champagne, poured, then offered caviar to Mrs. Roosevelt and Gutiérrez.

In the rear cockpit, the duke talked to Commander Mac-Gruder—

"The waters between New Providence Island and Eleuthera Island are quiet shallow. You can be several miles off the west coast of Eleuthera and still be in waters of three or four fathoms. Not suitable for submarine operations, obviously. Tricky for surface operations, in fact. On the eastern side of the island, it's quite different. There you have soundings generally of a hundred fathoms within a mile offshore, and two thousand fathoms within five miles."

Commander MacGruder nodded. "But there have been submarine sightings," he said.

"Yes. Five miles off Nassau you have a thousand fathoms. There are other deep waters nearby. And, of course, beyond Eleuthera—the open Atlantic. Oh, they're out there. And they're all but invincible, too. The Germans knew what they were doing when they built a fleet of U-boats. They're still building them, of course. Hundreds a year. You sink a few—" He shrugged. "They have five times as many to replace that few."

" 'Invincible,' " Commander MacGruder mused. "You think so?"

The Duke of Windsor nodded.

"U-boats operating at this range have to be serviced by surface vessels," said MacGruder.

"Tenders," said the duke. "They're out there, too. The British navy looks for them, but it's a big ocean. Also, they call at neutral ports. I need hardly tell you, there's a great deal of sympathy for Germany in many of the Latin American countries."

"Pleasure yachts act as tenders, you suppose?"

The duke shook his head. "No. They're not big enough to carry the fuel and food the U-boats need."

Commander MacGruder turned his head and stared at the shoreline of Eleuthera as the runabout raced south, parallel to that shoreline. Either the duke was innocent of what *Christina* had been doing, or he was a consummate actor.

The sun was low when the runabout re-entered the harbor at Nassau. Even the duchess, whose girlish enthusiasm for the boat ride had not flagged, was weary from the buffeting and noise and showed her relief when Gutiérrez at last pulled back on his throttle and *Maria* settled into the water and churned toward the yacht club with only a low rumbling.

"Oh, look!" the duchess shouted as she spotted a new yacht in the harbor. "The *René*!" She turned to the duke and pointed, wagging her finger in her excitement. "Look, David! Alfred is here!"

The *René* was the yacht owned by Alfred P. Sloan, chairman of the board of General Motors. Mrs. Roosevelt remembered that when the duchess used the name Alfred.

Isidro Gutiérrez guided the runabout alongside the big

yacht and signalled with his horn. There was a scurrying on board, and in a moment the white-haired tycoon appeared at the rail, grinning and waving.

"And look who's with him!" the duchess exclaimed happily. "Errol Flynn!"

VII

Alfred Sloan, chairman of the board of General Motors, was by most people's consent a handsome man. His gray-white hair had long since abandoned his forehead, but on top it flourished in waves. His lined face was long and strong, with a defiantly jutting jaw. His lips were thick, and behind them he had big white teeth he showed when he smiled. His blue eyes were extraordinarily large, and he had a habit of lifting his eyebrows and showing his eyes in a look of amused skepticism. He carried a pince-nez, which he shoved onto the bridge of his nose when he wanted to read. Above all, his face was mobile and expressive. It telegraphed his changing moods.

He had peremptorily overruled Isidro Gutiérrez's suggestion that the Windsors and Mrs. Roosevelt dine at the Emerald Beach Club as the guests of Gutiérrez and insisted that they dine with him and Errol Flynn aboard *René*.

Mrs. Roosevelt's staff was invited—excluding of course the uniformed maid and the secretary.

* * *

"Parties . . ." breathed Mrs. Roosevelt in her bedroom in Government House. "Don't these people think of anything at all in this world but parties?"

"Obviously they don't," said Jean King.

Back in costume for her role, Jean wore the black dress and white cap and apron. She stood just outside the bathroom door, where Mrs. Roosevelt soaked in the big, rusty tub.

"Miss King . . ." said the First Lady wearily. "Who killed Gunnar Torstenson?"

"Do we care?" Jean asked.

"I think we have to care. As a personal matter, as a matter of ethics, morals . . . as a matter of national policy. It may be significant. I have to report to the President—"

"All right," said Jean. "First of all, there's me. Did I do it, do you suppose?"

"Did you?"

"Since you ask, I judge you're not confident I didn't."

"Jean . . . If you did, I know you did it in your country's service, and—"

"I didn't."

"I accept that. Then . . . ?"

"Then British intelligence," said Jean. "Her Highness, the duchess, accuses the British government. I can't say they didn't. I can say I doubt it."

"Which leaves . . . ?"

"The captain of the yacht," said Jean. "Or some member of his crew. Start with them. They had motive. Then any one of several Nassau businessmen. Chapman and others. They had motive. Then you have foreigners, like Gutiérrez. *They* had motive. Beyond that, Torstenson's property dealings may have been threatening to some local, maybe even some Negro."

"I think it is important," said Mrs. Roosevelt, "to begin

identifying the whereabouts of some of these people at the time when the murder occurred. If nothing else, we can eliminate some people."

"Alibis," said Jean. "As for me, I don't have one. I said I was soaking in your rusty bathtub. But who was witness? I hope no one was."

"I don't really suspect you," Mrs. Roosevelt called through the bathroom door.

"Chapman was aboard the *Christina*," said Jean. "Where was he when Torstenson died?"

"I don't know," said Mrs. Roosevelt. "Maybe Mr. Krouse does."

"What about Captain Lindeblad?" asked Jean.

"I don't know where he was."

"And Lieutenant Valentin?"

"No. I don't know where he was."

"The duke?"

"You *don't* suspect the duke!"

"No, but where was he?"

"Oh, I think he was where I could see him. The whole time. As best I recall."

"Okay. Who else?"

"Señor Isidro Gutiérrez," said Mrs. Roosevelt. "I would like to know where he was and what he was doing when Mr. Torstenson was killed."

"I'll do what I can to find out," said Jean King.

"Yes. I understand that you and Mr. Krouse and Commander MacGruder have your assignments, separate from what was communicated to me. But I think we will do well to work together rather than independently, Miss King."

"I will cooperate with you, Ma'am."

Mrs. Roosevelt was due aboard *René* at eight o'clock. By seven Jean King was on the waterfront, still dressed as a maid, in black dress, starched white apron and cap, but carrying a small pair of binoculars provided by Commander MacGruder. She found herself a hidey-hole between two huge baskets of bananas and stationed herself to observe the yacht through the glasses. It was anchored no more than fifty yards from the dock, and she had a good view.

Traffic on and off *René* was heavy. Small boats pulled up to deliver food to the yacht. Another boat brought wine and liquor in cases. A boat accepted a large load of laundry.

Several others brought visitors.

Jean could see Alfred Sloan at the rail of his yacht, greeting his visitors with hearty grins and waves as their boats brought them alongside. The movie star Errol Flynn was beside him part of the time, also grinning and waving.

An odd pair, that. Odder yet was Alfred Sloan's collection of visitors—

Jean recognized Henry Chapman. Another small boat brought out his friend Curtis Wyler. Two other men came aboard. Jean did not know them.

It was apparent, anyway, that Sloan was holding a business meeting aboard. That it was a business meeting and not social calls became even more apparent when—as the hour for the party approached—all these men returned purposefully to their boats and were taken ashore.

Jean had borrowed a bicycle. She rode back to Government House, with information she would give to Krouse and MacGruder before they went aboard *René* for the party.

Isidro Gutiérrez waited at the dock, aboard his Chris-Craft runabout, ready to ferry Mrs. Roosevelt and the Windsors out to *René*. Ken Krouse and Commander MacGruder were with the First Lady for this evening. Gutiérrez brought the runabout alongside the yacht, where two crewmen helped Sloan's guests from the boat to the platform at the bottom of the gangway ladder. When the guests had gone up to the deck, the crewmen anchored the runabout a few feet away, where it would not be in the way of other boats arriving with other guests but could be reached with a boat hook.

"Mrs. Roosevelt, this is a real honor and pleasure!" Sloan beamed as she reached the main deck.

"It is an honor and pleasure for me, too, Mr. Sloan."

"And Your Royal Highnesses! How good to see you both again."

"Alfred!" laughed the duchess.

The duke allowed Sloan to incline his head in the brief semblance of a bow, then took his hand, smiled shyly, and murmured a greeting so softly that it was incomprehensible, probably even to Sloan.

"And let me present Errol Flynn," said Sloan.

Flynn was as flamboyant a character as his reputation made him out to be. While all the other men wore white dinner jackets and black tie, Flynn wore a violet-colored silk dinner jacket with black satin cuffs as well as lapels. The stripes on his black trousers were also violet, as was his loosely knotted bow tie. On his feet he wore crocodile pumps with two-inch heels. His pencil mustache was neatly trimmed, his hair was slicked back with oil, but his face was flushed; it was plain that he had already consumed a considerable amount of alcohol.

"Charmed," he said to Mrs. Roosevelt and the Duchess of Windsor; and to the duke he said, "Good to see you again, old boy." He nodded at Ken Krouse, Commander MacGruder, and Isidro Gutiérrez, but it was only a perfunctory acknowledgment; he did not speak to them.

René was a newer yacht than *Christina*, but not as big. Sloan led his guests aft, where a bar was set up in the open on the rear deck. Just forward of this deck was the main lounge, and the wood-and-glass doors had been folded back so the lounge was entirely open to the deck. Tables were set up both inside and out.

One guest had not come out to the gangway to greet the new arrivals. Flynn introduced her—

"Everybody say hello to Judy," he said.

Judy could not have been more than sixteen years old, a diminutive, youthful figure simply and unstylishly dressed in a straight gray skirt, white blouse, and shoes of knitted straw in the shape of ballet slippers. Her face was flawless but plain, her light-brown hair hung straight to her shoulders, something else that was unstylish that year. She had a martini in her left hand, and she nodded at the people who had come to the rear deck. If she knew who they were, she was not impressed.

Mrs. Roosevelt would have liked to avoid champagne. She'd had it at breakfast, for lunch, during the run out to Eleuthera, and now was confronted with it again. She accepted a glass and, since Sloan was watching, apparently curious to see how she would judge it, took a sip and nodded appreciatively.

"Well, the newspaper boys would love to see this," said Sloan with a grin. "Mrs. Roosevelt and Alfred Sloan hobnobbing on a yacht."

"It might be destructive to your reputation, Mr. Sloan," she said. "A wealthy industrialist and Republican . . . and the wife of *'that man* in the White House.' "

"Yes, I think my membership in several clubs is at hazard," said Sloan, his grin broadening.

"Including the Liberty League, Mr. Sloan?"

"Ouch!" Sloan laughed, and the Duchess of Windsor winced, tried to smile, and shook her head.

Mrs. Roosevelt smiled. "Reasonable people can disagree reasonably, can they not?" she asked.

"Of course," he said, conspicuously relieved.

"Certainly," she said. "So, being a reasonable man, you will probably disassociate yourself from the Liberty Leaguers, who are unreasonable."

"Yes. Of course. Why not?"

"You have a beautiful yacht," said Mrs. Roosevelt.

"Oh, I thank God, we are going to talk about boats," said the duchess.

Another boat had pulled alongside, bringing Henry Chapman and Curtis Wyler to the *René.*

"Curious," said Krouse quietly to MacGruder. "According to Jean, that pair was aboard less than an hour ago. Why do you suppose they left and are returning?"

Flynn intruded on their conversation. "They tell me you fellows work for the government," he said.

Krouse nodded. "State Department," he said.

"Think your boss is going to be elected for a third term?" Flynn asked.

"We can hope," said Krouse.

"Yeah. Well, let's hope he doesn't let the Jews drag us into their war," said Flynn. He tipped his glass and drank a slug of gin. "Or let Churchill drag us in to pull his irons out of the fire. This is a pretty damned good world we've got. We could lose it if FDR lets us get involved in that war over there."

"That's Mr. Sloan's opinion, too, I imagine," said Krouse.

"Damn right."

Ken Krouse judged Flynn was drunk—and probably not

too bright when he was sober. "I suppose the murder of Gunnar Torstenson has upset Mr. Sloan's plans. I mean, his chief reason for coming to the Bahamas."

"Yeah . . . Word came by radio when we were off the Cuban coast. I thought he might not come on to Nassau, but . . . Well, he did. Here we are."

Flynn turned, snapped his fingers, and raised his empty glass in the direction of Judy. She hurried to the bar to get him another drink.

"I suppose, he wanted to meet with the others," said Krouse quietly.

"Yeah . . . I s'pose. Me, I want to get back to Havana. That's where the fun is."

The Duke of Windsor, at the same time, was having a rare moment of private conversation with Mrs. Roosevelt.

"The métier of a businessman is hard-headed practicality," he said. "A man like Alfred Sloan must make decisions without letting sentiment or emotion interfere. That's what I admire about a man like him. I'm sorry to speak of my admiration for a man who opposes your husband politically, but I do admire him. I think we all can learn much from Alfred Sloan."

"You are a man who allowed sentiment to influence a judgment," said Mrs. Roosevelt.

"You mean the abdication," said the duke. "Yes. I was influenced by sentiment, the most noble sentiment of which mankind is capable. And those who opposed me were influenced by emotion and sentiment—base emotions, ignoble sentiments."

"And you think Mr. Sloan is influenced exclusively by rational analysis?"

"Yes. In opposing President Roosevelt, as an example, Alfred Sloan is moved only by his analysis of what impact the New Deal has on General Motors. The Roosevelt presidency has cost G.M. money, *ergo* G.M. opposes Roosevelt."

"And for a like reason Mr. Sloan wants the United States to remain aloof from the war in Europe," said the First Lady.

"General Motors has immense investments to protect, huge business interests in Germany."

"And opposition to the inhumanity of Herr Hitler—"

"Is emotionalism," said the duke flatly, raising his whisky to his lips. "Once Winston Churchill's crusade is over, the world will be able to get along with the things that count."

"Like General Motors profits?"

"Among other things."

"I am surprised," said Mrs. Roosevelt, "to discover that our values differ so widely."

The duke flushed. "Oh, I should not like to think they do," he said. "I would rather say our *perceptions* of things differ."

"Why is Mr. Sloan in Nassau?" she asked, pressing the advantage of the duke's momentary embarrassment.

"A business meeting," said the duke ingenuously.

"About opportunities in Mexico," said Mrs. Roosevelt.

"Yes," said the duke. "Or, more correctly said, opportunities in Latin America. Business money is retreating from Europe. The Western Hemisphere will become the financial center of the world. The political center. Social center. Cultural center. The Old World is destroying itself. The New World will inherit everything."

Mrs. Roosevelt shook her head, but the duke was wound up and continued—

"When the war is ended, a new order of social justice will prevail in the world," he said. "A new order. I will return to my throne, as king of a much diminished British nation. I—"

"They will call you back?" Mrs. Roosevelt asked, surprised. She had heard this was his ambition; still, she could not help but be astounded at the idea—and that he should so openly express it.

"Yes. My brother, poor Bertie, will have to go into exile, maybe in Canada. He allowed our kingdom to be dragged into an impossible war, and—"

The duchess interrupted him. "David, we are being seated," she said.

By the time everyone was seated at the tables inside and outside the aft lounge of the yacht, it was obvious that Errol Flynn was irretrievably drunk. Like any other drunk, he didn't know it. Sloan knew him well enough not to seat him with Mrs. Roosevelt or the Windsors. He was seated at a table with Kenneth Krouse, Isidro Gutiérrez, and his teenaged plaything, Judy.

At whatever table he sat, his conversation was audible to everyone aboard.

"To Pres . . . dunt *Roosevelt,*" he yelled, raising a glass of gin. "Th' arsenal of . . . *democracy.*"

Mrs. Roosevelt sat between Alfred Sloan and the Duchess of Windsor. She looked out toward the dark harbor and the brightly lighted boats.

"My apologies," said Sloan. "He is usually a very entertaining fellow."

Flynn rose and again lifted his glass. "Toast to Win . . . son Churchill, Adolf Hit— Hil . . . ler. An' Ol' Ben . . . Ol' Ben Moosle . . . Y' know who I mean. Ol' Ben. The bald wop. Toast to him, too."

"Odd combination," remarked Krouse.

"Yeah, well . . . You ever done any . . . boxin'? I like to

strip down and trade a few . . . *fists* with you, State Department."

"Fine," said Krouse. "After we get ashore. Maybe on the dock."

"Umm, *yeah*. Like . . . Jus' . . . frien'ly. 'Kay?"

"Oh, no way but friendly," said Krouse.

Flynn chuckled and grinned. "Okay. Hey, Judy. Ol' Uncle Errol got to go. Horsie, baby . . . ?"

"Errol . . ."

"Well, I don' think I . . . C'mon, baby."

The girl rose reluctantly. Flynn stumbled up. She planted her feet firmly and wide apart, and bent forward, and Errol Flynn stumbled against her and climbed on her back. It was all the slip of a girl could do to bear his weight. She strained and grimaced and staggered toward the exit from the lounge, carrying Flynn toward the bathroom. Climbing on her, he had shoved up her skirt, exposing her muscular legs above her stockings—in fact all the way to the garter belt that held up her stockings. Her agony of effort was apparent to everyone, and no one was amused; no one was anything but shocked by the cruel show. Grunting, Judy carried Flynn from the lounge.

The people at the tables were silent, most of them staring down at their plates, their silverware.

Suddenly, an unnatural glow of dull red light flashed across the decks, and an explosive shock struck the hull of the yacht like a huge fist. *René* shuddered. An instant later, with the roar of the explosion, came an eruption of water that flew over the rail and drenched the decks, the tables, the diners. After another instant, echoes of the blast rippled the awnings and shook the air like repeated shots from heavy guns.

The Duchess of Windsor screamed. Just out of sight

from the lounge, Judy shrieked in terror. Several of the men ran to the rail.

Off the starboard side of the yacht, and toward the stern, the water churned with mud brought up from the bottom of the harbor by the force of the explosion. High-flung bits of debris splashed into the water. Small pieces hit the yacht with a clatter—none of them big enough to break through the awning over the rear deck.

A launch had been swamped by the explosion and sat deep in the water, slowly sinking.

The Christ-Craft runabout, *Maria*, was gone. It had been blown to bits.

Commissioner of Police Edgar Hopkins had accepted rum over ice from Alfred Sloan, and he leaned back comfortably against the rail on the rear deck of *René*.

"Not gasoline fumes," he said. "No. Definitely not gasoline fumes. The handsome little runabout was blown up with dynamite. You can still smell it."

Mrs. Roosevelt stood beside him, Alfred Sloan to his other side. Both of them were watching police boats dragging nets, picking up debris from the surface and below. Just before he came aboard, Commissioner Hopkins had paused for several minutes and talked to the uniformed officers on a net-dragging launch. He had examined bits of flotsam they displayed to him in buckets.

"What is more," said the commissioner, "someone was aboard the boat when it was blown up. Someone was killed in the explosion."

"Your nets have brought up pieces of . . . of a person?" Sloan asked.

"Yes," said Commissioner Hopkins. He used his handkerchief to wipe perspiration from his broad black face.

Then he sipped rum. "I am afraid so," he said to Mrs. Roosevelt. "I am sorry, Ma'am, but we are finding remains."

"Can you make any guess as to who it was?" she asked.

"Not yet," said Hopkins. "No bits of hands, no fingerprints. No face. Clothes . . . nondescript. As we keep dragging, we may find something on which an identification could be based."

"Why?" asked Mrs. Roosevelt grimly. "Why in the world would anyone want to blow up that little boat?"

"At the moment, we can only speculate," said Hopkins. "I suppose someone might have wanted to frighten Señor Gutiérrez. Or . . . I am reluctant to mention this speculation, but someone may have accidentally killed himself while wiring a charge to go off when Señor Gutiérrez tried to start the engines on the runabout."

"In which case, I should have been killed with him—as would the Duke and Duchess of Windsor and two members of my staff," she said solemnly.

Hopkins nodded. "Yes, but he may not have known that. In fact, I very much doubt he knew that."

"Or he may have chosen the wrong boat," said Sloan. "The other would have carried Chapman and Wyler."

"He might actually have thought *you* would come ashore in so handsome a launch," said Hopkins to Sloan.

Sloan's chin came up fast. "Yes . . . Yes, I suppose so."

Errol Flynn lurched across the deck, not carried by the girl, but leaning on her so heavily that she staggered.

"Hey! Who gonna pay for my dinner jacket? Ruin . . . Salt water on silk . . . Big BOOM throw sal' water—No funny. No funny."

"Bicycle," said Jean King quietly to Mrs. Roosevelt. "I can ride a bicycle, but—"

"*I* can ride a bicycle," said Mrs. Roosevelt.

"But—"

"I don't want the duke and duchess to know I'm leaving Government House," said the First Lady, "and I don't see how I can gain access to a car without their knowing. A bicycle will be perfect. It's but a short distance."

Five minutes later the two of them walked their bicycles, which belonged to members of the household staff, through the pillars in front of Government House. Jean King was still dressed like a maid, in black and white. Mrs. Roosevelt wore a white summer dress and had tied a silk scarf over her head.

"Well . . ." she said tentatively as she put her hands on the handlebars. "It has been some years. But they say if you've learned once, you can always do it."

She stepped through the frame—it was a woman's bicycle with no top tube—and lifted herself to the saddle. With her right foot she pressed down on the pedal. The bicycle moved forward, wobbling and swerving from side to side but staying erect. As it gained speed, it straightened up. Mrs. Roosevelt frowned and gripped the handlebars anxiously. She had a moment of panic as the front wheels hit a hole in the road, but the bicycle bounced out of the hole and rolled forward.

"Uhmm . . ." she grunted.

Jean caught up with her. "Okay?"

"Well . . . Not quite okay, perhaps. But adequate. I think I shall not fall on my face."

In bright, post-midnight moonlight, they rode toward the center of the town. Mrs. Roosevelt had told Commissioner Hopkins she would come to his headquarters before two A.M., one way or another. She wanted, she had told him, to talk to him out of the presence of the duke and duchess, emphatically out of the presence of any of the Bay Street boys.

Their wheels splashed through mudholes and ruts filled with muddy water. Fortunately, the moonlight was just bright enough for them to see the holes and ruts and steer between them, but when the moon abruptly sailed behind a cloud they were left in almost total darkness. Mrs. Roosevelt's front wheel plunged sideways into a rut, and in an instant the bicycle fell over to the left and threw her into a deep puddle.

"Damn . . ." she muttered.

"Oh, my God!" Jean yelled. She could hardly see what had happened but had heard the clatter and splash. "Are you hurt?"

The First Lady sat in oozy mud, with water around her legs. "In my dignity only," she said ruefully. "In that, I am fatally injured. Not otherwise."

"We should go back," said Jean. "You may be hurt."

"I shall not go back. I am fifty-five years old, not *quite* yet senile. And I am sure Commissioner Hopkins has seen mud before."

Jean picked up the bicycle, and Mrs. Roosevelt mounted it again. The moon was out again, and she peered ahead at the pattern of ruts and puddles, then set out determinedly.

As they reached the center of the town of Nassau, they cycled along between waterfront bars that were still lively. Through the open doors issued a rhythmic, plaintive music: tropical, African, yet distinctively American—American in spite of the Union Jack that floated in the glare of floodlights over a few government buildings.

Police headquarters and the office of the commissioner of police shared a building with other government offices. Like British-empire buildings in many tropical outposts, it was characterized by high ceilings, lazily turning ceiling fans, open windows, spare furniture in rooms without carpet or drapes—what Whitehall supposed served to keep interior spaces cool.

On learning who had arrived, Commissioner Hopkins rushed out. Shortly after him came Kevin Hammet, overtly solicitor's clerk, covertly lieutenant, Royal Navy, intelligence section.

"Mrs. Roosevelt! You have suffered an accident!" exclaimed the commissioner.

"An incident," said Mrs. Roosevelt.

Her white dress was brown with mud and hung in wet wrinkles. The commissioner took her hand gently, and Hammet took the bicycle and wheeled it aside.

"What can I do for you?" asked Hopkins.

"If some sort of robe can be provided, I will wear it," said Mrs. Roosevelt. "Otherwise . . ." She shrugged. "If you can bear the sight of me, we shall ignore the incident and get on with our meeting."

The commissioner of police grinned, showing great white teeth. "I have heard that America's First Lady is not easily discouraged. But . . . by bicycle! I would have sent a car."

"And the governor would have known I was coming. No. The bicycle is—"

"You don't trust the governor?"

Hopkins and Jean introduced Kevin Hammet, and Mrs. Roosevelt said to him, "It is not a question of trust, I think. The issue is dissemination of information."

Hammet, whose sense of humor was ordinarily deficient, seemed to think he should be amused by this comment and laughed nervously.

Calls were made. A black policeman came bearing a gray wool robe. Mrs. Roosevelt went in a bathroom and took off the dress, and the policeman said he would wash it and iron it dry.

They sat down in the office of the commissioner of police, where they made a picturesque group—Mrs. Roosevelt in the long gray bathrobe, Jean dressed as a lady's maid, Commissioner Hopkins in his shirtsleeves and unbuttoned vest, which hung loose over his ample belly, exposing a sweat-stained shirt, Hammet in a white linen suit, totally buttoned and totally limp.

Coffee steamed in a stoneware pot on an electric hotplate on a table to one side. Bottles of rum, gin, and brandy sat beside the coffee pot. Mrs. Roosevelt accepted a little brandy. Jean took brandy and a cup of coffee.

On another large table on the opposite side of the room, bits of debris and flotsam were displayed.

"I have something to show you, Ma'am," said Commissioner Hopkins.

He stepped to the table and picked up a small bakelite cylinder to which wires were attached. "This . . ." he said.

Mrs. Roosevelt examined the object. It was sturdily made of thick Bakelite. Insulated wires ran out a narrow throat at the top—two of them heavily encased in rubber, two of them much less heavily encased. Though the object was sturdily made, it was cracked; and the wires had obviously been torn loose from something, not neatly cut.

"Do you see the point, Ma'am?" Hopkins asked.

"I'm afraid I don't."

"I think I do," said Jean King. "That's an ignition coil off a gasoline engine. But it has two wires too many."

Hopkins pried off the top. The two heavily insulated wires were soldered to their terminals. The two thinner wires had been attached to the same terminals by twisting and crimping. Conspicuously, they were a recent and temporary addition.

"Two extra wires," said Jean. "To the detonator."

Hopkins fingered the two thin wires. "We'll never know for sure where they led. I would guess to a bundle of dynamite sticks."

"More precisely," said Hammet, "to the detonator caps imbedded within one or more sticks of dynamite. The slightest electric charge will fire such detonators. They are effective but of course exceedingly sensitive and dangerous. And what our would-be bomber may have overlooked," he went on, "is that the boat's battery kept one of those wires hot, even if the ignition switch in the cockpit was turned off—*and* anything attached by a conductor to the block of either engine was ground. He touched . . . or a wire touched, and . . . Well, I am sure that you understand."

"Unless perhaps a timer failed," said Mrs. Roosevelt.

"A possibility," said Hopkins. "A remote possibility. I'm afraid, actually, the reason why we found no bits of hands, no bits of face, but only parts of the lower body, is that the would-be bomber was bent over his dynamite, concentrating on setting the charge—and it went off and blew him to bits."

Mrs. Roosevelt glanced at the table. "Pieces of . . ."

"Not here," said Hopkins quickly. "In the morgue. Bits are being laid out in some semblance of order. I need not describe."

"Clothes?" asked Jean.

"Suggestive," said the commissioner. "The parts covered with gore are in the morgue. But here, on the table—"

Bits of fabric caught in the net were laid apart, to one side of the table. Blue and white.

Mrs. Roosevelt picked up a piece. It was rough wool,

dark blue. Another piece was wool, too, white and a little lighter.

"A swim suit," she said.

"I agree," said Commissioner Hopkins. "The man blown up on the boat came to it in the water. Swimming."

"Carrying dynamite and detonators?" asked Mrs. Roosevelt.

"If you are thinking he should not have allowed them to get wet," said the commissioner, "I am sorry, but that would have nothing to do with anything. Dynamite, detonator caps, et cetera are entirely waterproof."

"It will be difficult, perhaps impossible, to identify the man," said Hammet. "No fingerprints . . . Nothing but bits of a swimsuit for clothing. No fingerprints, either. He was apparently wearing gloves, probably rubber surgeon's gloves. I doubt we will ever know who he was."

"Actually," said Mrs. Roosevelt, "I should think we *will* know in a day or two."

"How?" asked Hammet.

"We will observe that someone is missing," she said.

Commissioner Hopkins frowned, then grinned. "Simple," he said. "And correct. It's not likely that the dead man is a complete stranger to us. He was a white man, incidentally, which eliminates five-sixths of the population at a stroke. All we have to do is discover who is missing from among the remaining one-sixth."

"From among the business community, I should think," said Mrs. Roosevelt. "If it be assumed that the target of the bomb was Señor Gutiérrez, then the bomber almost has to be someone from the business community."

"Or an employee," said Jean.

"Or an employee," Mrs. Roosevelt agreed. "On the other hand, if—"

"I don't even want to think of that possibility," said

Hammet. "But if you were the target, Ma'am, then we are looking for a German agent, I should think."

"Don't forget that the duke and duchess, as well as two members of my staff, were brought to the *René* by Señor Gutiérrez. And presumably we would have returned to the dock the same way. Six of us would have been killed had the bomber succeeded—the Duke and Duchess of Windsor, Señor Gutiérrez, Mr. Krouse, Commander Mac-Gruder, and myself."

"We are dealing, then, with an extremely dangerous and desperate criminal," said Commissioner Hopkins.

"Who is at large, too—almost certainly," said Jean. "It seems unlikely that the principal himself swam out through the harbor to plant that bomb."

"That is speculation," said Mrs. Roosevelt. "I tend to agree, but we cannot base a criminal investigation on speculation."

Kevin Hammet shook his head somberly. He spoke directly to Mrs. Roosevelt and said, "I shudder to think what might have happened."

"Since I seem to have escaped a violent death only by the error of my would-be murderer, I believe I am entitled to take an active role in this investigation," she said.

VIII

While Mrs. Roosevelt was at breakfast with the Windsors in the dining room at Government House the next morning, a messenger arrived bringing the invitation the newspaper publisher, Junius Gerald, had said he would tender. The First Lady—and, significantly, not the governor and his lady—was invited to a luncheon party at the New Providence Club.

"New Providence . . . ?" The duchess frowned and shook her head. "I don't think you should go there. I know you are sympathetic to the problems of American Negroes, but that place is hardly respectable."

The duke, who had finished his spare breakfast and was thoughtfully smoking a pipe, drew in smoke. His cheeks collapsed as he sucked on the stem; then he pursed his lips as he let the smoke trickle out of his mouth.

"It is entirely possible," said the duchess, "that the explosion last night was set off by some dissident in the Negro community. We have expressed our sympathy to Mr. Gerald and told him we will look for ways to relieve the poverty of his people, but they don't accept our assurances very readily, and they maintain a sullen attitude."

The duke, whose eyebrows were lifted as if in an expression of innocence, wobbled his pipe as he nodded his agreement with the duchess.

"Well, I think I shall risk it," said Mrs. Roosevelt. "I did promise Mr. Gerald I would come."

The messenger waited, and she told him to tell Junius Gerald that she would attend the party.

"I believe," said the duke, "that I am going to have to tighten the security around us all. I've asked Brigadier Hilary-Percy to meet with me this morning to talk about establishing a better guard around Government House."

"We are the guests of Henry Chapman tonight, you know," said the duchess to Mrs. Roosevelt.

"We could all have been killed," said the duke.

"He has a lovely home," said the duchess. "We may in fact live there during part of the remodeling of Government House."

"Bombing is a cowardly way to—"

The duchess interrupted the duke. "We can tour the harbor and see some more of the yachts this morning, if you like," she said to the First Lady.

"I should like that," said Mrs. Roosevelt. "However, I did promise to pay a call at Commissioner Hopkins's office this morning. I shan't be there more than an hour, I should think."

"Hopkins?"

"To talk about the murder. And about the explosion. He has some observations he wants to make to me alone. I have one or two I should like to make to him."

"Oh. Well. I suppose we could have the car drop you off, then pick you up in an hour."

"You have arrived at an opportune time," said Commissioner Hopkins to Mrs. Roosevelt. "Allow me to introduce

Mr. Mason Hupp. Mr. Hupp is the proprietor of Hupp Catering Services, Limited—the company that supplied the
food and drink served aboard *Christina* the night when
Gunnar Torstenson was killed. He has come in at my request to talk about the girl who walked out of the galley
and never returned."

Hupp was a florid man with a time-and-dissipation-
ravaged face. He stared at Mrs. Roosevelt through octago-
nal rimless glasses and blinked as though he could not believe he was actually seeing the famous wife of the
President of the United States.

"We would have questioned Mr. Hupp yesterday," said
Hopkins, "except that he was gone all day on a fishing
trip."

"I am pleased to meet you, Mr. Hupp," said Mrs. Roosevelt as she sat down.

"So . . ." said Hopkins. "Tell Mrs. Roosevelt what you
told me about how you came to hire that girl."

Hupp nodded and spoke to the First Lady. "A man came
to my shop. Said he had a girl that needed a job bad. I told
him I didn't need any girl, but he handed me a five-pound
note and said I should take the money and give the girl a
job. So I did. But, honestly, I don't know who the man was.
I never saw him before or since."

"This was when?" asked Mrs. Roosevelt.

"Monday. 'Bout two hours before I had to have people
on the Torstenson yacht. The girl showed up a little while
after the man left, and I told her she could wash dishes
that night. She said okay, and that was that. It was funny,
thinkin' about it later, that she never asked how much I'd
pay her or anything. She just said okay."

"Describe the man," said Hopkins.

"Like I said. Young fellow. Never saw him before."

"Could he have been an American?" asked Mrs. Roosevelt.

Hupp shrugged. "I suppose he could have," said Hupp. "But then . . . maybe not, come to think of it. He didn't talk funny, like an American."

"And the girl?"

"Well, she . . . She didn't say much."

"Describe her," said Mrs. Roosevelt.

"Young. Awfully thin. Looked like she needed a job, actually. Short hair. Kind of a pretty girl, I guess you'd say."

Hopkins stood. "Thank you, Mr. Hupp. Be where I can contact you for the next few days. If you decide to leave the island for any reason, let me know in advance, will you?"

When Hupp was gone, Commissioner Hopkins sat down again. "Well . . . Not very enlightening, was he?"

"Perhaps he was," said Mrs. Roosevelt. "Are you thinking what I'm thinking?"

"Yes, and I can find out easily enough. But I thought we ought to discuss it first."

"You would find out by having the two confront each other?" said Mrs. Roosevelt.

"Yes, plus Hannah, the woman who worked with her in the galley."

"I must confess," said Mrs. Roosevelt, "that the idea is so dreadful that I am not sure I want to know. If it proved untrue, I would be relieved. If it proved true—" She stopped and shook her head.

"I've been thinking it could be Miss King," said Hopkins. "When she was here last night, the thought ran constantly through my mind. When Hupp began to describe the man who paid five pounds to get a girl a job, I thought he might describe Mr. Krouse. But he didn't. I pressed him for a more thorough description than he gave you. His description of the girl could be of Miss Jean King. His description of the man could not be of Mr. Kenneth Krouse."

"Shortly before Mr. Torstenson was killed, Mr. Krouse came to me and told me there was a fire on board the yacht. I've wondered how he knew—since no one else seemed to. I've wondered from that hour if he and Miss King . . . And if they did, did they do it on authority of the government of the United States?"

"Or at the request of His Majesty's Government," said Hopkins. "It could be a matter of national security, on the part of either government, or both. That is one reason why I am reluctant to arrange a confrontation between Miss King and Mr. Hupp."

"The government of the United States does not commit murder," said Mrs. Roosevelt. "Even as a matter of national security."

She said it warmly, but she remembered vividly the words of the President's wire—MATTER MAY BE EXTREMELY COMPLEX AND SENSITIVE STOP MUCH INVOLVED THAT I CANNOT COMMUNICATE BY WIRE STOP. What could be so complex and sensitive?

"His Majesty's Government is at war," said Hopkins. "I suspect it is quite capable of committing murder, if there were definite information identifying Torstenson as someone whose continued existence would seriously damage the nation's chances of survival."

"Even if we were at war, I—Well, I don't know, actually. But the United States is not at war. The position of a friendly neutral is most difficult, Mr. Hopkins."

"I must say, on the other hand, that I would be much surprised if His Majesty's agents killed Torstenson. I . . . think they would tell me. I think someone would at least be warning me off the investigation."

"There are many other kinds of motives for the murder," said Mrs. Roosevelt.

"Yes. But none that I can think of for so expertly destroying the radio on *Christina.*"

"Well, Mr. Hopkins . . ." the First Lady sighed. "Just what are you going to do about Miss King?"

"For the moment, nothing," he said. "I keep thinking I will receive instructions."

"The duchess has not reported her jeweled clip missing?"

"No. On the other hand, she might not. I don't believe the Windsors are too pleased with their Commissioner of Police."

"She told me nothing was missing," said Mrs. Roosevelt.

"Maybe I should return the clip to her and explain where I found it," said Hopkins.

"I suggest you do that. I should like to be present when you do."

"The duke and I would like to own a boat of our own," said the duchess as she and Mrs. Roosevelt left the Rolls-Royce and began a stroll along the Nassau waterfront.

Alex Zaferakes walked a few paces behind, as did a British soldier in mufti, a bodyguard for the Duchess of Windsor.

"We have always wanted a boat," the duchess went on, "but unfortunately we have never felt we had enough money to own a suitable yacht. Perhaps a cabin cruiser . . . The duke does love to go boating."

"So does my husband," said Mrs. Roosevelt. "He used to own, in partnership, a very comfortable sort of houseboat and cruised the waters around Florida for weeks on end. I rarely went aboard, but he loved it. When he retires, I hope it will be possible for him to have a boat again."

"He will never know privacy again," said the duchess. "Neither will I. The duke has never known it and doesn't miss it, but for myself, I would welcome the opportunity to walk the streets of Paris or New York unrecognized—as I used to be."

"Señor Gutiérrez," said Mrs. Roosevelt, nodding toward the chubby little Mexican who stood on the wharf ahead of them, looking at a boat.

Gutiérrez turned and saw them, and he strode toward them, smiling widely. He was accompanied by two ominous-looking men. Apparently overnight he had hired bodyguards. Two of them.

"*Good* morning!" he cried. "It is the great pleasure. You find me contemplating the boats, thinking of buying another. Excuse me for not apologizing last night for the almost-tragedy which did not befall you."

"Our sympathy on the loss of your handsome boat," said Mrs. Roosevelt.

"Oh yes, Isidro . . ." said the duchess.

"It was not of mine," he said with a sad smile. "I have leased it. Even so . . . so beautiful a boat, they don't make them many anymore."

"Who did it, Isidro?" the duchess asked. "Who tried to kill us?"

"It was me, not you," he said. "They want to kill me. I am not surprised."

"You are not surprised?" asked Mrs. Roosevelt.

He shook his head. "They kill nations. Whole peoples. Why should they be reluctant to kill one Mexican banker?"

"Who are you talking about, Isidro?" asked the duchess.

"The Hitler gang," said Gutiérrez. "I warned Torstenson of them."

"You never talked this way before," said the duchess.

He shrugged. "They never tried to kill me before."

"Who tried to kill you?" the duchess demanded sharply.

"Your friends, Your Royal Highness," he said grimly. "And may I suggest to you, therefore, that you be more careful in choosing your friends?"

The duchess turned her back on Gutiérrez and stalked away. "I shall be," she muttered.

Errol Flynn came toward them. Dressed in a loose white shirt and white duck trousers, he wore sunglasses and a floppy straw hat. Judy was with him, wearing tight little shorts.

"Ah! My dear ladies! On your way out to the boat? We came ashore in the launch, and it hasn't gone back out, I think."

"No, Errol," said the duchess. "We're not going out to the yacht this morning."

"Just as well," said Flynn. "Sloan's having some kind of meeting. All very businesslike. Veddy, veddy businesslike. And boring."

"Will he be staying in Nassau long?" asked Mrs. Roosevelt.

"Longer than he planned. The big boom last night damaged the hull. Underwater. She took a thousand gallons or so in the bilge overnight and developed a list. Repairs start this afternoon."

"Things run downhill," said Judy. She demonstrated with her hands. "Anything round rolls off the table and across the deck. Weird."

"Chapman and Wyler?" asked the duchess.

"Right," said Flynn. "On board. Swilling coffee. Grim."

"Settling the problems of the world," said Judy.

"Yeah, right," said Flynn. "Say there, Mrs. R. Where's your man Krouse? He agreed to go a couple rounds bare-knuckle with me."

"As a favor to me, Mr. Flynn, would you forget all about that?"

He grinned. "Sure. As a favor to you. But why?"

"Well . . . Mr. Krouse was a university boxing champion. Besides that, he has studied jujitsu under a Japanese master in Washington. I am afraid, Mr. Flynn, you might be seriously injured."

"Oh. Well . . . Might be interesting, but—"

"I shouldn't like the publicity," said Mrs. Roosevelt. "I mean . . . a major motion-picture star injured, perhaps his nose or jaw broken, by a member of my staff." She shook her head. "I would be grateful if you didn't take the risk."

Flynn showed her a toothy smile, a trademark of his. "Sure," he said jauntily. "As a favor to you."

The First Lady returned his smile. "Thank you, Mr. Flynn."

Jean King, Ken Krouse, and Kevin Hammet sat down for lunch in a downtown restaurant, at a table on a shaded balcony overlooking the water.

Jean drank from a gin and tonic. "Damn," she said. "I am tired of playing lady's maid. The Windsor bitch shoots me one dirty look after another—because I don't know how to play the part to her standards."

"Sacrifices," said Ken. "Line of duty."

"Before food is served," said Kevin, "I need to talk a bit about the difficulty in identifying the various pieces of corpse that have been netted by the commissioner's men."

"Anything that helps?" asked Jean.

"No. Nothing, I'm afraid. Still, if we could identify the

bomber, we should have a good lead to the murderer of Gunnar Torstenson."

"Not necessarily," said Ken.

"We know a few things about the man," said Jean.

"Such as?"

She smiled wryly. "He didn't know how to plant an explosive charge."

"American humor!" exclaimed Kevin.

"On the other hand," she said, "he had access to dynamite and caps. Not everyone does. And, he had to be a reasonably strong swimmer, to swim out to *René*, ferrying his dynamite and caps, plus a coil of wire and some tools."

"The police have concentrated a part of their effort," said Kevin, "on finding out where he entered the water. It was dark, of course—or nearly so—and he must have swum very quietly among the boats and out. Still, he had to swim at least fifty yards, carrying a burden as you say."

"Who's missing?" asked Jean. "That's Mrs. Roosevelt's question. Is anyone concentrating on that?"

Kevin shrugged. "So far, no one seems to be missing. The police are checking on the employees of the various men involved in business relationships with Torstenson and Gutiérrez—but no one is missing, apparently."

"What do you know about Isidro Gutiérrez?" asked Jean.

"His government doesn't like him," said Kevin. "He is wealthy and probably evades taxes on the bulk of his wealth. He uses his wealth politically. He is opposed to your country or his becoming involved in the war, because he sees the war in Europe as an opportunity for the businessmen of neutral countries to make immense profits."

"A Latin American Torstenson," said Ken.

"Yes. I think that would sum it up."

"Nazi connection?" asked Jean.

"Not that we've been able to uncover. And I—Oh, I say! Isn't *Christina* moving? Yes! She is moving. She's underway!"

They stared at the Torstenson yacht. Crewmen cast off lines and leaped aboard. The bow swung out from the wharf, and the propellers churned up silt from the bottom. Two policemen ran along the wharf, yelling. They were ignored. The big yacht gained speed and moved authoritatively out into the harbor.

Small boats scattered as *Christina* bore down on them. The yacht moved past Sloan's yacht, *René*, and on toward open water, pursued now by a police launch that roared after her, a police officer yelling through a megaphone.

"I'll be damned!" said Kevin. "Captain Lindeblad is taking her to sea, impounded or no."

"He's getting away with it, too," said Ken.

The police launch was alongside now, but the yacht kept gaining speed, moving west. In minutes it would be beyond the barrier island that formed the harbor and would swing north into the open sea.

The Duke of Windsor stood with a pair of glasses pressed to his eyes and watched the yacht turning north. Brigadier Sir Edmund Hilary-Percy stood beside him, also with field glasses, watching the yacht pull away from the police launch, which lost speed as it had to cope with the swells off the open ocean.

"I shall notify command," said the brigadier. "We'll put aerial surveillance on her, and perhaps the navy has something in the area."

"No," said the duke, lowering his glasses. "Let her go. There is no point in creating an international incident."

The brigadier continued to watch through his glasses, and after a moment he murmured, "I suspect one is being created anyway."

When the duke lifted his glasses and looked again, he saw a fast patrol boat racing toward the *Christina*. It flew the British naval ensign, and the duke could see it flashing a signal at the yacht.

The yacht continued north, out to sea. Suddenly there was a flash and a puff of smoke from the bow of the patrol boat. Through their glasses the men could see the splash and small explosion as a shell hit the water.

"My God, he's firing on her!" yelled the duke.

"A warning shot across her bow, as they say," observed the brigadier insouciantly.

Christina slowed, and turned, and retreated slowly into Nassau harbor.

Junius Gerald met Mrs. Roosevelt at the door of the governor's limousine. He bowed, kissed her hand, and escorted her into the New Providence Club.

It was, as the duchess had said, a social club for the black population of Nassau, situated on a road a little out of town, on a small rise with a view of the harbor but with no frontage on the water. The rambling, one-story building was of weathered clapboard. The roof sagged. The broad rear porch, which afforded the view of the water, was a ramshackle structure that tilted outward.

Fortunately, the luncheon at which the First Lady was guest of honor was being held on the sloping lawn beyond the club building. There, forty or fifty people, most of them dressed in white, broke into applause as Gerald led Mrs. Roosevelt out the rear door of the club, across the porch, and down some wooden stairs.

A band to one side was playing rhythmic music, the

music she had heard last night as she rode the bicycle through Nassau. A young woman in a brightly colored costume danced sinuously on a small wooden platform in front of the band.

"We are honored," said Junius Gerald.

"I am honored," said Mrs. Roosevelt.

"Did you hear about the Swedish yacht?"

"No. Is there news about the *Christina*?"

"Yes, indeed. She cast off and tried to leave the harbor a little while ago. A patrol boat cut her off just beyond the tip of Hog Island and fired a warning shot across her bow. You can see her out there now, coming back to her mooring."

Mrs. Roosevelt looked down at the harbor. It was true. The yacht was moving very slowly back toward the wharf where she had been moored. "Strange, don't you think?" she asked. "I mean that Captain Lindeblad would try to elude patrol boats and go to sea illegally."

"The patrol boat is a British naval vessel," said Gerald. "It's on submarine-patrol duty in Bahamian waters and would usually be many miles from here. No doubt its skipper received a radio call from the Nassau police, and it's just a matter of good fortune that the boat was close enough to help. Once the yacht was outside Bahamian territorial waters, it would have been difficult to find—not to mention that different legal questions arise about stopping a neutral vessel on the high seas."

"What happens now?" she asked.

"You'll have to ask Commissioner Hopkins," said Gerald. "As I'm going to do. He would have been here by now, except for this incident. Let me, incidentally, introduce you to his wife."

Although no receiving line was formed, in the next half hour Mrs. Roosevelt met nearly everyone at the party.

They approached her—some of them shyly, all of them warmly smiling—and happily accepted the hand she offered them to shake. She was handed glasses of a punch they maintained in a large round glass bowl. One sip told her it was heavily laced with rum. Watching them replenish the bowl, she saw a whole bottle of rum poured in.

Seeing her observe this, Gerald asked, "Do you enjoy rum, Mrs. Roosevelt?"

"Ordinarily, I drink very little of anything alcoholic," she said. "My husband enjoys rum, though. His usual cocktail is gin, but from time to time he makes a cocktail from a recipe he learned in Haiti many years ago. He mixes equal parts of rum and fresh orange juice, puts in some brown sugar and part of an egg white, and shakes it with cracked ice. The several ingredients seem to disguise the taste of the rum, and you drink it without actually realizing there is much alcohol in it. In fact, I will accept a glass of it myself, as will my husband's mother." She paused to smile. "The President enjoys serving this cocktail to people who are a bit stuffy. He gives them several glasses of it and is amused to see how they loosen up."

Gerald laughed. Then he said, "You met Joseph Miller a while ago. I think you might talk with him again."

Miller was tall and slender, with gleaming chocolate-brown skin. His face was merry, as if everything amused him. He peered down at the First Lady through round, gold-rimmed spectacles.

"Joe buys and sells property," said Gerald. "He's the only man of our race on the island who does."

"I see," said Mrs. Roosevelt gravely.

"Let him tell you about a particular property deal he knows something about."

They sat down at a trestle table covered with a white cloth and set with paper plates and cups. The food Mrs.

Roosevelt had seen inside the clubhouse would be brought to the tables later—huge bowls of cold salads and great fish on platters. For now people were standing around sipping punch and chatting, and seeing Gerald and Miller having a solemn talk with the American lady, they kept away from that table.

"I buy and sell," said Miller. "Small properties, what my people can afford. Small houses with a little garden space. Little stores. That kind of thing. Property is cheap on Eleuthera. Life is lazy over there. Boats chug back and forth, bring people to Nassau to work, take them home at night. But most folks fish, garden a little . . . maybe steal a little now and again. You know. The easy life. I guess I've bought and sold fifty little properties over there. Fifty pounds a good price."

"Up till now," said Gerald.

Miller nodded. "Up till now. Now the word is, the government of the United States is going to build a naval base there, maybe an air base, chase after submarines. Lot that was worth fifty pounds six months ago is worth a thousand pounds today—more if they think it's on the land the government of the United States will buy. It's made me a rich man. I sold what I had there, before some smart white man figured out a way to take it away from me."

"Mr. Miller . . ."

"That's the way it is, Ma'am. Way it is. I sold four lots, all I had on Eleuthera. All to one man. As I was telling Junius here, the high bidder was Mr. Gunnar Torstenson. He bought four properties I had, all on Tarpum Bay. I know he bought at least twenty more."

"High bidder, you say. And who was the next-highest bidder?"

Miller smiled. "Henry Chapman. He bid five hundred. Not for himself, though. He was bidding for a group. Curtis Wyler. William Ashbrook. And . . . our learned governor, the Duke of Windsor."

"The duke would be a front man, lend respectability," said Gerald.

"You are suggesting, I suppose," said Mrs. Roosevelt, "that these men had motive to kill Mr. Torstenson. Their lost profits."

Gerald smiled slyly. "If, of course, the government of the United States decided not to build its base on Eleuthera but moved on south a bit, say to Cat Island, the speculators would be outfoxed."

"And no one will have gotten rich but me." Miller laughed.

"I will report the matter to the President," said the First Lady. "His first consideration must be the defense of the hemisphere. I know he would be delighted to frustrate the schemes of war profiteers, however, and I will put the matter to him in that light."

"The same thing is going on here on New Providence Island," said Gerald. "Here it involves expensive land. Whole cays. Beach frontage. What people of my race can't afford."

Mrs. Roosevelt frowned. "I'm afraid I have little influence here," she said regretfully.

The food brought to the trestle tables was even more delicious than it had looked in the clubhouse. The First Lady ate a large portion of flaky white fish, surprised to discover that it could be so palatable cold. The fruit and vegetable salads were delicious. She found on her plate a quivering white square of gelatinous, starchy paste which turned out to be savory, especially when eaten with the fish. It was made from rice, she was told. She ate fried bananas, which she had never tasted before. Some bits of meat defied identification, and she ate them and did not ask what they were.

While everyone ate, the band played on, and a pair of black dancers, a man and a woman, skimpily dressed, their bodies glistening with oil, entertained from the tiny stage.

Commissioner Edgar Hopkins arrived while she was eating. He saluted her and sat down with his wife. It was only when the meal was finished that he came across the sloping lawn to her table.

"Interesting things have happened," he said to her as he sat down beside her at a place vacated by Miller to make room for him.

"I heard that Captain Lindeblad tried to take the *Christina* to sea."

"More than that," said Hopkins glumly. "When we got men aboard the yacht, back in the harbor, we found Captain Lindeblad dead. A suicide, apparently."

"I suppose you are not prepared to accept that," said Mrs. Roosevelt.

"I don't know what to accept," said Hopkins. "He was in his cabin, just ahead of the room where the radio was burned out, dead of a shot to the head, a Luger pistol in his hand. If he was murdered, I know who murdered him, though."

"Who?"

"His lieutenant. Valentin. Missing. It could be that he shot the captain, then went over the side, maybe to a boat waiting for him. The crewmen we've questioned swear they haven't seen him since yesterday afternoon. Don't ask me why. I haven't reached a theory about that as yet."

Mrs. Roosevelt drew a deep breath. "*I* have," she said.

"I'd be glad to hear it."

"Lieutenant Valentin is the man who died in the explosion on Señor Gutiérrez's launch. Missing. We've been looking for a man who is missing. Missing since yesterday afternoon. Allow me to suggest, Commissioner, that you dedicate a great deal of effort to learning the identity of Captain Lindeblad and Lieutenant Valentin."

"Your theory?"

"Theory . . . Let me keep my theory to myself. It will be a great deal more persuasive if you examine the facts and arrive at the same or a similar theory. If I tell you what I think, you may be led to accept and follow the suggestion. I, uh . . . Well, that is one of the techniques of criminal investigation I have learned during my brief and occasional acquaintance with such matters."

IX

The Duchess of Windsor faced Jean King. "I have never seen a lady's shoes in so unkempt a condition as these," she said sharply, pointing to three pairs of shoes in Mrs. Roosevelt's bedroom closet. "And these clothes have not been brushed. How long have you been in service, Jean?"

"Not long, My Lady."

"Not long enough to have learned proper forms of address," said the duchess. "You will address me in future as 'Your Royal Highness.' Do you understand?"

"Yes . . . Your Royal Highness."

"Bring those shoes to the east wing," said the duchess. "My maid will show you how to care for shoes properly. And while you are learning, you can do some pairs of mine as well. If you do half a dozen pairs of mine, and those, you might become half competent."

"I hope so, Your Royal Highness."

The Duchess of Windsor raised her chin high. "If in fact you don't do shoes properly and don't brush clothes—and don't know forms of address—you leave me no option but to suspect you are no maid at all."

"I am sorry, Your Royal Highness."

"Forget the shoes, Jean," said the duchess. "I'm an American like you, and you can't fool me about being a servant. You can fool the Brits, but I know an intelligence agent when I see one. I was one once. For the United States Navy. In China. Thankless damned job. You're out of your league, you know. *They've* been at it for centuries. I mean the British and the Germans. We Americans are strictly amateurs when it comes to espionage and counterespionage. I suppose your assignment is the duke and me. You're wasting time and energy if it is. There's nothing to learn. Anyway, good luck to you."

Jean grinned. " 'Kay, Wallis," she said. "Good luck to you, too. Let's us Americans stick together when the chips are down."

The duchess shrugged. "I'm not really an American anymore, you know. I'm a British duchess. Well . . . I've said too much already. But I believe something, Jean. I *believe* it. The duke could have prevented the war, and he can end it honorably. Send the word back to your government—the salvation of democracy is in a negotiated peace. A war that somebody wins will destroy civilization as we know it."

"If somebody doesn't defeat Hitler, then what happens to civilization?" Jean asked.

"If somebody does defeat Hitler, then what does Stalin do to civilization?" the duchess asked in return. "Anyway, no one is going to defeat him. The only way to save civilization is to come to terms with him."

Jean smiled wryly at the duchess. "I may not be a maid, but making war and peace is quite beyond my scope."

"Just what is your assignment, may I ask?"

"Can you keep a confidence?"

"Of course."

"I'm simply Mrs. Roosevelt's second bodyguard. Alex Zaferakes is her public and official bodyguard; I'm the covert one."

The duchess smiled, genuinely amused. "Yes, of course. Anyway, send the word where you can. The duke can contribute importantly to ending the war. He's no insignificant man, you know."

Henry Chapman's home was situated at the top of a ridge, where homes had been designed and built to catch every cooling breeze that blew off the sea. The windows were large, screened, and wide open. Ceilings were high. Fans hung from the ceilings and turned slowly, stirring the air. Even so, the rooms were uncomfortably warm. Even in a well-maintained home like this one, the plaster flaked from the walls: the result of constant high humidity.

"The colonial splendor of a very small colony," the duchess remarked quietly to Mrs. Roosevelt as they entered the house. "Fortunately, Henry Chapman is a generous and genial host."

Cocktails were being served on a veranda lighted by candles in hurricane lamps. A felicitous breeze stirred the palms around the house and the tropical shrubbery near the veranda. The duke had elected to appear this evening in his white uniform, but the other men were wearing tropical-weight white dinner jackets and were undoubtedly more comfortable than he would be. The women wore white gowns.

Once again, Mrs. Roosevelt's staff was invited, so Krouse, MacGruder, and Zaferakes were with her. Alfred Sloan was there, as was Errol Flynn, with Judy; also Curtis Wyler, Chief Justice Sir William Melbourne, and Brigadier Sir Edmund Hilary-Percy. Once again too, as Mrs.

Roosevelt noted, no representative of the island's black community had been invited.

On the way to the party, the Duchess of Windsor had described the conversation they were likely to hear as "colonial" and "provincial." It was. Mrs. Roosevelt smiled and endured. Years of experience in politics had taught her to endure it.

As soon as the Rolls-Royce pulled away from Government House, Jean King changed out of her maid's uniform, into a bathing suit, over which she wore a pair of white slacks and a blouse; then she borrowed a bicycle and set out for the beach.

If New Providence Island lacked much, it did not lack for coral beaches: smooth white sand behind a pounding surf. They were to be found everywhere, it seemed to Jean. Oddly, most of the population of the island cared little for them. Tourists did. The local population, white and black, was bemused by the tourists' fascination with nothing more than waves lapping on sand and rarely visited the beaches. Especially at sunset and after.

She found Kevin where he had said he would be. She ran to him and threw herself into his arms for a lingering kiss.

"God, I thought we'd never—" she whispered.

He stopped her words with another fervent kiss. For a whole minute they did not break it off.

Kevin had gathered driftwood and had a fire going. The sun was setting as Jean pushed her slacks down and took off her blouse. West was behind them, so they saw the sun disappear behind high ground, not into the ocean horizon where it would rise. The tops of purple clouds caught the fading rays, though, and burned hot orange in contrast to the darkness below and above.

"I suggest we splash in the surf and not venture out into the water much," said Kevin. "I haven't experienced it, but the natives say the barracuda come close to shore once the sun sets."

She nodded and ran down to the edge of the water. It was warm, and she stood in the sand and let the waves rush up around her legs. Whether she swam or not was immaterial. She was on the beach and in the water—and with him—and that was what counted.

She wore a bathing suit that was considered bold in 1940—a light-blue, one-piece suit, its thin fabric tightly stretched over her body and molded to its every curve, deep-cut in front, and exposing her whole back. Kevin was not subtle in his appreciation.

Standing in the sand that shifted under her feet as the water rushed around them, she found it difficult to believe this beach was in a colony of a nation fighting desperately for its survival, that under that darkening sea, only a few miles out—and within the distance she could see—an enemy submarine might be lurking.

Kevin stepped up behind her. He had perhaps read her thought, because he said, "The lights are kept on in Nassau, as if the war were thousands of miles away."

"How long will you be stationed here, Kevin?" she asked.

"I've wondered," he said. "It must seem like privileged duty. It *is* privileged, in fact. My father and mother have seen more of the war than I have."

"How are they?" she asked.

"They're at our country place in Kent. The flat in London has been damaged. Dad goes into town during the week and stays in the undamaged room, but Mum hardly ever ventures in. You remember the boat? Dad made three runs across the Channel to Dunkirk with it, to bring back wounded lads. It was strafed on the last run. Two lads were killed. Dad wasn't hit, but the boat was chopped up rather badly, so he couldn't make the fourth run. She sank overnight."

"Americans can't imagine that kind of thing," she said.

"God forbid they should have to," he said solemnly.

Impulsively she reached out and touched his arm. He reacted. He bent down and kissed her on the forehead. Then he put his arms around her.

"Kevin . . ."

They kissed. Then simultaneously they broke off and walked back up the beach to his fire.

He spoke very quietly. "I've tried to do something American," he said. "Commander MacGruder told me how to cook an American hotdog—that is, on pointed sticks over a small fire. I brought bread. You can't buy American hotdog buns here. I brought mustard and catsup. And beer."

"You are a wonderful man, Kevin," she said simply.

They had to go up the beach to the edge of a palm grove before they found the green sticks they would need to sharpen for hotdog spits. She taught him how to cook a hotdog, holding the spitted wiener into the flame as long as she dared before the stick caught fire. The grease oozed out and dripped into the flames, and the smoke that rose brought saliva to their mouths. His mustard was brown and piquant. The beer was warm but English and dark, heavy, and delicious.

"I have a bit of information," he said as he ate. "I hate to bring it up, but Commander MacGruder should know."

"All right."

"I wired the morgue photos of Lindeblad to London, together with images of his fingerprints. You know—radio transmission to Miami, then wire to New York and cable to London. They've returned a tentative identification. It seems Captain Eric Lindeblad was really *Hauptmann* Heinrich Hardegen, *Kriegsmarine.*"

"Captain in the German navy," said Jean, frowning.

"More than that. A dedicated Nazi, as relatively few German naval officers are."

Jean drew a deep breath. "How does that relate to the murder of Gunnar Torstenson and the attempt to murder Isidro Gutiérrez?"

Kevin shook his head. "I don't know. There will be time to think about all that later, will there not?"

As she nodded, he leaned toward her and drew her into his arms.

"I am curious to know," said Mrs. Roosevelt to the Duke of Windsor, "why Señor Gutiérrez is not a guest this evening. I understood he is one of the business associates of Mr. Chapman and the others."

The duke shrugged. "I think it is possible they are rivals, actually," he said.

"Indeed. Rivals for what?"

"Investment capital," said the duke. "All of them are wealthy. Like all wealthy men, they want to become more wealthy. No one ever thinks he is rich enough, you know."

The duke, she observed, drank a good deal of whisky but held it well. It generated a change in his voice, and his eyes glittered when he had been drinking, but otherwise he showed no sign of intoxication. The duchess drank more and became a little louder, a little shrill. Possibly Errol Flynn had been admonished about last night. After dinner he settled into a huge peacock chair in a corner of the veranda, let Judy bring him drinks, and quietly lapsed into a stupor. The girl, who herself was staggering, sat down on the floor at his feet and fell asleep, leaning against his legs.

Mrs. Roosevelt nodded to Commander Wilson Mac-Gruder to indicate that she wanted a word with him, aside. When they could step apart from the others for a moment, she said to him—

"I assume you can send a coded message to Washington and receive a coded reply. Can you not?"

He nodded. "Yes, Ma'am."

"I want some information," she said. "Send word to Washington that we want—whether you say you want or I want is immaterial, whichever will produce quicker results—a summary of the financial position of Mr. Henry Chapman. He is Canadian, I believe. I don't need a great deal of detailed information, but I should like to know if his affairs are in a sound condition."

"Immediately?"

She nodded. "If you please."

When Mrs. Roosevelt returned to her room in Government House, she found Jean King there, asleep on her bed.

"Oh, I'm sorry!" she said when the First Lady wakened her. "I was waiting for you, and—"

"It's quite all right, my dear. Did you have a pleasant picnic with Mr. Hammet?"

Jean smiled. "Very pleasant, thank you. I—Well, very pleasant. But I have to report to you something that he told me."

"And what is that?"

"Captain Eric Lindeblad was in fact Captain Heinrich Hardegen of the German navy."

Mrs. Roosevelt raised her eyes to the ceiling. "Ah. Significant," she said.

"There is a car waiting for us on the road. If you want,

Kevin will meet with us tonight, and with Commissioner Hopkins. Both of them understand your close interest in the murder of Gunnar Torstenson."

"It might be well, then, if Mr. Krouse joins us."

Parked on the road a hundred yards from Government House was, not a car and driver, but a car. Hammet had provided it earlier, and Jean had driven it. She drove it now, along the same road where she and the First Lady had bicycled the night before. It was, again, after two in the morning; and Ken Krouse, who had difficulty remaining awake in the back seat, even for this five-minute drive, wondered aloud how Mrs. Roosevelt managed to function with so little sleep.

"I am all but asleep during these interminable parties," she said.

Jean laughed, but she was instantly solemn again. "I must tell you both something," she said. "The duchess knows I am not a maid. I guess I didn't play the part well enough. She confronted me on it late this afternoon, and I told her I am a bodyguard."

"Well, if she knows, everyone knows," said Ken. "The woman is incapable of keeping a secret."

"I had as soon we dropped the pretense anyway," said Mrs. Roosevelt. "I've found it awkward."

"Does this mean I don't have to wear a cap and apron anymore?" Jean asked, chuckling.

"You look lovely in what you're wearing," said Mrs. Roosevelt.

Jean was wearing the white slacks and blouse she had worn over her swimsuit. It was in dramatic contrast to the First Lady's party gown and Ken's white dinner jacket.

The commissioner of police was waiting for them in his

office. He made a call and said Hammet was on his way and would not need five minutes to arrive there.

"Thanks to Secret Intelligence Service, we now know who Captain Lindeblad really was," said Hopkins.

"Mr. Hammet really is—?" asked Mrs. Roosevelt.

"Lieutenant Hammet, Royal Navy," said Jean. "On assignment to Secret Intelligence Service. He's a Cambridge graduate and was on his way to a career as a barrister when the war came."

"How many people know who he is?" asked Mrs. Roosevelt.

"*We* do," said Hopkins, making a circle of the room with a finger. "Commander MacGruder knows. There are other intelligence officers in Nassau, I am sure, though I don't know who all of them are, and I doubt all of them know all of each other. A couple of naval officers know. Otherwise—"

"The Duke of Windsor?" asked Mrs. Roosevelt.

"Emphatically not," said the commissioner.

"Are we to understand," she asked, "that the *Christina* was in effect a German naval vessel?"

"I think it would be better to let Lieutenant Hammet explain that."

In a very few minutes Hammet was there, and he did explain—

"We didn't really know, you see. We suspected. So—"

"Who sabotaged the yacht's radios?" asked Mrs. Roosevelt.

Hammet flushed and frowned. "I did," he said brusquely. "Technically a violation of Swedish neutrality—"

"But necessary if you had good reason to believe the

yacht was being illicitly used in the German interest," said Mrs. Roosevelt.

He nodded. "I appreciate your understanding," he said.

"I am very curious about something," said Mrs. Roosevelt. "Just what was Mr. Torstenson's role? What was his attitude?"

"His company, Vellinck-Torstenson, is selling war materiel to Nazi Germany," said Hammet. "Their profits are immense. It is possible Mr. Torstenson was, in effect, hostage to those profits."

"It's possible they had something else on him," said Ken Krouse. "It is possible he was being blackmailed."

"In any event," Hammet went on, "we saw no evidence that he was raising any strenuous objection to the use being made of his yacht."

"It is possible then, is it not? . . . that the late Captain . . . uh, Hardegen, killed Mr. Torstenson," said Mrs. Roosevelt. "At any rate, his identity makes him a prime suspect."

"We have, I think, a *list* of suspects," said Commissioner Hopkins.

"Perhaps we can limit the list, if we put our minds to it," said Mrs. Roosevelt. "Shall we begin by making a list? Should we write it down, actually? I have had some success in these matters by making a chart of suspects. Do you have a blackboard handy, Commissioner?"

He had one brought in by a policeman and propped up on a tripod. Mrs. Roosevelt stood beside it with a piece of chalk.

"Write my name on there first," said Kevin Hammet. "I've admitted I was secretly on board and destroyed the radio. Perhaps I committed a political assassination."

"I will write your name as you suggest, Mr. Hammet," she said. "But I do it only because if what you suggest proves true—which I much doubt—it would establish the innocence of others whose names are about to be written."

She wrote his name in the upper left corner of the board.

"By the same token," said Ken Krouse, "I could have killed him. Are you absolutely certain, Mrs. Roosevelt, that *our* government didn't order a political assassination?"

"I am absolutely certain," she said curtly. "Even so, I will write your name. And beside it I will write that you were in the lounge and within my sight for the quarter hour preceding the discovery of the body of Mr. Torstenson." She smiled ironically at him. "That is what is called an alibi, Mr. Krouse."

"I have a question," said Jean. "How much time elapsed between the last time one of you saw Gunnar Torstenson alive and the time when you discovered the body?"

Mrs. Roosevelt looked to Ken Krouse. Of those together now in the commissioner's office, only she and Krouse had been guests at the party aboard *Christina*.

"Torstenson was there," said Ken, "when he went around introducing the captain. I remember he was rather forceful in saying that Wilson MacGruder should become acquainted with the captain. The duke was emphatic about that, too. And, as I recall, Torstenson left the party shortly after he introduced the captain."

"I can't recall seeing him," said Mrs. Roosevelt slowly, hesitantly, "during the last few minutes of the party—say ten or fifteen minutes."

"All right," said Ken. "Then Captain Hardegen—as we now know him—left the party not long after Torstenson left. I remember thinking he was in something of a hurry."

Mrs. Roosevelt wrote the name Hardegen on the blackboard. She wrote nothing to the right of the name, no alibi.

"I have a question for you, Mr. Krouse," she said. "You

warned me that there was a fire aboard. You said the crew was trying to keep it secret. Still, you knew it. You—"

"I knew the radio was going to be destroyed," said Krouse briskly. "I'm sorry, but I couldn't tell you. I was afraid there would be panic if the flames were seen beyond the confines of the radio room, so I wanted to move you to a place where it would be easy to get out."

"I see . . . Thank you."

"I can name someone else who was on board," said Krouse. "Someone who wasn't invited, I suspect. Curtis Wyler. Not only was he on board, he was wearing dungarees. He wasn't there for the party."

"How do you know?" asked Mrs. Roosevelt.

"I told him," said Kevin Hammet. "I saw Wyler."

Mrs. Roosevelt wrote the name Curtis Wyler on the blackboard. Then she said—

"There is reason to suspect that Mr. Henry Chapman may have had motive to kill Mr. Torstenson. I myself was talking with him shortly before the body was found. But I suppose he had time to go out and commit the murder."

She wrote that name.

"There is also reason," she said, "to think Señor Gutiérrez may have wanted Mr. Torstenson dead. If Mr. Wyler was aboard surreptitiously, then perhaps Señor Gutiérrez was, too. It seems to have been easy to walk on and off the *Christina.*"

"I suggest another name," said Commissioner Hopkins. "Lieutenant Valentin."

Mrs. Roosevelt nodded and wrote the name.

"Well . . ." the commissioner said. "We—"

"We are forgetting the first suspect," said Mrs. Roosevelt. "The young woman who left the galley and disappeared from the yacht about the time when Mr. Torstenson was killed. We don't know who she was, do we?"

No one spoke.

"Very well," said Mrs. Roosevelt, and she wrote MISS X. Her blackboard now looked like this—

MR. HAMMET

MR. KROUSE   REMAINED IN LOUNGE.

CAPT. HARDEGEN

MR. WYLER   WHY IN DUNGAREES?

MR. CHAPMAN

SR. GUTERRIEZ

LT. VALENTIN

MISS X

"I think you can erase Miss X," said Ken Krouse. "You yourself said that a young woman probably would not have had the strength to lift a man Torstenson's size over the rail and drop him into the water."

"What proves, Mr. Krouse, that only one person was involved in committing the murder?" she asked. "A young woman could have captured Mr. Torstenson's attention while his assailant came up behind him and hit him. For that matter, she could have hit him, then had the assistance of someone else in throwing him over."

"So the list remains as it stands, then," said Krouse. "Too many suspects."

"And the culprit," said Commissioner Hopkins, "may not be on the list."

Mrs. Roosevelt looked at the blackboard, sadly. "I might almost hope the killer is not one of these people," she said soberly.

X

Kevin Hammet left the little black car for Jean's use. She could drive around the island all she wanted, now that it was understood she was not Mrs. Roosevelt's maid. It turned out handy for Mrs. Roosevelt, too. On Thursday morning she took it and drove to a meeting with Commissioner Hopkins, leaving just after breakfast. She had earlier spoken with the commissioner on the telephone, and he was expecting her call.

The Windsors, she suspected, were relieved that she was away on some adventure of her own. Neither of them were entirely at ease in her presence, and both of them had agendas of their own. The duchess this morning wanted to spend two hours, at least, with a hairdresser she'd brought down from New York, and having Mrs. Roosevelt away was convenient. The duke wanted to play golf with Alfred Sloan. He was pleased not to have to stay at Government House and play host.

The commissioner had asked the First Lady to meet him, not at his drab headquarters, but at an outdoor *café* that faced the waterfront. When she arrived, he had a pot of coffee on the table, with croissants and marmalade, and was eating breakfast. She sat down and accepted a cup of coffee.

The sun beat down on a morning mist that swirled over the waters of the harbor. The waterfront was bustling— porters carried loads to small boats pulled up to the docks, bicyclists hurried along the quay, fishing boats edged up to the docks and unloaded fish, shellfish, and squid. The *Christina* lay alongside a wharf a little distance from the restaurant: a glum, unhappy boat, guarded by Nassau policemen. *René* lay at anchor fifty yards out. People shouted. Horns tooted. Gulls screamed. The air was heavy with the mixed odors of raw fish, fruit, and engine fumes.

"After you left last night," said Commissioner Hopkins, "I wrote a change on your blackboard. I had it covered then and locked in a closet. We may want to refer to it again."

"A change?" she asked. She paused with her coffee cup just short of her lips. "You've learned something more?"

"I *knew* something more," he said. "I didn't think I should mention it in front of the others."

"What is it?" she asked, then took a sip of rich black coffee.

"I wrote something beside the name of Kevin Hammet. 'Perfect alibi.' He was not aboard *Christina* that evening. He couldn't have been. He was sitting right here, at one of these tables. I saw him. He was sitting here drinking a whisky. Looking thoughtful. Staring at the yacht. When I began to sort out in my mind the circumstances surrounding the death of Gunnar Torstenson, it occurred to me, as it did to the Duchess of Windsor, that Secret Intelligence Service might have sent a man to assassinate Torstenson. I came here and asked the waiters and bartender about

Hammet. He sat here for two hours, during which time he drank four whiskies, and he left when he saw the police cars arrive at the yacht. They are quite positive he did not slip away for ten minutes, go down to *Christina*, and return."

"How very interesting," said Mrs. Roosevelt. "Then he was lying last night. Have you any idea why?"

"I can think of several reasons. But I'd rather not speculate."

"Also, why do you suppose he sat here for two hours nursing whiskies? Was he alone all that time?"

Hopkins nodded. "So they say."

"Then he did not sabotage the radio, he did not kill Mr. Torstenson, and . . . and let us not forget, he did not see Mr. Wyler aboard the yacht in dungarees."

"Yes. I scribbled a question mark over that."

Mrs. Roosevelt shook her head. "Distressing," she said. "Why do you suppose that young man lied to us?"

"I can only suppose it was to protect someone else," said the commissioner.

"You are thinking of . . . ?"

"Miss X," said Hopkins. "Whoever she was."

"Jean King," said Mrs. Roosevelt glumly.

"Well . . ."

"It raises a great many questions. In the first place, *why* would he protect her? And if she killed Mr. Torstenson, why did she do it? Commissioner, I am utterly certain the United States government did not send Miss King down here to commit a political murder—no matter what Mr. Torstenson was and what he was doing."

Commissioner Hopkins shrugged. "His Majesty's Government have no such scruples. Of course . . . We are at war, as you are not."

Mrs. Roosevelt sighed. "Mr. Krouse said last night that

he knew the radio was going to be destroyed. If he didn't know it from Mr. Hammet, then how did he know it?"

"Another question for which I have no answer," said the commissioner of police.

She looked out across the harbor, mostly at the Sloan yacht. Boats were drawn up alongside, suggesting that *René* might be in the process of reprovisioning, in preparation for a return to sea. Deep in thought, she stared at the big yacht for a long time

"It all fits together some way," she said finally. "It's not a series of coincidences. The murder of Mr. Torstenson, the explosion that destroyed Señor Gutiérrez's runabout, the fire that destroyed the radio aboard *Christina*—all of it fits together in some way. I am afraid—I am afraid, Commissioner, we may have to think the unthinkable to proceed toward a solution to the mystery."

"We have to arrange a confrontation between Miss King and Mason Hupp," said Commissioner Hopkins. "And one between her and Hannah. Also, one between Hupp and Hammet. We've avoided that, but we can't avoid it any longer."

"I agree. Let's arrange it. And while we are on the subject of what we have avoided, let's confront the Duchess of Windsor with the three-feather clip you found in Mr. Torstenson's pocket. I think we have postponed that long enough."

They returned to Government House, to be told that the Duchess of Windsor was with her hairdresser and had left explicit instructions that she was not to be disturbed.

"Tell the duchess that Mrs. Roosevelt will be sitting in the garden and would like to see her as soon as possible," said Commissioner Hopkins coldly to the maid who brought this word.

The gardens had been neglected. The pool was empty of water and the bottom littered with debris—dried palm fronds and other tropical detritus. Lizards skittered through the untrimmed shrubbery.

"I must say something for the duchess," Hopkins remarked. "It is totally unnecessary for me to like the governor or his lady—or for them to like me, which I suspect they do not—but I must say something in the woman's favor. There is no reason why the mansion of a colonial governor should have been allowed the fall into decay as this one has. It was full of the most *grotesque* old wicker furniture. Within three days after the duchess arrived, much of that was piled up and burnt. In the drawing room there were perfectly offensive portrait paintings—bad reproductions, of course—of Queen Victoria and Queen Mary. The duchess sent them to the attic. And the duke didn't say a word. Whatever the Windsors are, the islands were a backwater before they arrived. Bad as they may be in some respects, their presence here will be a benefit to the Bahamas."

"I hope it may be," said Mrs. Roosevelt. "They seem, though, to have befriended the worst elements."

Commissioner Hopkins laughed loudly. "The millionaires! The worst elements! Spoken like a democrat—I mean, a democrat with a small 'd.' Bravo, Mrs. Roosevelt! Bravo!"

"Millionaires, yes," said she. "But there are millionaires and millionaires, Commissioner. The ones who have gravitated here seem, frankly said, mostly fugitives from justice."

"Do you include the chairman of General Motors in that?"

She smiled. "I do."

"I find myself in a situation more awkward than I can explain," said Hopkins. "Relative to the Windsors—"

"Commander MacGruder," said Mrs. Roosevelt quietly, stopping him before the American naval officer came close enough to hear what the commissioner was about to say.

MacGruder was wearing white uniform, with his ribbons on his chest and boards on his shoulders. He nodded to Hopkins and spoke to Mrs. Roosevelt—

"I sent the radiogram you asked for. This is the reply, decoded."

She scanned the decoded message. It read—

SUBJECT OF INQUIRY ONE HENRY
CHAPMAN WELL-REGARDED CANADIAN
BUSINESSMAN STOP HAS EXTENSIVE
INTERESTS IN LAND OIL MANUFACTURING
STOP SOME DATA SUGGEST HE MAY BE
OVEREXTENDED AND IN DANGER OF
SEEING LOANS CALLED STOP SHOULD BE
REGARDED AS VULNERABLE TO POSSIBLE
FINANCIAL DISASTER STOP HAS
SIGNIFICANT INTERESTS IN GERMAN
MANUFACTURING AND IS THEREFORE
SYMPATHETIC TO GERMAN CAUSE
ANXIOUS TO SEE QUICK NEGOTIATED
PEACE STOP PRESENCE IN BAHAMAS
MYSTERIOUS STOP EXPECTED TO MOVE
ON TO NEUTRAL NATION WHERE HE CAN
WORK TO SALVAGE GERMAN
INVESTMENTS STOP

To Commander MacGruder's obvious surprise, Mrs. Roosevelt handed the message to Commissioner Hopkins.

" 'Overextended,' " she said. "And outbid on Bahamas properties. I find that significant, don't you, Commissioner?"

"Possibly highly significant," said the commissioner.

"I am afraid I am in left field, as we Americans sometimes say," said Commander MacGruder.

"Well, let us not worry about that for the moment," said Mrs. Roosevelt. "I have a question for you. More than one question."

"I will answer to the best of my ability," said the mustached officer.

"You came with me on the basis of written orders, did you not?"

"Yes, Ma'am."

"If I were to ask to see those written orders, could you show them to me?"

"Yes, Ma'am, I could. I would have no problem in showing them to you."

"Do you have them with you?"

"They are in my luggage, Ma'am. If you are not willing to accept my word as to what they contain, I will be glad to show them to you."

"Commander MacGruder . . . I will accept your word. Gladly. All I want to know is, did your orders include authority to act in any way against Mr. Gunnar Torstenson?"

"To kill him, you mean, Ma'am?"

"No, Commander. You need not be so stiff. I have no doubt on that score. Were you, though, authorized to destroy the radio equipment on his yacht?"

"Absolutely not, Ma'am."

"Did you know the nature of the radio equipment on the *Christina*?"

"Yes, Ma'am."

"Were Mr. Krouse or Miss King ordered—or authorized—to destroy that equipment?"

The commander sighed. "We compared orders," he said. "I am betraying a confidence, in a sense, but I can tell you that none of us were ordered or authorized to commit any aggressive act against Mr. Torstenson or his yacht." He sighed again. "Whatever the temptation may have been."

"By which you mean?"

"He was working in the Nazi cause," said Commander MacGruder bluntly. "To be altogether frank with you, Mrs. Roosevelt, I do not regret the death of Gunnar Torstenson. The world is better off without him. I may almost say I regret that I didn't kill him."

"Are there others in Nassau of whom that might be said just as well?" asked Commissioner Hopkins.

Commander MacGruder shot a hard glance at the black police commissioner. "Several others, I would suppose," he said.

"It may be your recommendation that the Bahamas not be the site of an American naval base," said the commissioner.

"It may be," said the commander, "if this nest cannot be cleaned out."

"Whom do you trust, Commander?" asked Hopkins. "Mr. Hammet?"

"Yes, Sir. I trust Mr. Hammet."

"We have caught Mr. Hammet in a series of lies, Commander," said Mrs. Roosevelt. "Would that change your attitude?"

"Mr. Hammet is an intelligence officer, Ma'am," said MacGruder. "In the course of duty it is sometimes necessary to tell lies."

"Particularly to civilians," said Hopkins sarcastically.

MacGruder frowned at Mrs. Roosevelt. "I find myself placed in an untenable position, Ma'am."

She shook her head. "Never mind, Commander," she said. "I thank you for taking care of my message to Washington. I am sure I can count on you if it should be necessary to look to you for other services."

"Thank you," said MacGruder curtly. He nodded—almost a bow—and turned and walked away.

"I didn't ask him something I might have asked," Mrs. Roosevelt muttered to Hopkins. "So . . . Do we sit down here and observe the beauties of nature and wait for the duchess? Or do we go bait her in her den?"

They had no need to ponder the question. A servant appeared almost as Mrs. Roosevelt spoke, bearing iced champagne and a tray of hors d'oeuvres. The Duchess of Windsor, he said, would join them in a few minutes.

In a few minutes, she did. She was elegantly dressed—far too elegantly, in Mrs. Roosevelt's judgment, for a late-morning meeting in a somewhat seedy garden behind a deteriorating colonial mansion—in a handsome dark-blue linen suit, with spectacular jewelry at her throat and on her wrists.

"We may join Alfred Sloan for lunch aboard *René*, if we wish," she said. "The invitation has been extended to you as well, Commissioner."

"I am honored," said the commissioner dryly.

"It has been extended to your staff, Mrs. Roosevelt—including the one-time maid, Miss King."

Mrs. Roosevelt smiled broadly. "A graduate of Smith, Your Grace," she said.

"Indeed?" said the duchess, ignoring the fact she had been addressed as "Your Grace," not "Your Highness."

"Yes. She came with us incognito."

"Not very well disguised," said the duchess. "Americans—graduates of fine colleges in particular—don't mime servants very well."

The Duchess of Windsor was engaging in this dialogue in a smiling, amused humor, and Mrs. Roosevelt gladly adopted the same mood. "Americans," she said, "are not skilled in deception."

The Duchess of Windsor lifted her chin. "That is a skill acquired through long civilization," she said. "For my own part, I have found it difficult to lie as skillfully as the Europeans into whose company I am thrown do quite nonchalantly. Adroit lying, I am afraid, is a luxury acquired only through centuries of practice."

"It is called diplomacy," said Mrs. Roosevelt.

The duchess laughed. "Score one for you, Mrs. Roosevelt," she said. "Have you tasted the champagne? The duke had it flown in from Philadelphia. It seems none very good is to be had in Miami. It is difficult for us, even as royal governor and lady, to match the hospitality we are afforded by some of the—"

"For a town of only twenty thousand people, Nassau seems to have an exorbitant share of millionaires," said Mrs. Roosevelt.

The Duchess of Windsor laughed nervously. "How could a town have too many millionaires?" she asked.

"The commissioner has something to show you," said Mrs. Roosevelt. "Have you not, Commissioner Hopkins?"

The commissioner nodded, reached into the deep pocket of his white, double-breasted jacket, and fished out the jeweled clip in the design of the three feathers of the Prince of Wales.

The duchess blanched. "Wherever . . . Wherever did you find it?"

"You were aware that it was missing?" he asked.

"Of course. For a week. I supposed it had been stolen!"

Commissioner Hopkins glanced at Mrs. Roosevelt. He remembered that the duchess had assured her that nothing had ever been stolen from Government House—not since she and the duke arrived. He handed the valuable property to her, and she turned it over and over in her hand, as if she were fondling it.

"Where did you find it, Commissioner?" she asked.

"In a somewhat embarrassing place, Your Highness," he said. "It was in the pocket of the jacket worn by Mr. Gunnar Torstenson when he was murdered. It was found when the corpse was stripped for the autopsy."

"Oh, my God!"

"Can you offer any explanation as to why Mr. Torstenson should have had in his pocket so valuable a property, belonging to you?"

The Duchess of Windsor, visibly shaken and finding difficulty in saying anything at all, shook her head. "I . . . have no idea where he got it. I can only surmise that he learned it had been stolen, bought it from the thief, and . . . No. No. That is not a reasonable explanation. In the end, I . . . I simply do not know. Does this make me a suspect in his death?"

"Not at all," said Mrs. Roosevelt. "We did wonder, though, if it might not suggest to you some information you might be able to offer, that might lead the investigation in a useful direction."

The duchess drew a deep breath. She stared at the jeweled clip in her hand. "Gunny Torstenson was as good a friend as the duke and I had in the world," she said. "His death was a tragedy to us. If I had any evidence whatever as to who killed him, I would shout it at you. It is my opinion—as I told you before—that he was killed by British intelligence because of his known devotion to the concept of a negotiated peace."

"British intelligence . . ." murmured Commissioner Hopkins.

"Mr. Hopkins," said the duchess, in clipped tones through clenched teeth, "if you knew what 'His Majesty's Government' is capable of—as the duke and I know— then you would not imagine that government would scruple at murder."

Mrs. Roosevelt glanced at Commissioner Hopkins. The duchess had regained her composure and her aggressive stance. Short of a tough cross-examination, she was not going to reveal anything she did not choose to reveal.

"Let's hope no one tries to blow us up this time," said Alfred Sloan to Mrs. Roosevelt as she stepped aboard *René*.

"Let me introduce my staff," she said. "Mr. Kenneth Krouse, Department of State, Commander Wilson MacGruder, United States Navy, and Miss Jean King, naval intelligence officer. Commissioner Edgar Hopkins you have met."

Alfred Sloan shook hands with the men and bowed to Jean King as if he were a butler, not a multimillionaire. Like most highly successful men, he did not show his feelings, did not allow his face or voice to reveal his thoughts. So far as anything on his face or in his voice were concerned, he was welcoming new friends for an innocent luncheon on his boat.

He welcomed the Duke and Duchess of Windsor the same way, as if they were no one in particular, just friends come to spend a pleasant midday.

"I was sitting on the waterfront over coffee this morning," said Mrs. Roosevelt, "and thought I saw you preparing the yacht for departure. Are we soon to be deprived of your company?"

Sloan grinned. "If you are, it will be no surprise. I would guess you are not often surprised, Mrs. Roosevelt."

"Mr. Sloan, I never cease to be surprised," she said.

As they talked he had subtly stepped away from the others, so that he and she could have words together. "Have you any clue as to who killed Torstenson?" he asked quietly.

Curious that he should ask, she frowned and shrugged and said, "Clues, yes. Persuasive clues, no. I don't know, really."

"Nor do I," he said. "I came here to meet the man, only to find him dead, the victim of murder. Mrs. Roosevelt, I have been an aggressive businessman all my life and have destroyed men's careers; but I've never witnessed murder before."

"Perhaps, Mr. Sloan, you have never encountered Nazis before—I mean, not in any realistic way."

"Your judgment is that—"

"I make no judgment," she said. "But what we are looking at is not just business ventures. We are involved, Mr. Sloan, in the life and death of nations."

Sloan looked around—and by his hard glance discouraged others from coming near them. "I came here," he said quietly to her, "to investigate the possibility of putting some money into a Latin American business venture. Some money . . . I mean a great deal of money, Mrs. Roosevelt. So did Torstenson. Nothing illegal. A straightforward business proposition—"

"I know, Mr. Sloan," she said.

"You know?"

She smiled. "We of the New Deal are not ignorant of business considerations," she said.

"Mrs. Roosevelt—"

"I should like to know," she said, "what, if anything, Mr. Torstenson was advising you to do."

"To invest," said Sloan. "But I had a radio message from him, saying don't decide finally until we talk."

"But before you could talk—"

"He was murdered."

"Do you consider that significant, Mr. Sloan?"

The tycoon nodded. "Damned right I do," he said. "Damned right I do. I'd give anything to know what Torstenson had in mind."

When Mrs. Roosevelt and her party were carried by boat back to the wharf, three uniformed policemen were waiting for Commissioner Hopkins. What they wanted to report to him had happened half an hour or so before. She and the commissioner walked a little distance away from the Windsors and the other Americans, while one of the policemen made his report—

"There has been a shooting, Sor. In fact—" He glanced at Mrs. Roosevelt. "Like in American movies. I mean . . . like gangsters."

The uniformed officer, a red-headed, freckled man, was conspicuously upset by what he had to report. Sweat poured from under his cap and down his forehead, and he took the cap off and stood with it in his hand.

"Go on, Brittigan," said the commissioner.

"One man is dead," said the policeman. "He had a gun. He fired shots. The man he was shooting at returned his fire, apparently, and was a better shot than he was."

"Have you anyone in custody, Brittigan?"

"No, Sor. The man fled. But we know who he was. That is to say, we know how to find out. He works for Señor Gutiérrez, the Mexican."

"Have you spoken with Señor Gutiérrez?"

"Yes, Sor. He offered his cooperation immediately."

Commissioner Hopkins looked at Mrs. Roosevelt, shook his head, and said, "A seamless fabric, you think?"

She nodded gravely.

They sat in the duke's office. He insisted that as governor he was entitled to know what was going on. In a small room with an overhead fan turning, with glass-fronted cases of unused law books around the walls, with a worn oriental carpet on the wooden floor, the duke, the commissioner, and Mrs. Roosevelt faced Isidro Gutiérrez.

"The matter is of the simplest," said Gutiérrez. "When they have attempt to murder us all by exploding my boat, I am deciding to employ the bodyguard. I have two of them. This morning as I leave my hotel, two men have fired on me. My guards have killed one of them."

"What is the name of your bodyguard who killed the man, and where is he?" asked Commissioner Hopkins.

"His name is Perfecto Rojas," said Gutiérrez. "He is frighten for what the authority will do to him and has run away. I do not know where he is."

"A Mexican?" asked the commissioner.

"Cuban," said Gutiérrez.

"You say you decided to employ bodyguards," said Mrs. Roosevelt. "Was this man already in your employ?"

"He is before in my employ from time to time."

"How does this Cuban happen to be in Nassau?" asked the Duke of Windsor.

"After the explode of my boat, I am telephoning Havana and asking for him. He flies here yesterday."

"In other words, you imported a Cuban gunman," said Commissioner Hopkins.

"Two of them," said Gutiérrez. "And of the good luck for me that I am, hmm? In other case, I am being dead."

"Who is your second bodyguard, and where is he?"

"He is name Angelo Dioguardi. He waits outside."

The duke puffed thoughtfully on his pipe. "You say there were two of these assailants. What of the other one?"

"He has fleed," said Gutiérrez simply.

"My officers say four shots were fired," said Commissioner Hopkins. "Can you account for four shots? Who fired at whom?"

"Two shots are fired at me," said Gutiérrez. "One by each man. From across the street. You are finding evidence of them in the wall of the hotel, no?"

The commissioner nodded.

"Two are fire by Perfecto Rojas. Both are hit the man. He fall. The other man run."

"Then Dioguardi didn't fire a shot?"

"No. Jumped on me. Knocked me down, to protect me."

"And you really don't know where Rojas has gone?" the commissioner asked.

Gutiérrez shook his head. "I know where he is going. I do not know how. He is going back to Cuba."

"By boat, do you suppose?" asked the duke. "Have we patrol boats out looking for him?"

The commissioner shrugged. "Where would we search? By now he could be on a fishing boat, even on a plane. There're thousand boats at sea. We can be sure he was carrying plenty of money, can't we, Señor? Likely too, he has friends. His kind always have their contacts."

"Has no one the interest about the other question?"

asked Gutiérrez. "Who is firing shots at me? Who is trying to kill me? Who is the man killed by Perfecto Rojas?"

"And why?" asked the duke excitedly. "This is the second attempt on this man's life. The duchess and I and Mrs. Roosevelt could have been killed in the first attempt. Why, Commissioner? Why, Isidro? Who would want to kill *you*?"

"I assume," said Mrs. Roosevelt, "that you have not yet identified the body. I assume also that it will not be difficult to do, since you have a body with fingerprints and perhaps identification in the clothes. When we—"

"We are checking the fingerprints, of course," said Commissioner Hopkins. "There was, however, no identification on the body. The pockets were empty. The man was not even carrying money. Not even a key. Nothing. He is a white man, about thirty years old, I would judge. More than that . . . we know nothing. Not yet, anyway."

"If we can find out who he was, then we should be able to find out who hired him," said Mrs. Roosevelt.

XI

"Damned nice shooting," said Kevin Hammet. "He needn't have fired the second shot."

Jean King nodded. Her stomach was churning, and she was fighting against a drift toward fainting.

They were in the Nassau morgue, staring at the body of the man shot by Perfecto Rojas. While Mrs. Roosevelt and Commissioner Hopkins were down the street in the governor's office, talking to Isidro Gutiérrez, they had come here to the morgue to see if they could identify the gunman who had attempted to kill Gutiérrez.

"I don't know him," said Kevin.

"Neither do I."

The stark-naked body was a Caucasian male, still young, muscular—in fact, athletic looking. Two bullets had punched through his chest, obviously killing him instantly. He had a long white scar across his upper thigh: an old wound, long healed. Apart from that, he had no identifying marks.

Kevin turned over the right hand. It was not calloused, except for a pronounced small callous on the left side of the middle finger, which suggested the man had done a lot of writing with a pen or pencil. Kevin stepped down and looked at the feet.

"He didn't do much physical labor and not a lot of walking, either."

"Not a sedentary man, though," said Jean, nodding at the flat belly.

Kevin blew a sigh. "Well . . . They'll open him up. We'll find out what he's been eating, maybe what he's been drinking. There may be something suggestive in that." He reached for the sheet. "Finished with him? Shall I cover him up?"

She gestured that Kevin should throw the sheet over the corpse—glad enough not to have to look at it anymore.

They went outside. A uniformed police officer was waiting for them.

"Ah," said Kevin. "Brittigan, isn't it?"

"Yes, Sor. Mark Brittigan, Sor."

"Well, Brittigan. Looking at the body wasn't particularly enlightening. Do you have his clothes, his weapon?"

"Yes, Sor. If you'll come with me—"

The man's bloody shirt bore a label from a Nassau shop. It was a common kind of shirt, with short sleeves—the kind favored by natives and tourists. The pants were similar: khaki, common.

"No underclothing, Sor," said Brittigan solemnly.

"And nothing in the pockets," said Kevin. "Nothing whatever?"

The policeman shook his head emphatically. "Not a cigarette, not a book of matches. Nothing."

"Which means," said Kevin, "that the man went out to kill and carried nothing, so he would be difficult to identify if . . . if something happened."

"*Did* he go out to kill?" asked Jean. "Tell us, Brittigan—

What happened on the street? Do witnesses confirm that the dead man fired the first shot?"

"Yes, Mum. Exactly that. Half a dozen witnesses saw the entire incident. This man and another drew pistols and began to fire at the Mexican gentleman. The first shot— fired by the dead man, all but one of the witnesses say— missed the Mexican gentleman, and the man beside him knocked him down so that the second shot, fired by the other man, missed him, too. But another man pulled a pistol and fired on this man. And hit him. Then he took aim on the other man, but that one was already running."

"What kind of weapon did you find?" Kevin asked.

"I can show it to you, Sor. It's an American pistol, what's called a Smith and Wesson pistol. A revolver. Odd. A five-shot revolver, not a six-shooter. American cowboys wouldn't like that, would they, Mum?"

Jean tried to smile. "No," she said. "No, they wouldn't."

"One shot fired from it," Brittigan went on. "The witnesses were right. The dead man only fired one shot."

"A botched murder . . ." Kevin mused.

"What little I know about firearms, Sor, I'd say the first mistake was in the choice of weapon. The pistol is light and has a short barrel. Firing from across a street, a man could well miss. A weapon like that is meant to be fired from close range."

"Which suggests," said Jean, "that the man in there was not a professional killer. If he had known what he was doing, he would have moved in closer before he fired. I'd guess he was nervous."

Kevin nodded toward the closed door of the morgue. "He had reason to be," he said.

Assistant Secretary of State Adolf Berle maintained an informal intelligence network through American consu-

lates. In mid-afternoon, that Thursday, Mrs. Roosevelt encoded a message in the special code she used to communicate with the President—which she and the President
had confided to Berle before she left for the Bahamas—
and sent Tommy Thompson to the American consulate to
have it transmitted. It read—

> I FIND MYSELF IN EXTREMELY AWKWARD
> POSITION STOP AM COMPELLED TO
> SUSPECT THAT STAFF ACCOMPANYING ME
> IS ACTING INDEPENDENTLY OF ANY
> INSTRUCTIONS I CAN IMAGINE THEY WERE
> GIVEN STOP IMPOSSIBLE FOR ME TO
> STAND AROUND SMILING
> DIPLOMATICALLY IF STAFF HAS GRIM
> INSTRUCTIONS NOT DISCLOSED TO ME
> STOP ASK YOU SEND IMMEDIATELY
> COMPLETE BACKGROUND INFORMATION
> ON MISS JEAN KING STOP

Commissioner Hopkins arrived at Government House a
little after four in the afternoon. He had come to see Mrs.
Roosevelt of course; but the duke continued to insist that
the governor should take an active role in the investigation of a major crime committed in his territory; and the
duchess, who had been offended by her exclusion from
the meeting in the duke's office, made her wish to be present at this meeting so ostentatious that it would not have
been possible to exclude her, except rudely.

For the duchess, being a proper and charming hostess
was as important as the investigation, and she led the
party into the sparsely furnished drawing room and sum-
moned the butler to take her orders for refreshment.

"You must excuse this place," she said. "Until furniture

arrives, we must live like Spartans. I suppose we are fortunate not to be sitting on the floor."

They did in fact sit on some rather threadbare silk-covered chairs, which bore the stains of water that had dripped from the ceiling. She had brought this furniture in from various rooms, after she had thrown out the wicker, and it did not match. An oil portrait of King George IV smiled down from a wall. ("The only Hanoverian who knew how to smile," the duchess had remarked to Mrs. Roosevelt earlier, "and the only one except David I find particularly attractive. Look at the mischief in that face, though. I think I'd have liked George the Fourth.")

"I have the report of the autopsy," said the commissioner. "And we still don't know who the dead man is."

"What facts do we have that we didn't have before?" asked Mrs. Roosevelt.

The commissioner sighed. "Only that he drank coffee before he set out to attempt murder. And ate porridge. And, uh, he had fortified himself with brandy."

"Brandy," said the First Lady. "Brandy, indeed! That is suggestive, don't you think?"

"Of what?" asked the duchess.

"Tell me, Commissioner," said Mrs. Roosevelt, "could the man have bought a drink of brandy in any of the waterfront bars in Nassau?"

Hopkins frowned. "No. It wouldn't be impossible to find brandy, but, no, you couldn't get it in most bars."

"So he drank it in a hotel or in some private place."

"And wouldn't it be unusual for a bar to serve brandy before noon? If you sent—"

"There aren't more than half a dozen bars in town where you could get brandy," Hopkins interrupted. "So if I sent two or three officers to those to ask, we could find out if our man . . . Well, maybe we can find out if he had a room in a hotel. The hotel bars are the ones where you can get brandy. Excuse me. I'll make a call."

While the commissioner left the room to use the telephone, the duchess shook her head and marvelled. "You have a certain turn of thought that amazes me," she said to Mrs. Roosevelt. "As though you were a professional detective."

"Not actually," said the First Lady modestly. "These things are just little puzzles of logic. I'm afraid I give too much thought to them, the way some people do to crossword puzzles."

"Well then, what motive do you deduce anyone might have for wanting to kill Isidro Gutiérrez?" asked the duke. He was smoking his pipe again. "He seems such a likable fellow."

"Oh, David, Mrs. Roosevelt couldn't possibly know!" the duchess protested. "How can you ask her such a thing?"

"Actually," said Mrs. Roosevelt, "I am reasonably confident I know why Mr. Torstenson was killed and why two attempts have been made to kill Señor Gutiérrez. Perhaps I should say it this way—I have two alternative theories on the subject, and I am reasonably confident one or the other is correct."

"Please disclose them to us," said the Duke of Windsor.

"Oh, please!" Mrs. Roosevelt exclaimed with a broad grin. "I couldn't. They are mutually exclusive propositions, and when one proves to be correct the other will be left as nothing but a horrible slander on the names of the people I have in mind."

"You are going home tomorrow," said the duchess. "Do you expect the mystery to be solved before you leave?"

"I hope it will be. I need a few more facts, only a few more facts. The mystery is not so very mysterious, really. Indeed, few of them are. Solving these puzzles is only a matter of assembling facts, then putting them together in the correct combination."

"How was it Sherlock Holmes put it?" the duke asked. "I can't quote the statement, but it was something to the effect that when you eliminate the impossible, what remains, however improbable, is the truth."

"Yes," said Mrs. Roosevelt. "I can't quote it exactly either, but it was something very much like that."

The butler returned, bringing iced champagne and a tray of canapés. The duchess poured.

"I regret," said the duke to the First Lady, "that your visit has been marred by this horrible sequence of events."

"Your hospitality has been simply marvelous," said Mrs. Roosevelt. "You couldn't have been more gracious. And I've enjoyed the hospitality of your friends, too. I . . . I, of course, regret the tragic events that have happened."

The Duchess of Windsor smiled. "I suspect," she said, "that you would have been bored without them."

"Oh, please . . ."

"You are not a woman who can be content with eating and drinking and chatting," said the duchess. "It is of course too bad that all this had to happen, but it has made your visit more memorable, has it not?"

Mrs. Roosevelt shook her head. "The visit would have been memorable in any case."

A kind breeze stirred the thin, sheer curtain at the window. Jean lifted herself on her elbow and smiled at Kevin. He had gone to sleep. She was moved to wake him. They had too little time together to waste any of it with one of them sleeping. On the other hand, he was living through an utter horror, and a few minutes' sleep he could snatch from any hour could refresh and strengthen him.

She rolled off her side of the bed and stepped to the window, letting the wind off the harbor cool her damp skin. She remembered all the times she had been cold with Kevin, when he had supposed it was tolerably comfortable.

God! They'd lost the boat! They had been so proud of it. Kevin's father had taken it to Dunkirk. Of course. Could she have supposed he would do anything else? No wonder Kevin had hated the *Christina*—luxury yacht of a treacherous profiteer. It was for damned sure that boat would never have gone to Dunkirk!

She looked down fondly on Kevin. He was ashamed, almost, for this apparently comfortable berth. It was temporary, of course. And it was dangerous. The gunmen on the streets of Nassau this morning could just as well have been out to kill *him*.

They knew who he was. For today, they had judged Isidro Gutiérrez more dangerous. Tomorrow they might decide Kevin Hammet was worth their attention.

Fifty miles north-northeast of Nassau, Lieutenant Manfred Luth, commanding U-231, turned his periscope and surveyed the sunlit surface of a wide strait the Englanders called the Northeast Providence Channel. His listening equipment had picked up the sound of the screws of a medium-sized boat, and he had risen to periscope depth to have a look at it.

Tuesday night the yacht had failed to appear. Nor had it appeared Wednesday. The navy had no explanation and had ordered him to remain on station at the rendezvous point and see what happened. He had been happy enough to do that. They were supposed to get fresh fruits and vegetables from the Swedish yacht, and for that he would have waited a week.

Whatever was on the surface, it was slow; it was not an English patrol boat. The English worked these waters. He was eighty kilometers north-northeast of Nassau but also only thirty kilometers south-southwest of Great Abaco Island and sixty kilometers west of Spanish Wells, the northern tip of Eleuthera.

Hunting was not good here. U-231 had sunk a couple of small, rusty freighters this cruise, but it had been more for psychological effect than any other purpose—to show the English and Americans who controlled the seas. A commander could make no reputation in these waters.

Ah. A fishing boat. Nothing but a wooden-hulled fisherman, making its way due north, maybe toward Grand Bahama Island, maybe on its way to the Gulf Stream off Florida. Well—

"Er funkt, Herr Leutnant." He's transmitting, Sir.

"What?"

"He sighted our periscope, Sir. He's giving our position to the English patrollers."

So . . . Lieutenant Luth drew a deep breath and blew it out in disgust. So . . . Signalling our position . . .

"Surface! Deck-gun crew to the hatch. Prepare to fire."

The U-boat broke the surface less than a hundred yards from the fishing boat. The deck-gun crew fired two shots. The fishing boat was blown to splinters. Only two of the ten men aboard survived.

Lieutenant Manfred Luth would never know that he had just killed a man very much wanted by the authorities on New Providence Island. His leg shattered and bleeding, Perfecto Rojas was thrown into the water and drowned within three minutes.

* * *

The Duke of Windsor returned to the drawing room, where Mrs. Roosevelt, the duchess, and Commissioner Hopkins waited for him. The commissioner was enjoying the champagne and canapés that the two women only tasted.

"An interesting call," said the duke when he resumed his seat and reached for the bottle to chill the champagne left in his glass. "A fishing boat out of Nassau sighted a periscope between here and Great Abaco. A firm sighting. A periscope. And—And since the initial signal, the boat has not responded to signals from here. Patrol boats are on their way. But—" He turned down the corners of his mouth and turned up his palms. "Ominous."

"The duke keeps telling the admiralty there are U-boats in Bahamas waters, but no one wants to believe it," complained the duchess.

"Oh, they believe it," he said. "They are just so heavily engaged on other seas that they can't expend men and materiel here. So what do we have? A few patrol boats to cover thousands of square miles of sea."

"Perhaps American ships before long," said Mrs. Roosevelt.

"I must hope not," said the duke.

Jean picked up a pair of binoculars from Kevin's dresser and squinted through them at the Sloan yacht. She twisted the wheel to adjust the focus. It was always interesting to see who was going aboard.

Now who?

Gutiérrez. Señor Gutiérrez was at the foot of the ladder. Sloan waved at him, and the pudgy little Mexican waved back and climbed toward the deck. At the rail they embraced.

A man climbed just behind Gutiérrez. Sure. The body-guard. The Italian of the pair. What was his name? Angelo Dioguardi. Kevin had put in an inquiry about him. The response hadn't come back yet. She had suggested he tell SIS to ask the FBI what it had on Dioguardi.

Sloan led Gutiérrez into the lounge at the stern. Old buddies, by the look of them.

She'd report this information to Mrs. Roosevelt.

Tommy Thompson had accepted the coded message delivered by courier from the consulate and had decoded it. When Mrs. Roosevelt came up to her room, Tommy handed her the missive from Adolf Berle—

DISTRESSED TO HEAR YOU SUSPECT
STAFF ACTING CONTRARY OR
INDEPENDENT ORDERS STOP ASSURE YOU
NOTHING IN ORDERS AUTHORIZES
ANYTHING OF WHICH YOU WERE NOT
FULLY INFORMED PRIOR TO DEPARTURE
STOP AM INFORMED OF MURDER OF T AND
ATTEMPT TO BLOW UP G STOP WORD HAS
COME ALSO OF A SHOOTING ON NASSAU
STREET TODAY STOP OUR PEOPLE HAVE
NO AUTHORITY TO BE INVOLVED IN
ANYTHING OF THIS NATURE STOP AM
TRANSMITTING EMPHATIC SUPPLEMENT
TO THEIR INSTRUCTIONS STOP J KING IS
TRUSTED INTELLIGENCE OFFICER WITH
GOOD RECORD STOP BACKGROUND IS
THAT SHE HAILS FROM PITTSBURGH
ORIGINALLY ALSO GREENWICH,
CONNECTICUT WHERE SHE GRADUATED
COUNTRY DAY SCHOOL STOP GRADUATED

SMITH AS YOU KNOW STOP SPENT ONE
YEAR AT CAMBRIDGE UNIVERSITY STOP
THAT WAS 1938 STOP SHE ASKED FOR THIS
ASSIGNMENT EXPRESSING WISH TO
BECOME ACQUAINTED WITH YOU STOP
WILL MEET YOU IN MIAMI TOMORROW
AFTERNOON FOR FULL DISCUSSION STOP
BRITISH CABINET SEEMS TO BE DRAGGING
FEET ON ELEUTHERA STOP WOULD BE
HELPFUL IF YOU CAN GAIN ANY
IMPRESSION AS TO WHY STOP PERISCOPE
DEFINITELY SIGHTED 50 MILES NORTH
NASSAU TODAY STOP THREE DESTROYERS
HURRYING INTO AREA STOP CONSIDER NO
DANGER BUT TAKING NO CHANCES STOP
YOU MAY SEE OUR SHIPS OFF COAST BY
TIME OF YOUR DEPARTURE TOMORROW
STOP SAY THEY ARE ON NORMAL
MANEUVERS SCHEDULE STOP BEST
REGARDS STOP

"I . . . I am sorry, but in decoding that for you I detected something that concerns me," said Tommy Thompson.

Mrs. Roosevelt sat on the bed, thinking of lowering her hot and weary body into the cool water of the rusty tub. "Don't be sorry," she said. She smiled. "If I wanted to send or receive something I did not want you to read, I would tell you."

"I am aware," said Tommy, "that some odd things have happened during this visit. I, uh, supposed you would tell me why when and if you wanted to."

Mrs. Roosevelt focused her thoughts on Tommy, who had been her completely loyal, hard-working secretary for many years, and she was seized with a pang of regret. Immersed in the demands of these busy days and late nights, she had neglected to talk to Tommy as she should have, to brief her about the strange concerns that had arisen during this visit.

"I am sorry, Tommy," she said. "I should have taken the time to tell you what is going on. Nothing is secret from you."

"Miss King . . ." said Tommy. "You seem to be concerned about her."

"Yes. She is a lovely young woman, but I have reason to suspect she has not been entirely truthful about some things."

"I know some things about her," said Tommy innocently.

Tommy Thompson was Mrs. Roosevelt's own age: a capable, honest woman who—as the First Lady had once put it—"makes life possible for me." She was no gossip. There were plenty of opportunities for a member of the White House staff to gossip, and Tommy never did. If she had anything to say, it was worth hearing.

"Anything you want to tell me," said Mrs. Roosevelt.

"I . . . I am most reluctant to say anything that might cause trouble for anyone," said Tommy.

"I appreciate that."

"You are concerned, I suppose, with where everyone was at the hour when Mr. Torstenson was killed."

"Yes."

"I can tell you where *I* was."

"I don't need to know, Tommy. You are not suspected."

"I can't stand the tropical heat," said Tommy. "Frankly, this is the worst assignment I've had since I began to travel with you. I don't like the beaches at night. They are infested with mosquitoes, and I understand the barracuda come in at night. I spend my evenings, when you are out, soaking in cool water in that rusty bathtub."

"I would do it myself, if I could," said Mrs. Roosevelt.

"But I overheard Miss King telling you *she* was soaking there at the hour when Mr. Torstenson was killed. I don't mean to suggest that she had anything to do with the death of Mr. Torstenson, but I can tell you she was not in your bathtub. *I* was."

"For how long, Tommy?"

"For an hour. Two hours. I don't know. But I was in your bathroom or in your room—mine is a hole, you know—that entire evening. Miss King was not here. I don't know where she was, but she was not here—as she said she was."

XII

"This house is so impossible that we are compelled to look to others to entertain for us," said the Duchess of Windsor. "We really do apologize, Mrs. Roosevelt, but we haven't had time to do anything about the place."

"I have been entertained beautifully," said Mrs. Roosevelt. In fact, for her own taste she had been entertained too much and would have welcomed a light snack and no numerous company on this her final evening in the Bahamas. "I am very grateful."

"Fortunately," said the duchess, "we have good friends who are honored to be your host during your visit. I was a little concerned about this last evening, but this morning I received a call from Mr. Wyler, who has invited us to be his guests for dinner. He has no yacht, and his home is not grand, but he has asked us to be his guests for a private dinner at the Imperial Hotel."

"How very nice," said Mrs. Roosevelt.

"All of the American party," said the duchess. "All your staff. The duke and I. Henry Chapman. And Alfred Sloan and Errol Flynn. It should be a pleasant group."

"A very pleasant group," said Mrs. Roosevelt, success-fully concealing her want of enthusiasm.

The Imperial Hotel might have been in Washington, or in Florida—indeed anywhere with a hot, damp climate. The floors were all of marble. Potted palms sat everywhere. Ceiling fans stirred the air. The lobby was crowded with leather chairs, where men sat smoking cigars and reading newspapers. It differed from an American hotel lobby in that the British colonials had never adopted the American habit of chewing tobacco, so it was not necessary to sta-tion cuspidors around the chairs. Black waiters carried drinks to the men in the lobby chairs. On two straight chairs near the elevators, a pair of prostitutes sat and waited for trade.

The entrance of the governor and his party disturbed the tranquility of the lobby. The duke, in the dress uniform of a major general, would have had, in an American hotel, the aspect of a gaudy doorman come into the lobby from the street, but here he represented colonial dignity; his practiced mastery of the role enabled him to carry it off with impressive dignity. Men stood, bowed, and smiled. The duke returned their smiles and brought his party to-ward the marble staircase that led to the ballroom tonight reserved as a private dining room.

The dining tables occupied only a small part of the broad floor of the ballroom. Here the floor was wood, and the ceiling was a full two stories above. Marble columns supported a balcony that overlooked the ballroom floor on all four sides. A forest of potted palms and other tropi-cal flora cluttered the periphery of the dance floor. Here again, the ubiquitous ceiling fans turned lazily and kept the air in motion.

Curtis Wyler waited for them. Smoking a cigar that he

quickly put aside as the party entered, he nodded to several men around him before he strode toward the door to greet his guests.

"My very great pleasure!" he said. "Your Royal Highnesses! Honored First Lady! How very gracious of you to be my guests!"

His other guests, except for Sloan and Flynn, had already arrived. Among them was William Ashbrook, the Bay Street businessman said to be a part of the consortium established by him and Chapman to buy Bahamian land.

"We have some exceptionally fine champagne," said Wyler. Then he addressed Mrs. Roosevelt and said, "But perhaps the First Lady would enjoy instead some very dry Spanish sherry."

"I would enjoy that," said Mrs. Roosevelt.

"Allow me," he said, offering his arm. "Someone told me you are an *aficionada* of the fine sherries."

"I can't claim that," she said.

"I like that a lot better than the black dress with white cap and apron," said Ken Krouse wryly.

Jean King wore a floor-length white satin dress. Hung from her shoulders by spaghetti straps, it fell over her thin body like water, clinging to her and revealing every subtlety of her body.

"So do I," she said.

"I am interested in an apparent omission from the invitation list," he said.

She glanced around the room. Alfred Sloan and Errol Flynn had now arrived, with Judy, and the party seemed to be complete.

"No Señor Gutiérrez," he said.

"Not surprising," said Jean.

"No, but it confirms something, doesn't it?"

She nodded. "No love lost. But Gutiérrez was aboard *René* this afternoon—received by Sloan like a long-lost brother."

Ken nodded at Wyler who was approaching. "Our gracious host," he said to Jean.

"Miss King, Mr. Krouse. Thank you for coming," said Wyler with a warm smile. He fixed an amused eye on Jean and added, "I am glad you were able to drop the pretense of being Mrs. Roosevelt's maid. The last time I saw you, you were serving champagne from a tray."

"And carrying a gun under my apron," said Jean.

Wyler looked her up and down appreciatively. "I don't believe you are carrying one now," he said mischievously.

"In my bag," she said, raising her small, beaded handbag. And it was true. She was carrying a .25 caliber Browning automatic. "Never without it."

Wyler laughed. "Very good," he said. "Very good."

"I've visited your country, Mr. Wyler," she said. "I understand you are Irish."

"Well . . . Ireland is my native country. I haven't spent much time there of late years."

"Graduated university there, though?" she asked.

He shrugged. "Well, yes. Dublin."

Jean smiled and nodded. "I was able to spend only about two weeks in Dublin. A beautiful city."

"It is," he said. "Very beautiful."

"I was able to get a ticket for a play at the Lantern Theatre," she said. "Though, I must say, I couldn't hear very well. My seat was far back, the twenty-fifth row or something like that."

"Yes," said Wyler. "The acoustics could be better. I've had that experience myself, being unable to hear well from one of the back rows."

"Yes. But it was a wonderful experience," she said. "I'd like to go again."

"I wish I could see you there sometime," said Wyler. "Perhaps I could get us better seats for a good play."

"If ever I am in Dublin again, I will make a point of looking you up," she said. "If by chance you are in town—"

"I hope I will be," he said. "Excuse me. Mr. Sloan . . ."

As Wyler walked away toward Alfred Sloan, Jean turned to Krouse and murmured, "He's never been in the Lantern Theatre. There are only six rows of seats. I doubt he's ever been in Dublin."

Errol Flynn crossed the room toward Jean King. Grinning, he outpaced little Judy, who trotted after him. Tonight he was dressed like the other men, in a white dinner jacket, and though his face was blotched and puffy, he was very much the dashing actor who played the swashbuckling roles. Judy, dressed again in her long gray skirt, followed him like a puppy.

"I must confess," he said to Jean. "I asked who you are. It's a pleasure to see you."

Even though she had heard of his drunken antics aboard Sloan's yacht, it was difficult for Jean not to be dazzled by the handsome, personable, famous movie star. She had seen him on the screen. She had read about him. She could not but be elated by his making a point of approaching her. She had no illusions as to what he had in mind, but she couldn't find it in herself to be offended.

"They tell me you're carrying a gun," said Flynn.

"Well, I imagine you have a sword somewhere," she said.

"Ha! Very good! Can I call you Jean? This is Judy. She'll be glad to get us some drinks. Something besides that

Alka-Seltzer grape juice? Champagne gives me a head-ache, doesn't it you?"

"I suspect Wyler has some whisky on hand," she said.

Judy took her cue and went off toward the bar.

"So you will be flying home tomorrow," said Flynn. "Could I encourage you to quit your job and come with Sloan and me? We're going back to Cuba. Havana. Now, there's a town . . ."

Jean laughed. "Just like that? Quit my job and go on a cruise with a famous movie actor and a multimillionaire?" She shook her head. "I must say, it's enticing."

"The best things happen to the brave and impulsive," he said. "Anyway, I've never been with a girl who carried a gun."

"Oh, I'd have to give that up. It belongs to the government."

"I'll buy you a new one," he said. "In Havana. I'll buy you a cannon."

"I'll settle for a machine gun."

Flynn's broad smile faded slowly. "I'm quite serious, you know," he said. "The invitation is real."

"I didn't take it otherwise," she said.

"A fantasy cruise . . . To the islands of our dreams."

"Somehow I had a different impression of a cruise hosted by Alfred Sloan. Why did he bring you to this back-water place? And don't I see a lot of grim business meetings going on aboard *René?*"

Flynn turned down the corners of his mouth and shrugged. "He has to make some money, I guess. Never has enough—particularly at the rate he spends it."

"Is he going to put some money into Mexico?"

Flynn showed her the trademark smile, flashing his teeth. "The girl with the pistol in her handbag," he said. "You really are a sleuth, aren't you?"

"I would need to know what I'm getting into," she said, adopting his facetious style. "If he's sailing off to Mexico, I'm not sure I want to go there."

"I don't think he's going to Mexico," said Flynn. "The Mexican made quite a pitch this afternoon, but I don't think Sloan bought it. I wasn't listening, really, but I gathered from the long face on Gutiérrez when he left that he hadn't sold any stock."

"Maybe Sloan's already decided to put his money in the other deal."

Flynn laughed again. "I shouldn't even talk to you," he said. "Honestly, I don't know what *is* going on. But it hasn't spoiled the cruise so far, and I don't think it's going to."

"Torstenson's cruise was rather spoiled," said Jean.

"Ooh . . . You do bring up unpleasant things."

"There is a real possibility," she said, "that Torstenson was murdered because of something to do with the investment Sloan is or is not going to make. There have been two attempts to kill Gutiérrez. What's going on? Are we absolutely certain Sloan is not the next target?"

Flynn frowned. "Are you serious that you might go with me?"

"That's what we're talking about, isn't it?"

For a long moment he stood and stared at her, silent, uncertain. She could all but read his thoughts as he glanced toward Judy, who was trying to get close to the bar and pick up two Scotches, then ran his eyes up and down the clinging white dress. The man was transparent. And he wasn't too bright, she judged.

"Jean . . . Alfred's made his decision. I've no idea what it is, but he's made it. I know something of the man. He's been pondering. Tonight the pondering is over. He's decided and is relieved. He sent a long cable to New York this afternoon. Encrypted. The hull repairs are finished, and he's about ready to sail."

"Are you sure he's going to Havana?"

"Havana. Absolutely."

"You say Gutiérrez left the yacht with a long face, as though he hadn't sold any stock. What about Chapman and Wyler? What about the Duke of Windsor, for that matter?"

Flynn tipped his head toward the duke and duchess, who were engaged in animated conversation with Sloan. "They look happy enough, wouldn't you say? And Chapman and Wyler don't look gloomy. Oh—One more thing, we'll be a party of five aboard the yacht—that is, we will if you decide to come. Wyler will be coming with us."

"Really? Why?"

Flynn shook his head. "How should I know? Now . . . Before Judy returns, are you serious? Will you come?"

Jean smiled. "Probably," she said. "I'll have to somehow break the news to Mrs. Roosevelt."

It was Curtis Wyler who broke it. "I hear some interesting news," he said to the First Lady. "Mr. Sloan tells me that your female bodyguard is going to resign her job and come with us to Havana, aboard *René.*"

"Really? She's said no such thing to me."

"Apparently she's fallen under the spell of Errol Flynn, who made her the proposition. I suppose—" He paused to smile. "I suppose the Flynn charm has claimed another victim."

"Miss King," said Mrs. Roosevelt, "is an exceptionally intelligent young woman, with a strong personality. I would be surprised if she has fallen under Mr. Flynn's charm. Perhaps she has other reasons."

"Yes. I wouldn't be surprised."

"But you said coming with '*us*' to Havana. Does this mean you are going to Havana with Mr. Sloan, aboard his yacht?"

"Yes. For a short visit. It's a kind invitation, don't you think?"

"Very kind indeed. Have you and Mr. Sloan been friends long?"

"Actually I never met him before he arrived in Nassau the other day. I've grown to admire him. He's a shrewd businessman."

"Yes. Very shrewd. Very shrewd . . ."

A few minutes later she joined the duke and duchess, who were still chatting happily with Alfred Sloan.

"Mrs. Roosevelt! I understand from Errol that your Miss King is coming to Havana with us."

"Yes, I'd like to speak with you about that," said Mrs. Roosevelt grimly. She looked at the duke and duchess. "Would you excuse us for a moment? It appears I have a staff problem."

Sloan stepped apart from the Windsors, and the First Lady frowned and began—"I find—"

"Mrs. Roosevelt, I won't permit it if it offends you," Sloan interrupted.

"Actually, I'm skeptical that the girl will really do it; but if she does, it's her business. I'd like to ask you about something else, if you don't mind. This is prying, Mr. Sloan. Officious intermeddling, my husband would call it. I imagine you will understand the motive behind my question and won't be offended."

Sloan's mobile, flexible face shaped a smile of real amusement. "Ask me anything you wish, and I won't be offended. I promise. I may decline to answer, but I won't be offended."

"It is about Mr. Torstenson," she said gravely. "You

came to Nassau to meet him. But he was murdered before you arrived here. Do you think it at all possible that he was killed to prevent his talking to you?"

Sloan's smile disappeared and was replaced by an expression that communicated disquiet. "The thought occurred to me," he said. "Quite frankly, I've wondered if Isidro Gutiérrez didn't kill Torstenson. His reputation back in Mexico is that he is capable of murder."

"You told me," she said, "that Mr. Torstenson sent you a radio message, saying you should not invest in a certain proposition until he'd had an opportunity to talk to you. Would you mind telling me what proposition that was?"

"Not at all. It's the proposal to fund a bank in Latin America, probably in Cuba, maybe in Panama. Torstenson and I were to have heard two competitive propositions, one from Gutiérrez, the other from Henry Chapman and Curtis Wyler."

"Is it improper for me to ask what you have decided to do?"

"I'm going forward with the Chapman-Wyler proposal. I may in the end decide not to invest in any major way, but I'm cooperating with them in establishing a seed fund and making preliminary plans."

"Which means you have rejected Señor Gutiérrez's proposal."

"Yes."

"I find it impossible to understand, then, what motive anyone has for twice attempting to kill Señor Gutiérrez."

"It is not beyond the realm of possibility," said Sloan, "that the attempts have been made by agents of the Mexican government. Gutiérrez is regarded as a threat to that government—which is one of the reasons why I lost interest in his investment proposal. I have no interest in becoming involved in an attempt to overthrow a government."

"I see," said Mrs. Roosevelt. "Well . . ."

"Would I be doing you a service if I refused to let Miss King come with us to Havana?"

"No, Mr. Sloan, you wouldn't. If she is prepared to abandon her responsibilities and go off on a romantic escapade with Mr. Flynn, then she is of no further value to me."

Sloan nodded gravely, but his eyes betrayed him. He was amused.

"I don't believe it for a minute," said Ken Krouse to the First Lady. "A little while ago she caught Curtis Wyler in a lie. She's *working*, Mrs. Roosevelt. She's doing what she was sent here to do: gathering information. If playing along with a proposition from Errol Flynn is what she has to do to get some information out of him, then she's doing just that—I have no doubt. But she won't sail for Havana with him, I can promise you."

"You seem quite certain."

"I am quite certain."

"She has lied to me, Mr. Krouse. More than once."

"And to me," he said. "At least once. But I know why, and I think you'll forgive her when you know."

"You might tell me."

He smiled wanly and shook his head. "Please let me do a little more checking before I speak."

Mrs. Roosevelt could not be pleased. A minute or so later she gently excused herself and went off to find a telephone.

*   *   *

"I hope you will forgive me," she said to the duke and duchess. "I have to make a short visit to Commissioner Hopkins at his office. I'm asking Mr. Krouse and Miss King to come with me."

"We are invited for breakfast on Alfred's yacht," said the Duchess of Windsor. "And after that, I'm afraid, we will have to drive you to the airport."

"Then we shall have time in the morning to chat and review the delightful time I've had," said Mrs. Roosevelt.

"Please let us drop you at headquarters," said the duke.

Mrs. Roosevelt smiled broadly. "It's only half a block," she said.

"Then we'll send the car for you when you're ready."

"If we need it, I'll call," said Mrs. Roosevelt. "But I am sure the commissioner will provide a car."

The three—Mrs. Roosevelt, Ken Krouse, and Jean King—walked the short distance along the muggy street, under a black sky where orange lightning flashed and thunder muttered. Ken and Jean were glum. The First Lady had been firm in summoning them to accompany her to police headquarters. As they reached the building, a sharp white flash of lightning must have shaken a cloud, because a torrent of rain accompanied the thunder, and they barely made it inside before they would have been drenched.

Commissioner Edgar Hopkins waited for them in his office—with Kevin Hammet. The commissioner deftly stepped into the hall, separating himself and Mrs. Roosevelt from the others for a private word with her.

"He promised to be here at eleven. I suppose he'll show up—though he's fifteen minutes late."

"With the woman."

"Picking her up may be what's delaying him."

Mrs. Roosevelt sighed. "Well—We have no option but to wait, I suppose."

"I have one or two other things to talk about," he said. "Unless you don't want to talk in front of—"

"It will be all right," she said. "We can talk in front of them."

They went into his office, where the others were sitting, having left a chair for the First Lady.

"A few things to talk about," said the commissioner as he lowered himself heavily into the chair behind his desk. "For one, Kevin asked for a more complete report on the autopsy on Captain Hardegen. I have to conclude that Hardegen was a suicide. The muzzle of the Luger that killed him was held close to his head. There are no other fingerprints on the pistol or on the ammunition. What is difficult to understand is, *why?* Why would the man kill himself?"

"Why did he try to take the yacht to sea?" asked Mrs. Roosevelt. "That was a reckless thing to do."

"There is still no sign of Lieutenant Valentin," the commissioner continued. "I am ready to believe that your theory is correct, Mrs. Roosevelt—that he was the man blown up in the attempt to set a dynamite charge in Señor Gutiérrez's runabout. And there is some additional evidence that supports that theory."

A clap of thunder shook the windows and interrupted the narrative.

"There is another crewman missing from *Christina*," said Commissioner Hopkins. "A man named Kohler. He is missing from the yacht because he lies in our morgue. He's the man killed by the Gutiérrez bodyguard this morning."

"How do you know?" asked Ken.

"Fingerprints. On the wheel. On the engine telegraph. On charts. On coffee cups. And so on."

"*Christina* is no longer temporarily impounded," said Kevin. "It's been seized by the admiralty. We opened the safe in the radio room this evening and found a German naval code book."

Mrs. Roosevelt was frowning, and she ran her finger over her lips and down over her chin. "This man Kohler did not receive orders from Captain Hardegen," she said. "I mean orders to murder Señor Gutiérrez. Captain Hardegen had been dead a whole day before the attempt on Señor Gutiérrez. Either he worked independently or—Or he received orders from someone else."

"What is more," said Jean, "the second man involved in the attempt to kill Gutiérrez is almost certainly another member of the crew."

"In fact, he isn't," said Kevin. "We took witnesses from the street aboard and lined up the crew for them to look at."

"Maybe there is another crewman missing," suggested Mrs. Roosevelt.

"The ship's papers indicate the contrary," said Kevin. "Of course . . . the papers could be false."

Mrs. Roosevelt sighed. "The *Christina* is, then, a German ship, a Nazi ship, with killers among the crew, and probably spies as well." She shook her head. "And Mr. Torstenson had to know that. Mr. Torstenson had to be . . . Well, at least he had to consent, if he was not a participant."

"That is true," said Ken Krouse.

"Which you knew when we came here," said Mrs. Roosevelt, nodding at him, then at Jean.

"Yes," said Jean. "We knew."

"So—"

"So you think one of us killed him," said Jean.

Mrs. Roosevelt shook her head sadly. "I don't know. I do know you have lied to me, Miss King. I don't know why."

"Mrs. Roosevelt—"

"Have our witnesses arrived yet, Commissioner?" asked the First Lady.

"I'll check," said the commissioner. He picked up the telephone, then nodded and said, "Yes. Both of them."

"Let's resolve this matter anyway, then."

Commissioner Hopkins spoke an order into the telephone, then went to the door and opened it. In a moment Mason Hupp, the caterer, and Hannah, the cook, walked into the office.

"Dat's her," said Hannah immediately, nodding at Jean. "She the one that walked off and left me with all them dishes to wash."

"Yes," Mason Hupp agreed. "She's the one I hired. I—" He frowned at Kevin Hammet. "Yeah. I hired her because *he* asked me to."

"Thank you," said the commissioner. "I appreciate your coming in on such a night. You've solved a problem for us."

When the two witnesses had gone out and the door was closed, Commissioner Hopkins looked at Mrs. Roosevelt, smiled faintly, and shrugged. "The answer," he said.

"Which of us is going to explain?" asked Jean.

"Let me see how much of it I can guess without your explanation," said Mrs. Roosevelt. "You went to school in England in 1938, met Mr. Hammet, and . . . And—"

"Fell in love with him," said Jean. She stood up and stood beside Kevin's chair, to put her arm around his shoulder. "We planned to be married. But—Well . . . You know. The war. I hate Hitler and all the Nazis stand for. I hate them for very good reasons apart from what they have done to my personal life. I volunteered for intelligence work. They laughed at me at first, but when they found out I speak fluent German and French and have some athletic ability besides, their naval highnesses changed their minds."

"Very well," said Mrs. Roosevelt. "What were you doing aboard Mr. Torstenson's yacht the night he was killed?"

"Destroying the radios," said Jean.

"That was my job," said Kevin. "But she insisted she—"

"This island is swarming with Nazi spies," said Jean. "Some of them know who Kevin really is. If he had gone aboard that boat that night, they'd have killed him for sure. But they didn't know me. The powerful radios on *Christina* were being used to send information to Berlin, also to direct U-boats to promising targets. Destroying those radios was a job that had to be done."

"But you work for the government of a neutral nation," said Mrs. Roosevelt. "If it became known that you committed an act of sabotage against the German navy, there could be grave international complications. What is more, you were associated with me on this visit. For you to involve yourself in such an activity was wholly in violation of your instructions."

"I'll resign."

"Well . . . Let's don't be hasty."

"I'm going to marry Kevin," said Jean. "Probably I'll be going back to England with him."

Mrs. Roosevelt nodded. "Mr. Krouse . . . ?"

"I didn't know in advance what she planned to do, but the night she did it she called Wilson MacGruder and me out on the lawn at Government House and told us what she'd done. She said we would probably want to disassociate ourselves from her."

"And this is what you couldn't tell me earlier this evening: that she is in love with Mr. Hammet and—"

"That's what I couldn't tell you," said Ken.

Mrs. Roosevelt rose and stepped to the window. She looked down on a street flooded by torrential rain, lighted in the blue light of constant lightning. The building rattled under the thunder.

With her back to the people in the office, she spoke regretfully—"No one has told me yet who killed Mr. Torstenson."

"I didn't," said Jean. "I swear I didn't, and I don't know who did."

"There was something wrong about Torstenson," said Kevin. "We don't know what. He was pro-German. That was understood. He was making huge profits by selling munitions to Germany, illegally. We knew that. But in letting his yacht be turned into a Nazi spy vessel, even a submarine tender, he surrendered to the Nazis more than the facts we know would justify. Jean didn't kill him. British intelligence didn't kill him. I don't know who did."

Mrs. Roosevelt turned and faced Jean. "You say you saw Mr. Wyler on board the yacht that night."

"Yes."

"In dungarees."

"Yes."

"Are you suggesting he killed Mr. Torstenson?"

Jean paused for a moment, then nodded. "Yes."

"But you have no evidence of it?"

"No."

"Obviously he didn't make the attempts on the life of Señor Gutiérrez."

"Not personally, he didn't."

Mrs. Roosevelt shook her head. "It would be convenient, wouldn't it, to suspect Mr. Wyler. It would be convenient to have *someone* to suspect. But—Evidence. Evidence. Incidentally, Miss King, have you explained to Mr. Flynn that you really are not going off on a romantic idyll with him?"

"If that drunken egomaniacal boob hasn't figured it out for himself, he wouldn't believe me if I told him."

"I am very much afraid," said Mrs. Roosevelt to Commissioner Hopkins, "that we will fly back to the States tomorrow without knowing who killed Mr. Torstenson."

"I won't be going with you," said Jean. "I'll give my resignation to MacGruder if that's all right."

Mrs. Roosevelt nodded. "And turn over your pistol, which is government property," said Ken Krouse with an ironic little smile.

"I believe we shall be able to provide her with another," said Kevin. "I shouldn't, after all, want to marry a woman who wasn't carrying a pistol."

Everyone rose. They began to make their way toward the door.

"I will speak with you before I fly back to Miami," said Mrs. Roosevelt to Commissioner Hopkins. "Indeed, I hope you will let me know how all this turns out."

The commissioner nodded. "Excuse me a moment," he said. His telephone was ringing.

The First Lady could not help feeling depressed. She looked around the drab colonial office for what she supposed must be the final time. She was oppressed with a disquieting sense of abandoning an unsolved problem—something she had never liked to do. Her mind was filled with facts and questions, and she kept mentally cross-referencing them, in spite of a sense of futility.

She had a sense also that her visit to the Bahamas had been worthless. Actually, she realized, her official visit had been chiefly a means of getting American intelligence personnel ashore in Nassau, for a look at the situation, and that she'd had no real purpose here. She'd attended more parties, eaten more food, drunk more champagne, and engaged in more idle chatter than she liked. It had been—

"Mrs. Roosevelt—" The commissioner put down the telephone. "There has been more shooting. Señor Gutiérrez again. This time they seem to have gotten him."

XIII

"I am sorry, Sor," said Officer Brittigan to Commissioner Hopkins. "A standing order you know. He is to be notified of any violent crime of a major nature."

The governor, the Duke of Windsor, stood beside his official car, the Rolls-Royce, in the diminishing rain. He wore the uniform of a major general, not the dress uniform but a khaki uniform that the drops of rain were gradually spotting. His knee-high boots were varnished, so that the water stood on them in drops. He smoked a cigarette in the European manner, between thumb and index finger—carefully, not inhaling, with the manner of a man who did not smoke cigarettes often and looked to this one maybe to settle his nerves.

They were on the wharf beside the moored *Christina*. The yacht was dark, as if the electric power aboard had failed. Policemen with long flashlights prowled about the decks, probing the corners with their sharp beams of light. What remained of the crew—ten bedraggled, rain-soaked men—stood on the dock, grimly stamping their feet, glancing angrily around them, staring at the armed officers who held pistols levelled at them.

"A very odd thing, Sor," said Brittigan. "The call came when the storm was at its awfullest. The report was that there was heavy firing aboard the boat. And in fact there has been. There's bullet holes all around, Sor."

"And who was doing all this wild firing?" asked Commissioner Hopkins.

"Them, I figure," said Brittigan, nodding toward the crew. "I also figure we'll dredge a few pistols out of the drink, come morning. I have it in mind they threw them overboard when they saw the police cars comin'."

Mrs. Roosevelt stood by Commissioner Hopkins, listening to this conversation. Someone had brought an umbrella for her, and she stood under it. She had invited Jean King to join her under it, but Jean stood in the warm rain, the dress that had already clung to her now wet and clinging all the more. Kevin Hammet kept his arm around her, protecting her the little he could from the rain. Ken Krouse stood to one side, having taken on something of the aspect of a wet chicken. Water trickled down his forehead.

"The report was," said Mrs. Roosevelt, "that probably Señor Gutiérrez had been shot. What information do we have that makes us think so?"

"Mum . . ." said Brittigan. "We fished the second Gutiérrez bodyguard out of the water. Angelo Dioguardi. Quite dead, Mum."

"They had been aboard the yacht?" she asked.

"Must have been," said Brittigan. "That's where all the bullet holes is."

Mrs. Roosevelt glanced at the sky, where the retreating storm had degenerated into distant rumblings, orange flashes that silhouetted tall, ominous, billowy clouds over the ocean.

"But you've not found Señor Gutiérrez?"

"No, Mum. No sign of him."

The Duke of Windsor tossed away his cigarette and walked over to the assembled crewmen held under police guns. He walked up to the first man in the line.

"Wie heissen Sie?" he asked curtly.

"Ich bin Schröder, Mein Herr."

"Was ist Ihr Vorname?"

"Reinhard, Mein Herr."

"Reinhard—Wo ist Herr Gutiérrez?"

"Ich weiss nicht, Mein Herr."

"Was ist Ihre Staatsangehörigkeit?"

"Ich bin Schwedisch, Mein Herr."

The duke shook his head curtly and glanced back over his shoulder at Mrs. Roosevelt and Commissioner Hopkins. *"Nein. Sie sind Deutsche, Schröder. Jetzt . . . Wo ist Herr Gutiérrez?"*

"Ich weiss nicht, Mein Herr."

The duke glanced again at the Commissioner of Police. *"Vielleicht wen wir jemand hängen . . . Sie, Schröder?"*

"Nein, Mein Herr!"

"What's he saying?" asked Commissioner Hopkins.

Jean translated. "The sailor says he doesn't know where Gutiérrez is. The duke says maybe he'll hang someone."

The Duke of Windsor walked along the line. *"Vielleicht wir losen ziehen,"* he said.

"Maybe we'll draw lots," Jean translated.

He had stopped before a sailor. *"Sie,"* he said to that man. *"Sie sind hässlich. Vielleicht Sie . . ."*

"He says, 'You're ugly. Maybe you.' "

"Und Sie . . . weiblich . . . unmännlich." The duke spoke over his shoulder to Commissioner Hopkins. *"Der Galgen ist bereit?"*

"He called that one feminine, unmanly, and he asks if the gallows is ready.

"Bereit, Herr General," she reported to the duke, as if she were translating for the commissioner.

"Gut," said the duke. He walked back to Mrs. Roosevelt and the commissioner. "Question them one at a time. Don't let the later ones see that the earlier ones have survived the experience."

"Do you think they are deceived?" asked Mrs. Roosevelt quietly. "Do you think any of them is really afraid?"

"If not, hang one or two," said the duke, "and let the others see the bodies."

"Oh . . . Oh, no," said Mrs. Roosevelt.

"We can do better than that," said Jean. "Will somebody get me some dry clothes?"

Ten minutes later Jean and Kevin—volunteers—and Officer Brittigan began the rigorous interrogation of the crew of the yacht. The Duke of Windsor stood in the doorway for a minute, then shook his head and walked away to an anteroom where Mrs. Roosevelt waited with Commissioner Hopkins.

"I . . . cannot condone torture," said the First Lady.

"If we hear any screaming, maybe we'll interfere," said the commissioner.

There would be no screaming. Jean was dressed now in a police officer's uniform, with the trouser legs and shirt sleeves rolled up because everything was too large for her. She was necessary to the interrogation, because she and the Duke of Windsor were the only ones who could translate, and the duke chose to withdraw from the process.

For the first interview they chose the man the duke had called unmanly. He was stripped naked and fastened to a chair with handcuffs and a belt. In ten minutes they were finished with him, without so much as touching him, even without threatening him.

They had another one, Schröder, brought in next. He answered their questions within six minutes.

To be certain, they had a third one stripped and fastened to the chair. He was Horn, the man she had knocked out the night she had destroyed the radios. He confirmed what the first two had said. The three men were taken to separate cells, and the remaining crewmen were locked up in the drunk tank of the Nassau jail.

"There are four Swedes among them," Jean reported to Mrs. Roosevelt, Commissioner Hopkins, and the duke. "It doesn't make any difference; these Swedes are more dedicated Nazis than the Germans. There is a man missing from the crew—I mean, a man besides Kohler, the one who was killed in this morning's attempt to murder Gutiérrez. His name is Rudolf Dietrich."

"He is listed in the ship's papers," said Commissioner Hopkins.

"Anyway, what of Señor Gutiérrez?" asked the duke.

"They think Gutiérrez is dead," said Jean. "He came on board during the storm, so far as they know. He was in the aft lounge. There was loud talk and then shooting. They think Gutiérrez fired many shots—and another man, probably Dioguardi, I'd guess. Dietrich ordered the crew to join the fight. Only one of them did. I'd guess that one was Schröder. When police cars shrieked onto the wharf, several men went over the rail on the harbor side of the yacht. At least one of those was wounded. Maybe two. Someone fired at one of them in the water. Schröder would like for us to think that wasn't him, but I have a feeling it was. Schröder is still a little defiant, though he has been taught that the English are ruthless and quite capable of hanging men, just on general principles. The other two are scared out of their wits. Even so, all three of them tell essentially the same story."

" *'Several men'* went into the water," said the duke. "Aside from Gutiérrez and Dietrich, who?"

"They swear they don't know," said Jean. "After Valentin disappeared and Hardegen died, Dietrich gave orders. They think he took *his* orders from someone ashore, but all three swear they have no idea who."

"Something we have long suspected was confirmed during the interrogation," said Kevin Hammet. "Orders for *Christina* did not come from the *Kriegsmarine*, the German navy. Hardegen and Valentin were naval officers. Dietrich is not. Dietrich, these men say, is an officer of the SD—the *Sicherheitsdienst*, the foreign intelligence service of the SS, under the personal command of Reinhard Heydrich."

"And if that is so," said Jean, "then whoever gave Dietrich orders is also of the SD."

"This is . . . Oh, this is really altogether unbelievable," said the duke.

"Why should it be, Sir?" asked Kevin. "The Nazis are making war against us."

"How thoroughly has the *Christina* been searched?" asked Mrs. Roosevelt.

"There is no one hiding aboard, Mum," said Brittigan. "We've crawled over every inch of her."

"Have all of the ship's papers been read? Everything? You searched the yacht this evening, Mr. Hammet. How thoroughly?"

"We seized the ship's papers," said Hammet.

"Would it be inappropriate to look about?" she asked. "Whatever was going on aboard, it was rather abruptly interrupted."

"And maybe they didn't have time to hide something they wanted to hide," added Jean.

They went aboard—Mrs. Roosevelt, the duke, the commissioner, Jean, Kevin, Ken, Brittigan, and half a dozen policemen. The lights were out because the main switch had been pulled. Kevin switched them back on.

The aft lounge was a shambles. Gunfire had ripped through furniture as well as the walls, and chairs and tables had been turned over. The windows were shattered.

Mrs. Roosevelt knelt and frowned over an ashtray that had been spilled on the floor. "Chesterfield cigarettes," she said. "An American brand. And Players. English."

Automatic pistols had ejected cartridge casings, which were scattered everywhere. "Don't touch," Jean said sharply to one of the uniformed policemen who had squatted and was reaching for one. "Fingerprints. They are all nine millimeter, though. Or thirty-eight caliber."

"There is evidence here that will identify the people who exchanged this gunfire," said Mrs. Roosevelt. "Cigarette brands. Fingerprints on the cartridges."

Ken Krouse shook his head. "Suppose the fingerprints are those of Gutiérrez and Dioguardi, then Dietrich and, say, Schröder and one or two other crewmen. Then what do we know that we didn't know before? Gutiérrez is probably dead. And Dietrich is missing and may not show up."

"That is an assumption, Mr. Krouse," said Mrs. Roosevelt. "Let's at least find out whose fingerprints these are."

"Maybe someone of whom we have no record," said the commissioner skeptically.

"I should like to look around a bit more," said the First Lady. "The cabins . . . Have the cabins been searched?"

The captain's cabin was typical of the quarters of a career officer—neat and impersonal. If he had left behind anything suggestive, it had been removed. The same was true of the cabin that appeared to have been occupied by Valentin and another officer, probably Dietrich. If Dietrich was in fact an SD man, his quarters would contain nothing to suggest his status.

Mrs. Roosevelt opened the door into the luxurious master suite that had been Torstenson's. These quarters, too, appeared to have been gone over carefully. Torstenson's clothes were neatly hung. His toiletries stood in military order on his dresser and in his bathroom.

On his night table stood a leather double frame, containing two photographs. One was of a woman, a handsome blonde who appeared to be about thirty years old.

"His late wife," said Kevin, who had noticed Mrs. Roosevelt staring thoughtfully at the picture. "The SIS dossier on him says his wife died in 1927. The other picture is probably his son. We don't know much about him. He didn't live with his father. Sort of faded out of the picture some years ago."

"Does anyone have a magnifying glass?" asked Mrs. Roosevelt.

No one did. She said it might be important, and a policeman rushed off to headquarters to get one. They looked inside the drawers and closets while the man was gone—and found nothing. It was obvious that someone had been through everything. Mrs. Roosevelt kept to herself the thought that it might have been better if this yacht had been thoroughly searched the night of the murder. She remembered the captain insisting that the Bahamian police had no jurisdiction and wondered what evidence he had been intent on destroying.

"This is somewhat intrusive, isn't it?" asked the Duke of Windsor uneasily. "Gunnar Torstenson was a gentleman, and I am reluctant to ransack his rooms."

"They've been ransacked already, Sir," said Kevin. "And then put back together to look orderly."

The magnifying glass, when at last it arrived, was a powerful lens. She held it over the picture of the blond young man who was probably the son of Gunnar Torstenson.

"What is that?" she asked. "Look at the little button in his lapel. It bears an insignia." She was looking at two white slashes on black, each one something like a squarish *S* written backwards. "What is that? Does anyone know?"

Commissioner Hopkins, who looked next, could only shake his head. He did not recognize the insignia.

But Kevin Hammet did. "It's a Nazi Party badge," he said. "Worse than that. It's the insignia of the SS. If this is a picture of Torstenson's son, he's not only a Nazi, he's a Nazi fanatic."

"Which, I am afraid," said Mrs. Roosevelt, "solves nothing but instead deepens the mystery."

"I thought highly of Gunnar Torstenson," said the duke. He shook his head. "His son . . . Too bad."

"I had rather hoped," said Mrs. Roosevelt sadly, "that we would learn he was killed because he was doing something damaging to the Nazi cause."

"Afraid not," said Ken Krouse.

When they returned to the deck of the yacht, the rain had stopped. Only occasional orange lightning fires burned on the horizon, too far away for the sound of the thunder to reach the harbor. Mrs. Roosevelt stood on the deck and looked down at the water.

"Mr. Torstenson's body was floating when it was seen," she said. "Was Mr. Dioguardi's?"

"Yes, Mum," said Brittigan.

"Then . . . Señor Gutiérrez?"

"Could be a lot of reasons," said Commissioner Hopkins.

"Including that he is not dead," she suggested.

"We checked his hotel, then had it watched. He hasn't returned there. If he's wounded—Well, he hasn't gone to hospital."

She tipped her head to one side, and for a moment she pondered—drawing her hands down both cheeks. "Commissioner . . . Did you find any trace of the other bodyguard? What was his name?"

"Rojas," said the commissioner. "No trace. But we have an idea where he went. One of the small fishing fleets is short a boat. He may have hired it."

Mrs. Roosevelt nodded. "And possibly," she said, "he just came running to the dock, spoke to the first fishing captain he saw, and on the spur of the moment hired the boat. It is more likely, wouldn't you say, that he knew the captain beforehand. Now—If Señor Rojas escaped New Providence Island that way, isn't it possible that Señor Gutiérrez is trying to escape the same way? That is, if he's alive."

"A remote chance," said Kevin Hammet.

"What else are we doing?" asked the First Lady.

The duke said he could not go on any unlikely expedition in the middle of the night. The duchess would be angry now, that he had spent so much time at the waterfront.

The others, in three cars, drove out to the docks where a fishing boat was missing, on Goodman Bay, three miles west of Nassau.

Though it was by now almost two in the morning, the fishing docks were alive. Boats were out. They would return before dawn, bringing in the fish that would be on sale on the Nassau waterfront on Friday, more fish that would be packed in ice on small freighters that would sail for ports like Miami, Havana, and New Orleans before noon. The docks were brightly lighted and noisily peopled. Bars were open. Music rang from open doors and windows.

Commissioner Hopkins left the car and strode out on the dock. As a black man he could get a quicker answer than could anyone else, he said. In two minutes he was back.

"She hasn't returned. No radio message. They don't know where the *Athol Saint* has gone. They're willing to admit now, though, that a man came and chartered her."

"Señor Gutiérrez could be at sea, too, on his way to . . . Lord knows where," said Mrs. Roosevelt.

The commissioner shook his head. "Look at the docks. Not a boat in. They're all out fishing. They rode out the storm, and they're all out making tomorrow's money."

"Then—"

"If Gutiérrez came here, he's around somewhere waiting. He can't get away until a boat comes in."

Mrs. Roosevelt glanced around, at the bustling waterfront along the bay. "What do we do? Search?"

"Well . . ."

"Suppose he's wounded," she said. "A doctor?"

Brittigan laughed. "Where would a wounded man go, Sor?" He raised his eyebrows and grinned. "If he knows this waterfront . . . Where Doctor Sparks might be found. And a bed."

Hopkins frowned and shook his head. "No."

The policeman shrugged, still grinning. "I can, uh . . . find out, Sor."

The commissioner glanced at Mrs. Roosevelt, then nodded curtly and said, "Discreetly, Brittigan."

As Brittigan hurried off along the docks, Mrs. Roosevelt smiled at the commissioner and asked, "Where is he going?"

"Uh . . . a place, Ma'am. Not a very nice place."

"A place of bad repute?" she asked with mock innocence.

"A brothel," said the commissioner. "I'm sorry."

"Oh. Here? For the fishermen?"

"Yes . . ." He sighed. "A very well-known establishment, I'm afraid. The lower elements would know about it. Gentlemen and ladies—"

"Would know but might not visit it," said Mrs. Roosevelt.

"Uh . . . Something like that."

"And why, precisely, does Officer Brittigan think he might find Señor Gutiérrez in this particular place?"

"I can think of several reasons," said the commissioner. "To begin with, it is a place where the . . . uh, lower elements of our society collect. I mean, if a man wanted to rid himself of some ill-gotten gains—"

"Fence them, we would say in the States," Mrs. Roosevelt suggested.

"Yes, Ma'am. Fence stolen property. And the like. It's not that Sister Hades, as she's called, would take that property off the thief's hands; it's that she would provide a meeting place where thief and fence might meet—so to speak."

"A wounded man . . ."

"A man wounded in the commission of a crime—Please understand, Mrs. Roosevelt, that we watch this place closely. Little happens that—"

"That you don't know, Commissioner. But often effective police work requires a degree of tolerance for such establishments, since their proprietors will gladly give you leads on major crimes in return for a degree of tolerance about minor ones."

"Spoken like a true policeman," said Commissioner Hopkins with a bold smile.

"Effective crime prevention is based on law, not morals, Commissioner," she said.

He nodded. "You have experience. I wish more people did."

They walked slowly along the docks. Jean King, in her rolled-up policeman's uniform, drew more stares than Mrs. Roosevelt in her dinner gown. The upper reaches of Nassau society, the commissioner explained, often came out here—"slumming," some of them called it—to see the lively activity and to buy the first fish returned by the boats. Kevin held Jean's hand. Ken Krouse wandered off for a few minutes and returned carrying a magnificent pink and white conch shell he had bought for ten cents.

Young women squatted in the sand at the edge of the water, washing clothes. Others hawked slices of pineapple that they cut on the spot, with whacks of big knives. Young men took money from the milling people, with games of three-card monte, or shell games played by men squatting around them on the docks. Angry words were exchanged. Money passed hands. A few young women conspicuously offered themselves in prostitution. Dogs scampered about. Cats, more purposeful, watched for bits of fish. Everyone glanced out to sea from time to time, looking for the distant lights that announced the return of the first fishing boats.

"Sor . . ." said Brittigan. He had caught up with them. "Señor Gutiérrez is alive." He inclined his head toward a ramshackle building just behind the docks. "For the time being, anyway."

* * *

Mrs. Roosevelt changed her clothes in the back of the car. She could not enter the precincts of a West Indian brothel in the white dress she had worn to a formal dinner at the Imperial Hotel. The resourceful Brittigan had taken five minutes to find her something suitable: an ankle-length cotton dress in a gaudy, flowered pattern of orange, white, and blue. He carried along the same, in green and white and yellow, for Jean. And so dressed they walked into the bawdy house operated by a redoubtable woman called Sister Hades.

"Which isn't what I'm really called," said the big black woman. "That's just the polite word. Don't even tell me names for yourselves. If I were you, I'd lie. If you were me, you wouldn't believe it. Anyway, I see who one of you is, but don't worry, my lips are sealed. C'mon. I took the Mexican in." She winked at Commissioner Hopkins. "I'd have reported to you . . . in the morning."

"Doctor Sparks . . . ?"

"Sure. And says he's going to live."

The doctor was a black man, maybe seventy years old, gray and wrinkled, and dressed in black pants, an open-necked white shirt, and no shoes. He was, the commissioner told Mrs. Roosevelt, genuinely a physician and delivered half the babies born every year on New Providence Island. That his breath reeked of rum simply told how he fortified himself against the work he had to do nights on the waterfront.

"Your friend," he said in a gravel voice, "is the beneficiary of somebody's inexpert marksmanship. Mostly he's nicked. He's lost a finger, taken off by a bullet. He's got a shattered rib, caused by another bullet that said hello as it went by. Also, he was grazed on a shoulder and twice on his left leg. It was all an accident, he says. Somebody mistook him for somebody else."

"What can we do for him?" asked Mrs. Roosevelt.

Doctor Sparks shrugged. "Let him sleep, if you want to do what's best for him." He settled skeptical eyes on the commissioner, then on Mrs. Roosevelt. "Which I figure you're not going to do."

"We'll take Señor Gutiérrez to hospital, I think," said Commissioner Hopkins.

"I supposed you would. Okay. Tell the white boys to give him a blood transfusion. That's all he needs that I couldn't do for him here. He's lost a little, could use a fresh supply."

"How did he get here?" asked Mrs. Roosevelt.

"He walked," said the doctor. "Like I said before, the worst wound he's got is to his dignity—though he'll miss that finger if he wants to play the piano."

"He wants to go to sea, I suppose," said the commissioner.

"Oh, yes," said Sister Hades, who had stood by and listened as the doctor spoke. "First boat he can get. Soon as the fleet's back in."

"Where does he want to go?"

"Away," she said. "Anyplace. Just so long as he gets away from New Providence."

"Does he have money?" the commissioner asked.

Doctor Sparks grinned, then laughed. "Does he have *money?* Ladies and gentlemen, that man is *made* of money. He gave me money to pay for treatment, then a whole lot more to keep my mouth shut." The doctor winked at the commissioner. "I'd have reported all this to you—in the morning."

Commissioner Hopkins turned to Sister Hades. "I suppose you searched him?"

"Searched him? Man, we *stripped* him! His clothes were wet, and he was covered with blood."

"How much money was he carrying?"

Sister Hades glanced at Doctor Sparks. "A little more than ten thousand pounds. I took a hundred. He gave the doctor a hundred. The rest of it's in the bed with him. Folding money. Hundred-pound notes, mostly. Wet, like him. But it's just as good wet as dry. The ink's not running. Ten thousand pounds, about. Money . . ."

XIV

As the sun rose over the stern of his yacht *René*, Alfred Sloan stood with Mrs. Roosevelt at the rail, as she was about to descend the stairs to the launch that had brought her aboard and would return her to the wharf. Jean King and Kevin Hammet were with her.

"All I can say to you," he murmured as she stepped out onto the platform at the top of the stairs, "is that I am grateful to you for taking me into your confidence. I understand the delicacy of the situation. I will extend my complete cooperation."

She smiled warmly at him. "I am grateful for your cooperation, Mr. Sloan. I never for a moment doubted that you would give it."

"We understand each other," said Sloan.

She nodded.

He had been wakened when her launch came to the yacht, and he stood on the deck in a robe, with white silk pajama pants showing below. His thin hair, not yet combed, fluttered on the light morning breeze. Mrs. Roosevelt was dressed for the day—the day on which she

would later board a Pan Am amphibian for the return
flight to Miami—in a dress of yellow linen, and she had
bound up her hair in a yellow scarf.

Sloan glanced at the rising sun, then watched the First
Lady go briskly down the stairs. She was, he saw, an ener-
getic woman. He did not know that she had not lain down to
rest until almost four A.M. She'd had an hour's sleep, no
more.

She slept two more hours before it was time to leave Government House with the Duke and Duchess of Windsor
and go with them in the Rolls-Royce to the wharf for her
public and formal visit to the Sloan yacht.

"I regret," said the duchess in the car, "that you will be
leaving without discovering who murdered Gunnar Torstenson."

"So do I," said Mrs. Roosevelt.

"The duke tells me that Isidro Gutiérrez was murdered
last night."

"Well . . . That has not been established," said the First
Lady.

"You went off somewhere to find out," said the duke.
"So?"

"Actually," said Mrs. Roosevelt, "it is better that we assume he was killed. It is better that the people who tried
to kill him believe they did so."

"Are you saying he's alive?" asked the duchess.

"I'd rather not say," said Mrs. Roosevelt.

"Well, this is quite mysterious."

"It will all become clear."

The Duke of Windsor wore white trousers, a blue
blazer, and a white yachting cap. The duchess wore a
white skirt, blue blazer, and a similar cap. Pinned to the
lapel of her blazer was the three-feather clip that had been

found in Torstenson's pocket, that Commissioner Hopkins had returned to her. Mrs. Roosevelt wore the yellow dress she had worn earlier. She looked fresh and not in the least tired.

The sun was high over the harbor by now. Alfred Sloan, dressed in yachting clothes like the duke's, greeted his guests as they came aboard. Henry Chapman and Curtis Wyler were already there, standing on the deck near the stern, drinking coffee. Their business associate William Ashbrook was at the buffet table, picking up coffee. Chief Justice Melbourne stood chatting with Errol Flynn. Brigadier Hilary-Percy was talking with Judy. Jean King, Ken Krouse, and Commander MacGruder had come in a car ahead of the Windsors and Mrs. Roosevelt and were in the aft lounge, talking earnestly. Flynn cast hostile glances toward Jean, whom he could see through the door.

When Errol Flynn saw Mrs. Roosevelt come aboard, he broke away from the chief justice and strode toward her. "Well," he said brightly. "Do we know who killed Torstenson?"

She smiled at him. "The murderer is aboard," she said.

Flynn frowned and walked abruptly away, toward Judy and the brigadier.

Alfred Sloan greeted the duke and duchess, then turned to Mrs. Roosevelt and said quietly, "Everything is ready. And if you'll forgive me, it's the damndest business I ever saw."

"That expresses my thought, too," she said.

"It's going to be a bit dramatic."

"Yes, and a horrible farce if I'm wrong."

"I don't think you're wrong," said Sloan. "I've been doing some checking. I can't tell you how grateful I am to you. And . . . If you are wrong, I'll keep your secret. Even if I have to take Flynn and the Windsors out to sea and drown them."

"Let us hope *that* won't be necessary," said Mrs. Roosevelt.

The big yacht trembled a bit as its diesel engines came to life. Electric winches began to raise the anchors.

"Are we going somewhere?" Henry Chapman called to Sloan.

"Didn't you know? A short cruise with our breakfast. A little run around the island. We won't be out long."

René began to move. Slowly it pulled away from the launches that had brought the guests out from the docks and headed east into the wider harbor beyond the town and on into the bay. Stewards brought out iced champagne and trays of fresh oysters in beds of ice.

Alfred Sloan invited Mrs. Roosevelt to sit down with him and have oysters and champagne.

"I confess I'm a bit hungry this morning," she said. "And some nice oysters won't be a heavy breakfast like eggs and so on. It sounds delightful, Mr. Sloan."

Henry Chapman and Curtis Wyler walked over. "May we join you?" Wyler asked.

"By all means," said the First Lady.

Though others were picking up their food and drink at the buffet table, a steward brought a tray of oysters and a bottle of champagne to the owner's table. Another steward brought trays of bread and butter and of sliced melon.

"A beautiful morning for a cruise," said the flushed, round-faced Chapman. He seemed a little short of breath, and his face glowed pink, as though the champagne had already affected him. "That was an impressive storm last night."

"Wasn't it," said Sloan. He examined the oysters through his pince-nez. "I should not have liked to be out in that rain and wind."

"Surely no one was," said Wyler. His handsome, cleft-chin, youthful face betrayed a troubling uncertainty, per-haps about eating raw oysters, at which he stared with a degree of misgiving. "Surely everyone took shelter."

"Many fishing boats were at sea last night," said Mrs. Roosevelt. "They went out in spite of the approaching storm, rode it out, and went on with their fishing, so they could bring in their catch this morning."

"Really?" said Wyler. "That's remarkable."

"I regret that I've never visited Ireland, Mr. Wyler. I hear it is very beautiful."

"Yes. Actually I've not been back home much myself since I was a boy."

"You've family there, of course."

"Yes . . . Yes, in Dublin."

"Wyler is an unusual name in Ireland, isn't it?"

"Yes. I suppose it is."

"What is your recipe for Irish coffee, Mr. Wyler?"

"Well, I . . . To be truthful, Mrs. Roosevelt, I never drank coffee when I was in Ireland. As a young man, I preferred tea. My mother liked coffee and made it in an old tin pot. Maybe I didn't like coffee because she made it badly."

"But *Irish* coffee, Mr. Wyler. Did she make that?"

He shrugged. "I suppose it was. For breakfast every morning. With her porridge."

Mrs. Roosevelt glanced at Alfred Sloan, who had put his pince-nez in his breast pocket and was frowning doubt-fully. She let him see a small but decidedly ironic smile.

"I've been away from home a long time," said Wyler un-easily.

"Yes, of course," said Mrs. Roosevelt. "Indeed, Mr. Wyler, tell me—Have you in fact ever been in Ireland at all?"

Wyler clenched his teeth, and his jawline hardened and

trembled. "Of course. I spent my youth in Dublin. But I will not be cross-examined on it, Ma'am, even by you."

"And you, Mr. Chapman, are Canadian . . ."

"Born and bred," said Chapman with a broad but forced smile. "And ready to answer any question you would like."

"Not necessary, Mr. Chapman," she said. "Not necessary."

The yacht had passed beyond East End Point and now entered the shallow waters between New Providence and Eleuthera islands, south of the string of reefs that joined them. Eleuthera was beyond the horizon, but seas stirred by last night's storm broke heavily on the reefs and low islands just north of the yacht's course and well within view.

"We have some other guests on board," said Sloan to Mrs. Roosevelt. "It is perhaps rude not to welcome them to the buffet."

She nodded.

Sloan lifted a finger and signalled a yacht officer who had been standing apart, waiting for that signal. The officer strode away, along the starboard gangway. Alerted, Wyler stiffened. He stared after the officer, seemed about to rise from his chair, then apparently thought better of it and settled back.

A moment later six uniformed officers of the Nassau police walked out onto the rear deck and took up stations at the rail, three on each side. Commissioner Edgar Hopkins came out through the lounge, nodded greetings all around, and stepped casually to the buffet table to pick up a cup of coffee.

"I say, Sloan," said the Duke of Windsor. "What is the meaning of this?"

"Oh, I can explain it," said Errol Flynn. "Mrs. Roosevelt

told me when she came aboard that the murderer of Gunnar Torstenson is among us. Whoever did it"—he spread his arms—"is right here. He's one of us."

"Really," complained the duchess.

Kevin Hammet came out from the lounge. He, too, walked over to pick up a cup of coffee.

"Well—" muttered Henry Chapman. "Here's the representative of British Intelligence."

"An interesting admission," said Mrs. Roosevelt. "How do you know he's an intelligence officer, Mr. Chapman?"

"Everyone in Nassau knows it," said Wyler. "The British butchers—murderers of the Irish—have never been subtle."

The yacht officer had returned, and Sloan nodded to him. In a moment the doors at the forward end of the lounge opened and a wheelchair was pushed through. It was pushed by a grinning Doctor Sparks. Sitting in it, hunched and pale and glistening with sweat, but with fierce accusation in his dark eyes was Isidro Gutiérrez.

Alfred Sloan rose from his seat at the table with Mrs. Roosevelt, Chapman, and Wyler. He put his hand on Gutiérrez's shoulder.

"Would you like a glass of champagne, Señor?"

Gutiérrez nodded. *"Si . . ."*

Sloan spoke to a steward. "Champagne for Señor Gutiérrez. And for the doctor."

"A very fine melodrama," said the Duchess of Windsor coldly. "Is it going to be explained?"

"Yes, Your Grace," said Sloan. "From this point forward, I think Mrs. Roosevelt should act as chairlady of the meeting."

The First Lady smiled and shook her head. "Oh no, Mr. Sloan. The Governor of the Bahamas should preside."

"Perhaps so," said the Duke of Windsor. "But since I have not the remotest notion what I am supposed to be presiding over, I gladly defer to Mrs. Roosevelt."

"Are we going to hear the solution to the mystery?" asked the duchess.

"Part of it at least," said Mrs. Roosevelt.

"Is someone going to be accused here?" asked Chapman. "If so, I suggest it is a most improper time and place for such a proceeding. In any event, whoever is about to be accused should have his solicitor present."

"We are going to proceed, Chapman," said Sloan firmly. "All you need to do is listen."

"Mr. Chief Justice . . . ?" asked Chapman.

Chief Justice Sir William Melbourne shrugged and sipped champagne.

"Mrs. Roosevelt . . ." said Sloan.

She pushed her plate aside and used her big white linen napkin to wipe her mouth. "Well," she said, raising her eyebrows high. "It is difficult to know where to begin."

"If I may suggest," said Sloan, "everything perhaps begins with my reason for coming to Nassau. I came here to investigate what was represented to me as an investment opportunity." He nodded at Mrs. Roosevelt. "Do you want to be more specific?"

"Mr. Hammet can add some specifics."

"Oh, yes. Let's hear from British intelligence," sneered Wyler.

Kevin Hammet stood with his backside pressed to the rail of the yacht, a saucer in his left hand, his coffee cup in his right. "Mr. Sloan," he said, "was not averse to investing in a Latin American bank that he understood would be pro-German. He has business reasons for that attitude, and since the United States is a neutral nation, it is perfectly legal for him to invest in German securities, German businesses, or a bank that will have German officers and will act in Germany's economic interest."

"My company has a great deal of money invested in Germany," said Sloan.

"Yes," said Kevin. "So Mr. Sloan's interest is entirely understandable. What Mr. Sloan did not know was that this proposed bank was going to act as an agency of the SS and *Abwehr*—Nazi and German military intelligence. The bank would be a conduit for funds that could be used to finance espionage operations. More than that, its funds were to be used to corrupt Western Hemisphere politicians and turn Latin American governments toward the Nazi cause. We have one pro-Nazi government in South America—that in Argentina—and with appropriate bribes several others could be turned that way. They—"

"You are listening to an agent of British intelligence," said Chapman angrily. "Some of this is speculation. Some of it is outright falsehood."

"Is it?" grunted Gutiérrez.

"You warned me," said Sloan to Gutiérrez. "I was wrong not to believe you."

"A reasonable disbelief," said Kevin. "Señor Gutiérrez is no innocent. He was a competitor for the funds Mr. Torstenson and Mr. Sloan were to invest. He needs money for his project to establish a new government in Mexico. He—"

"A pro-business government," said Gutiérrez. "Not socialist. Pro-business. For free enterprise. So maybe pro-German. Yes. But not under the control of these Nazi lunatics."

"Which Nazi lunatics?" demanded the Duchess of Windsor.

"Plus morons . . ." muttered Gutiérrez.

"Mr. Torstenson," said Mrs. Roosevelt, "was for some

reason under the complete control of the Nazis—to the extent that he allowed his yacht, the *Christina*, actually to be used as a U-boat tender."

"Oh, *really!*" snorted the duchess.

"It was I, Wallis," said Jean King—earning an outraged stare from the Duke of Windsor for having called the duchess by her first name—"who destroyed the radios on *Christina*. I overheard conversation between the captain and lieutenant, discussing the rendezvous they would make with a U-boat, to deliver to it a supply of fresh fruits and vegetables that were to have been brought aboard the yacht the night Torstenson was killed."

"Fanciful . . ." said Wyler.

"Not fanciful at all," said Commander MacGruder. "German U-boat crews are at sea for months, and they very quickly use up all the fresh fruits and vegetables they carry from port. An American fleet submarine is more than twice as big and carries refrigerators in which fresh food can be stored. A U-boat does not, and the crew soon subsists on sausages, cheese, and bread—plus canned foods. A crew shortly shows the results of this. Reduced visual acuity is only one result. The German admirals enter into all kinds of arrangements for U-boats to be supplied with fresh food."

"We can only speculate as to why Mr. Torstenson was so subservient to Nazi masters," said Mrs. Roosevelt. "The crew of the *Christina* was and is mostly Germans, including naval officers. It is not fanciful to say the yacht was in effect a German naval vessel. We have a clue as to why he allowed all this. He—"

"He made immense profits from the illegal sale of munitions to Germany," said Sloan.

"Beyond that," said Mrs. Roosevelt, "we know that his

son was a member of the SS—the black-uniformed Nazi
fanatics. Maybe he was a hostage to their demands on his
father."

"But why did someone kill him?" asked the Duke of
Windsor. "If there was such a cozy relationship between
Gunnar Torstenson and the Nazis, then . . . then did British
Intelligence kill him?" He stared at Kevin Hammet. "Did
you . . . ?"

"A better question, Your Royal Highness," said Commissioner Hopkins. "Why the repeated attempts to kill Señor
Gutiérrez?"

"All right. Why?"

"*David!*" shrieked the duchess. "You are the governor!
Make them answer *your* questions."

The Duke of Windsor frowned and seemed confused.
"Well, I must say I . . . I—"

"I should like to ask Her Royal Highness a question,"
said Commissioner Hopkins. "With your consent, Sir?"

The duke shrugged.

"Your Royal Highness," he said to the duchess, "is wearing an extremely valuable jeweled pin—the three-feather
emblem of the Prince of Wales. Your Grace has offered no
plausible explanation as to why that pin was found by me
in the jacket pocket of Gunnar Torstenson after his death.
Are you prepared to explain that now?"

"You have the temerity to demand an explanation of
me?"

The duke shook his head. "I think we shall have to explain, darling. Sooner or later."

The duchess fixed a furious stare on the duke, then
drew a deep breath. "All right. If royalty is reduced to ex-
plaining to . . . If we are reduced—Let it be understood! If
the duke were to appear on the streets of London today,
he would be cheered by the people. He would be raised on

their shoulders and carried to Buckingham Palace, where a growing crowd would demand the restoration of their king, the deposition of his muddle-minded brother, and the dismissal of the Churchill clique. My husband is the lawful King of England! And we—We are *prisoners* in this squalid colony. If we should escape from here and appear in public in the United States or Canada, much less in London, where we could express ourselves and see our words broadcast worldwide . . . we would be returned to London by public demand. So . . ."

The duchess sighed and shook her head. "So. So, we have to seek our own means of escape from the Bahamas. Gunnar Torstenson was a possible means. But he was a mercenary man. With my husband's consent, I gave him the three-feather pin. It is worth tens of thousands of pounds. It was to buy his cooperation and support. When he left Nassau, we would have gone with him, on *Christina*, to Miami. Then—"

"A minor issue," remarked Jean dryly.

The group assembled on the stern of the slowly moving yacht almost uniformly stared at the boards of the deck. Even the uniformed policemen, who did or did not understand what she had said, recognized a painfully awkward moment and were unsure how to react, except by looking down and waiting for the moment to end.

Kevin Hammet broke the silence. "Your Royal Highness," he said gravely to the duke. "British intelligence did not kill Gunnar Torstenson. No agency of His Majesty's Government killed him."

"Gunnar Torstenson was killed by your friends," hoarsely whispered Gutiérrez.

"You said something like that before," the duchess grumbled.

Mrs. Roosevelt was now distracted by the appearance

of one of the uniformed policemen standing at the rail facing her. For a moment she focused her attention on the long, solemn black face under the oversized cap. The man—He *winked* at her!

Junius Gerald! The newspaper editor! He was standing there, witnessing everything said.

"Isidro," said the duchess sharply. "You are wounded, I suppose. Wounded by whom?"

"Whatever he says, who would believe him?" asked William Ashbrook, Chapman's business associate, who until now had stood aside, watching, listening, and apparently absorbing. He was a compact man, muscular, square of face and head, dressed in a beige suit with white buttons. "Señor Gutiérrez is a professional criminal."

"Maybe I am," Gutiérrez muttered. He nodded. "Yes, maybe I am. But what are you . . . *Dietrich?*"

Ashbrook reached inside his jacket, but before he could draw a pistol he was faced by half a dozen others, alertly drawn by Jean, Ken, Kevin, and two of the uniformed policemen.

Jean turned the muzzle of her .32 Colt toward Wyler and Chapman, and in a moment three other muzzles were turned that way.

Commissioner Hopkins walked around behind the men and reached over their shoulders to disarm them, pulling pistols from inside the jackets of Wyler, Chapman, and Ashbrook.

"Do I need to have you handcuffed, gentlemen?" he asked. "Or are you prepared to behave yourselves?"

"I hope," said the duchess grimly, "that this outrage can be justified. If it can't—"

"Wallis," said Jean. "You're a stupid broad, and you and your stupid husband are in trouble. Take a word of friendly advice, one American to another, and shut up."

XV

The tension on the stern deck of the big yacht was incongruous with the gleaming, peaceful morning scene: bright sun on shallow blue water, with faint images of reefs and even schools of fishes visible under the waves. The air was warm and fragrant, but a sensitive nose could detect a sharp odor of the sweat induced by fear and frustration. The assembled group was stunned, some by one thing, some by another. Mrs. Roosevelt was made uncomfortable by the drawn pistols.

Curtis Wyler spoke. "There seems to be some sort of accusation before the group," he said. "I am not sure what it is. Would anyone want to say?"

"Let's begin with the shooting of Señor Gutiérrez last night," said Mrs. Roosevelt. "He accuses Mr. Ashbrook. Uh . . . or is it Mr. Dietrich?"

"Dietrich!" Ashbrook laughed. "I have been—"

"Schröder talked," said Commissioner Hopkins to Ashbrook.

"You tortured him," said Wyler.

"We might not be inclined," said Mrs. Roosevelt, "to accept the word of Señor Gutiérrez over your own word, Mr. Wyler, or over that of Mr. Chapman—except for one thing. Señor Gutiérrez, when he wandered into an establishment on the waterfront last night, seeking to charter a boat but too badly hurt really to be able to go to sea—was carrying more than ten thousand pounds in cash."

"Which proves what?" asked Chapman.

"He was shot aboard the *Christina* last night during the storm," she said. "His fingerprints are on a glass, a bottle, and an ashtray found in the lounge where the shooting took place. Mr. Dioguardi, his bodyguard, was killed there. The body of that man was found in the water beside the yacht. Three pistols were dredged up from the harbor water a little after dawn this morning. Ballistically, one of them matches the bullets taken from Mr. Dioguardi. The others match bullets dug out of the woodwork of the *Christina.*"

"And you found some very significant fingerprints on the pistols, I suppose," said Wyler.

"In fact, we found none. Whoever fired the pistols wore gloves."

"I will tell you why I am aboard *Christina* last night," croaked Gutiérrez. "I am lured aboard. I am given the money. They thought to recover it off my body after they killed me."

"Tell the story, Señor Gutiérrez," said Mrs. Roosevelt. "Who lured you aboard the yacht, and why?"

"I have tried to discourage Mr. Sloan from the placing of money in the proposed bank talked about by Chapman and Wyler," said Gutiérrez. "I have tried to discourage Torstenson of it." He shrugged. "Yesterday I am forced to realize I am defeated."

"You wanted the money for your own banking venture," said Ken Krouse.

"Yes. So . . . Last night I am meeting with Chapman and

Wyler to discuss a little compromise—some money to me in compensation for my loss of the opportunity they have seized."

"Ten thousand pounds," said Mrs. Roosevelt.

He nodded. "I know they would like to kill me, so I have taken with me Angelo Dioguardi . . . and my own pistol. I did not think they would be so bold, so foolish, but—I am coming prepared."

"You walked into their trap," said Jean.

Gutiérrez turned down the corners of his mouth and shrugged again. "I am in possession of information they do not want disclosed. I told them it is written down and kept in a safe place. I think they didn't believe that."

"So you met with—"

"Those two," said the Mexican, pointing at Chapman and Wyler. "They gave the money. No hesitation. No argue. Then . . . Off the lights. First someone has shot Angelo. But Angelo is the brave man; he does not die so easy and returns fire. I am on the floor, my pistol ready. I fire."

"Did Mr. Chapman or Mr. Wyler fire at you?" asked Mrs. Roosevelt.

"Not at first. Maybe not at all. They throw themselves on the floor to be out of danger. The firing, it is much. Crawling around in the dark. Angelo lives a long time, fires much. I, too. I find a pistol someone has dropped. Fire more. Then the police come. Men run out and jump to the water." He stared hard at Chapman and Wyler. "*They* did. Into the water. Then I."

"Yes," said Mrs. Roosevelt. "And you managed to swim ashore and escape."

Gutiérrez nodded wearily.

"What was the information you had, that they did not want you to disclose?" asked the Duke of Windsor.

"Their identity," said Gutiérrez.

"How did you learn their identity?" asked the duke.

"Gunnar Torstenson has told me what I have already suspect. I am not a fool. I have already suspect."

"What *I* have suspected, indeed," said Mrs. Roosevelt. She turned to Wyler. "I don't know who you are, Mr. Wyler, but you are not an Irishman. As Miss King told me, you have never been in the Lantern Theatre, though you told her you had. And this morning you told me your mother drank Irish coffee for breakfast. I know the Irish have a reputation for drinking, but I somehow doubt your mother starts the day with a heavy shot of Irish whisky."

"I carry an Irish passport," said Wyler aggressively. He glanced at Kevin Hammet. "I imagine British Intelligence has checked on its authenticity."

"The Irish Republic is so obsessively Anglophobic it would give a passport to Beelzebub himself if he happened to be at war with Britain," said Kevin.

"So who are they?" asked the duchess excitedly.

"Chapman is Chapman," said Gutiérrez. "Ashbrook is Rudolf Dietrich, agent of the Gestapo. And Wyler . . ." He sneered. "Curtis Wyler is Kurt Weiller, another agent of the terrible Gestapo."

Weiller laughed.

"If what Señor Gutiérrez says is true, you are spies and will be shot," said the Duke of Windsor.

"I would not be too quick to believe it, darling," said the duchess. "Henry Chapman, after all, is as prominent a businessman in Canada as Alfred Sloan is in the States."

"Not really," said Chapman. "I am not a multimillionaire, just a man who is trying to make his way in life. If these accusations against Curtis Wyler and William Ashbrook are true, I am as much surprised as anyone."

Weiller tossed his head. "If we hang, you hang, Chapman," he said.

"If you have need to look for leniency, Mr. Chapman," said Mrs. Roosevelt, "it might come to you as a result of cooperation. It is not too late to tell the truth."

"And testify against us, Henry," said Dietrich. "But beware of what happens when the Führer rules Britain and Canada. Where will you flee?"

" 'The Führer,' " Kevin repeated. "I guess that answers the question."

Gutiérrez seized the wheels of his chair and rolled it forward, closer to the two Germans and Chapman. He looked up into the face of Sloan, who stood looking down quizzically into his face.

"Does anyone want to know what Torstenson has told me?" he asked.

"Of course," said Mrs. Roosevelt.

He spoke first to Alfred Sloan. "You are a fool. I *told you!*" He spoke then to the First Lady. "Torstenson and I . . . Sloan and I, Chapman and I, are the like men. We are moved by money. It is our first concern. That is why we have it." He glanced at the duke. "That is why you don't. If you had put aside this foolish, shallow woman, you would be King of England and *rich!*"

"Isidro . . ."

Gutiérrez cut him off with a curt gesture. "We care not that Hitler may be murdering people. Torstenson, Sloan . . . me. So long as he doesn't try to murder us, we can do business with him. No? And Chapman . . . Henry Chapman has great need of money. Is it not so?"

"It is so," said Mrs. Roosevelt. "He is in imminent danger of bankruptcy."

"Yes," muttered Gutiérrez. "And is it not possible this

justifies him? What, then, is Torstenson's excuse? Sloan's?"

"See here, Gutiérrez," said Alfred Sloan. "Be careful what company you put me in."

The Mexican managed to laugh. He handed his empty champagne glass to Doctor Sparks and gestured that he wanted it refilled. "Torstenson had an excuse," he went on. "His son—"

"A member of the SS," said Mrs. Roosevelt. "The black shirts. A fanatic Nazi."

"Let us be more precise in our terminology," said Weiller. "The SS is an elite corps. And Dietrich and I are not police thugs, not of the Gestapo. We are of the SD, the *Sicherheitsdienst*, elite of the elite. Young Torstenson earned his membership in the SS."

"And died in it," said Gutiérrez.

"Yes," said Weiller. "Specifically, he was of the Waffen SS, a Nazi soldier in a crack regiment. He was wounded in Belgium in May and died in hospital in August."

"His father has of this learned only after arriving in Nassau," said Gutiérrez. "They tried to keep it from him, but the big yacht was in fact equipped with big radio contrivances and could hear signals from Sweden. Business associates send Gunnar Torstenson a dreaded message, in code. Then the Nazis lose their threat over him."

"So he sent me a message," said Sloan.

"Yes. The message is, don't yet invest the large money until I tell you all."

"Gunnar Torstenson and I," Sloan explained, "had a secret code, unknown to our Nazi bully-boys here. What he radioed to me was, 'Don't delay your arrival here. The tarpon are taking bait.' "

"You mean," chirped Errol Flynn, "the tarpon were not taking bait? No wonder we didn't go fishing!"

"The afternoon when the day was he was murdered," said Gutiérrez, "Gunnar Torstenson has told me he will no longer invest the many millions in what he calls the Chapman proposition. He has no more the reason for doing. His son is dead. He cannot escape wholly the domination, but he can escape some."

"I should have listened to you," Sloan admitted. "Frankly, Isidro, you are such a slimy character . . ."

"I have . . . How you say? I have my agenda. You and I should be work together, not opposed."

Sloan frowned at Weiller. "Who set the explosive charge in the Chris-Craft runabout?" he asked sternly.

"Since you seem to know everything," said Kurt Weiller, speaking to Mrs. Roosevelt as well as to Alfred Sloan, "why should I answer?" He shrugged. "On the other hand, why not? It is no longer of any consequence. In any event, I dislike leaving an impression that the soldiers of the Führer are incompetent."

"Oh, don't leave us with any erroneous impressions," said Kevin sarcastically.

"Captain Lindeblad was, as you know, *Hauptmann* Hardegen. Valentin was Valentin—*Leutnant* Valentin. *Christina* was, as you have guessed, a radio ship for the intelligence services of the Third Reich—until someone so cleverly planted Thermit in the radio cabinet and destroyed its capabilities. It was also a supplier of necessities to U-boats."

"So . . ." said MacGruder. "As we thought."

"And you violated your neutrality to act against us," said Weiller.

"No," said Kevin. "*I* burned out your radios."

Weiller smiled. "Yes, of course. To the temporary victor belongs the story. When we hang you, Lieutenant Hammet, the story will be whatever we tell."

"The runabout . . ." Mrs. Roosevelt prompted.

"Planting a charge and eliminating Señor Gutiérrez by explosion was *Leutnant* Valentin's assignment. He failed, but we were extraordinarily fortunate that he did. He failed to realize that the same small boat would have carried Señor Gutiérrez but also Mrs. Roosevelt and the Duke and Duchess of Windsor! How very fortunate for us that the idiot mishandled the wires and blew himself up."

"The death of Captain Hardegen?" asked Mrs. Roosevelt.

"Valentin was his subordinate," said Weiller. "He was therefore responsible, not just for Valentin's death, but for the unutterably horrible consequences if Valentin had succeeded. This would have gone on his record. Then we ordered him to take *Christina* to sea, to escape what seemed to be a rapidly deteriorating situation. Not only did he fail to escape the Bahamas, he brought the yacht back in—when he should have scuttled it."

"And for his errors—"

Weiller shrugged and interrupted. "It was suggested to him that he could go home, eventually, and face a court martial, or—"

"And he chose 'or,' " said Kevin. "I can understand, in the circumstances."

"I am compelled to acknowledge, Mr. Hammet, that you have won this minor skirmish—"

"Not a minor skirmish," said Kevin. "The bank you planned to establish in the Western Hemisphere would have become a major asset to Nazi ambitions."

"We will defeat you in Europe first," said Weiller. "Then we shall see what happens in this hemisphere."

"Isidro," said the Duchess of Windsor. "If you knew everything you have told us this morning, since Tuesday, then why—"

"Why didn't he tell everyone sooner?" said Weiller.

"Precisely," she said coldly. "What was the game?"

"When I was aboard the Torstenson yacht last night," said Gutiérrez. "The transaction was—"

"We were paying him blackmail," Weiller interrupted crisply. "Sloan had chosen to ignore as much as Gutiérrez had chosen to tell him—which was good judgment on Mr. Sloan's part—but Gutiérrez had withheld much of what he has told you this morning. The heroic Señor Gutiérrez was holding back most of what Torstenson had told him—to see who would bid highest for it. We bid ten thousand pounds."

"And planned it should recover off from my dead body," said Gutiérrez.

Weiller chuckled. "Of course. How else does one deal with a cheap little blackmailer?"

"You tried to kill him twice before," said Mrs. Roosevelt.

"And twice failed," said Weiller. "We are soldiers. He is a gangster."

"Is anyone still interested," Jean asked, "in how Gunnar Torstenson was killed?"

"It has become rather obvious, has it not?" asked Mrs. Roosevelt. "Of course . . ."

"I think it might be interesting if Henry Chapman told us how it happened," said Jean.

"*I* . . . Why, how would I—"

"Herr Weiller," said Jean. "*I* destroyed the radios. In spite of what Kevin says, I am the one who did it. I acted totally in violation of my authority and instructions from the government of the United States, but I did it. I had my reasons."

"Which were," Weiller interrupted, "that we wouldn't have suspected you. Whereas we would have taken care of Mr. Hammet the moment he tried to board *Christina*."

"Something like that," she said dryly. "Anyway, I saw you on board that night. You hadn't been invited to the party—"

"Because there had been an angry exchange between me and Torstenson that afternoon."

"Yes. But you were on board. Wearing dungarees. I didn't see you kill Torstenson, but—"

"But I did," said Weiller. "Since I am to be shot as a spy, what difference does it make that I tell you that?" He looked toward Chapman. "Henry? How noble do you wish to be?"

"I knew nothing of it," protested Chapman. "If this admitted Nazi spy says anything different—"

"You engaged Mr. Torstenson in conversation," said Mrs. Roosevelt, "while Herr Weiller stepped up behind him and struck him on the head. Then you helped him lift Mr. Torstenson over the rail."

"That's a guess!"

"We'll let a jury decide if it's no more than a guess," said Sir William Melbourne.

"We are here," said Weiller. "What has been said here is confidential, except only to those who are aboard this yacht. An opportunity is here for every one of you, to associate yourselves with the New Order. We put the Mexican over into the water. Maybe a few others, as necessity may suggest. Then—Well—The victory of the Third Reich is inevitable! I die. Others will surely die. But in the end, the kind of world the Führer has ordained will prevail!"

Mrs. Roosevelt turned toward Junius Gerald. "I believe you are a man he means to throw overboard," she said. "A newspaper publisher. Who could be more dangerous to his new order?"

Everyone fell silent. Only Errol Flynn spoke—

"We *will* be on our way to Havana this afternoon, won't we?" he asked Alfred Sloan. "Personally, I find Nassau depressing."

"So do I," muttered the Duchess of Windsor.

EPILOGUE

The Pan American World Airways flying boat took off from New Providence Island, the Bahamas, a little after one o'clock that afternoon. It carried Mrs. Roosevelt and her party, short one member—

Jean King sent back with the First Lady her letter of resignation from the service of the government of the United States—and her government-issue pistol, as Ken Krouse continued laughingly to insist.

Mrs. Roosevelt expressed her regret at being unable to remain for the wedding of Jean King and Kevin Hammet. She had a silver tea service sent from Washington immediately on her return. It arrived at Nassau ten days after the marriage and was shipped on to London, then down to Kent, where Jean and Kevin took up temporary residence in a small cottage not far from Knole House. They never saw the tea service, actually, until late in 1945 when at long last it caught up with Sir Kevin and Lady Jean Hammet.

Kevin Hammet served aboard His Majesty's Ship *Repulse* but happened to be ashore recovering from a bout of malaria when *Repulse* was sunk off Malaya in 1942. He escaped capture by the Japanese, too, and went on to serve under Mountbatten in Burma for the rest of the war. He returned to England only in 1945, about the same time when the tea service reached him and Jean.

Jean went to France as a British intelligence officer in 1941, was captured by the Gestapo, escaped, and made her way to Portugal, where she was interned by the neutral country. After fourteen months living as a prisoner in a Lisbon hotel, she escaped that, too, and returned to London. She was in Paris when the Allied forces arrived in the summer of 1944.

Kevin was knighted. Jean was decorated for heroism. Sir Kevin Hammet stood proudly beside his wife when she was awarded the Victoria Cross by King George VI.

Kenneth Krouse remained with the State Department. He accompanied President Roosevelt to the Casablanca and Teheran conferences. Assistant Secretary of State Krouse was among the first mourners to arrive at the White House when the President died. In the 1950s he was accused by Senator Joseph McCarthy of being a "dupe" of the Communist Party. He retired in disgust rather than defend himself and became a wealthy corporation lawyer in New York.

Commander Wilson MacGruder rose to the rank of vice admiral before his retirement in 1949.

Errol Flynn's little friend Judy bore his illegitimate child before she was eighteen. With the money he settled on her and her child, she established a gift shop in Palm Beach. It was immensely successful, and its success was in part due to the fact that the Windsors made a point of visiting it and buying from it during their every visit to the United States for the next twenty-five years. Judy's daughter married a distant cousin of Henry Ford.

Flynn died of what Flynn was bound to die of, before many more years.

The Duke and Duchess of Windsor served out their term of exile in the Bahamas, then began the lifeless travels that would occupy them for the rest of their years. They could never admit the futility of their existence, but it was their lifelong tragedy that they were always painfully conscious that their lives had no meaning.

Isidro Gutiérrez recovered from his wounds, returned to Mexico, and was murdered there in 1944. His murderer was never found—or at least never arrested.

Kurt Weiller and Rudolf Dietrich were returned to London to face a military court as German spies. They were not shot. They were hanged in February 1941.

Henry Chapman was returned to London on the same ship. He was sentenced to life imprisonment. He was released from Dartmoor Prison in 1957.

The Germans and Swedes of the crew of *Christina* were spies. They were sentenced to long prison terms, but all were released and repatriated when the war ended.

Commissioner Hopkins retired in 1954. He travelled to Britain and then to the States, where Mrs. Roosevelt received him as a weekend guest at Val-Kil cottage.

Several times during the 1950s, Mrs. Roosevelt saw Sir Kevin and Lady Jean Hammet, during visits she made to London. In 1956 she saw them for the last time, at a dinner at the Dorchester, held by the Duke and Duchess of Windsor. That evening the duchess offered a toast—

"It is not well known, but in 1940, when the duke and I were first in Nassau, a despicable Nazi spy plot was discovered and terminated. The duke has been given great credit for his perspicacity in discovering that plot and bringing it to the attention of the authorities. I would like to acknowledge now that Mrs. Roosevelt contributed sev-

eral ideas to the duke and me on that occasion and was of
significant assistance to us in uncovering and smashing a
dangerous Nazi scheme to turn the Bahamas Islands, and
indeed all of Latin America, into a Nazi base. That is but
one reason that I now say to Mrs. Eleanor Roosevelt—

"God bless you, dear lady, and thank you from all of
us!"